INSTRUMENTS OF PLEASURE

'What do you suggest, Maestro?' Holger asked, his thick voice displaying his delight.

'Oh, the whip. The cat, I think.'

It was a short-handled instrument, with a number of tails of thin supple leather, and was already to hand. Holger watched while the Maestro wielded it. Labat struck expertly, with a flick of the wrist, in a practised economy of effort. The tails fell first on Max's quivering behind. It felt as though myriad hornets had stung her all at once. Her head swung wildly, she shrieked and bucked, but at his snarled order to 'Keep still!' she found herself fighting against the torment in order to obey him, and somehow managed to do so, except for the involuntary clenching of her muscles and the drumming of her legs against the bed beneath her, proffering her scorched backside for the next swingeing blow.

T0316377

INSTRUMENTS OF PLEASURE

Nicole Dere

This book is a work of fiction.
In real life, make sure you practise safe, sane and
consensual sex.

First published in 2007 by
Nexus
Thames Wharf Studios
Rainville Rd
London W6 9HA

www.nexus-books.co.uk

A catalogue record for this book is available from the British
Library.

Typeset by TW Typesetting, Plymouth, Devon

Penguin Random House is committed to a sustainable future for
our business, our readers and our planet. This book is made from
Forest Stewardship Council® certified paper.

MIX
Paper | Supporting
responsible forestry
FSC
www.fsc.org
FSC® C018179

Printed and bound in Great Britain by Clays Ltd, Elcograf S.p.A.

ISBN 978 0 352 34098 6

One

'Keep playing, my dear. Don't stop!' Aunt Charlotte's voice, for all its softness, was like the hissing caress of a whip, and Max concentrated fiercely on the music. She knew she was playing far below her best, though, to a layman, the soaring notes she was producing from the violin would be considered exquisite. She closed her eyes and pressed her chin down more firmly on the vibrating instrument, its delicate quiver transmitting itself through her bone, through the slender column of her neck, her slim shoulders, to the very centre of her. Still she failed to block out the intrusion of that strange hand, its invidious softness, the cold dry fingers on her skin as they toyed with the back of her slender bent neck and the stray tendrils of loose dark hair at its base.

'How charming!' Professor Labat's deep murmur vibrated within her like the strings across which she drew her skilful bow. 'So wonderfully old-fashioned, and so elegant.'

'I thought you would approve.' Aunt Charlotte's voice, with its silky huskiness, was scarcely higher than the professor's. 'I've never liked the modern lack of style of young females. Such ugly garments, don't you think? No girl can look anything but ugly in them, no matter how shapely she might be. I said don't stop, girl!'

1

The last sentence was snapped out incisively, for Max had indeed faltered, as she felt the professor's close proximity, the warmth of his breath wafting across her face as he bent towards her. She had carefully eased off her smart heeled shoes before she began playing, and she could feel the cold smoothness of the polished wooden floor on her soles through the sheer nylon mesh of her stockings. She liked to be as free as possible when she played. The fewer and looser the clothes the better. In fact, when she practised alone, she often stripped to her underwear. She had even, on the rare occasions when she could be sure she would not be interrupted, dispensed with even these last scraps of attire. She almost lost concentration at the irreverent image of this eminent figure's reaction to such a spectacle. From what she could see and judge from those stroking fingers, that pent-up breath and the piercing gaze, such a display would not meet with the great man's disapproval.

His sleeve brushed the music stand and caused the sheets of music to tremble slightly. The vigour of her movement as she approached the crescendo of her performance pushed the hem of her dress further, to midway up her thighs. She felt those eyes like a caress following the silk's motion. She lowered her long dark lashes, and she faltered again, missed a note. The colour flooded her face. She had to pause, pick up the melody. 'I'm sorry,' she whispered.

'Stupid girl!' She could almost hear her Aunt Charlotte hissing. 'She's not used to being around men, as you can see,' the older woman said aloud, with a low laugh.

'I have your word for that?' Professor Labat asked, also with amusement, though Max could detect the seriousness behind his light tone. She experienced, as she so often did, that warring sense of devaluation and of her own complicity in it, while her two elders discussed her as if she were invisible.

'Of course. As you well know, Wolfgang, I've kept her *and* the boy in virtual isolation since they came to me. Apart from their music lessons, and their school tutors, they've had little contact with the outside world, except under my strict supervision.'

'Perfect!' Carefully, he picked up Max's dainty shoes and placed them neatly side by side. 'I can tell she's nervous of me. Aren't you, Max?'

Max started at the sudden increase of hearty volume when he addressed her directly. Those strong fingers rested lightly on her wrists, preventing her from continuing. He was kneeling still closer to her, and his hands now rested blatantly and heavily on her legs, just above her knees. She met his gaze, maintaining the carefully studied appearance of artlessness, and saw those flashing dark eyes resting on hers with sardonic amusement. The complexion was brown, adding to the foreignness of his appearance. His face was lined, his jaw long. The features were distinguished rather than handsome, the hair an iron grey overlaying the traces of black. Though prominent in the centre of the large brow, it receded considerably at either side. She had little idea of his age, except that he was surely older than her aunt, who was forty-one. She observed all this in that one quick glance, before her own gaze modestly lowered. Despite herself, the hot colour mounted at the penetrating quality of his steady observance, the knowledge of the world, and, maybe, even of her inner thoughts, in his curving lips.

Aunt Charlotte began to excuse the untypical flaws in the performance, but the professor's hands pressed down in brief hardness on Max's thighs as he levered himself upright. 'No, no, it's all right. She's done very well, the poor lamb. You've passed your first test with flying colours, my dear.' His laugh rumbled. He reached out and ruffled her soft dark hair as though he were caressing a pet animal, and the muscles of her neck grew rigid with her effort not to pull away from the playful caress. 'Now, why don't you put that lovely instrument away, and run along to Holger? My man. You'll find him downstairs somewhere. He'll show you where your room is. Your bags will be there. You can unpack, settle in. I'll send for you when I'm ready. Off you go.'

Feeling uncomfortably embarrassed under their gaze, she put her violin in its case and quickly folded the music sheets away. She looked down at her feet, her toes with their dark nails showing through the sheer material, and slipped them quickly into her shoes, shaken by a sudden feeling of relief at having them hidden once more, as though there had been something shameful in their exposure. She could still feel the pressure where those strong hands had rested on her legs. She wondered if they had left a red branding mark on her pale skin. As though he could read her mind, the professor's deep laugh rumbled again. 'You don't have to bother about formality in this house, my dear. Go barefoot by all means if you're happier that way.'

She looked now uncertainly towards her aunt. 'Run along!' Charlotte said, with just a hint of impatience.

'Will I – I wondered – will I see you . . .?'

Charlotte chuckled. 'Good God! I'm not kicking you out of my life! You'll see plenty of me, don't you worry! You won't get rid of me so easily. However, perhaps not this evening. I have things to do. Come here.' Max moved across to her, head down. Charlotte crooked a finger, lifting the bent head by the

4

chin, and kissed her lightly on the lips. 'Be good. Do everything you're told. Remember. You belong to the Maestro now.'

The last strange words echoed in her brain as Max left the music room and headed for the wide staircase of this unfamiliar house. She felt a little sick, and nervous at what lay ahead. This was a watershed in her young life, she knew. Though she had been prepared for it for some time, she nevertheless acknowledged her fear now that it had come. Since the sudden death of her parents, she had been under the sole jurisdiction of her aunt, Charlotte Behr, her mother's sister. It had been a tyrannical rule, and had come as a sudden shock to the twelve-year-old after the easygoing, almost careless, disregard of her parents. As talented professional musicians, both had spent large periods of time away from their only child, leaving her in the care of a succession of nannies and tutors in more than a dozen homes around the world. The only thing her mother and father had not neglected was her musical education, with the result that, even when she came to Aunt Charlotte, she was already an extremely competent performer.

Music had always been the centre of her young life. To it she owed even her name – to that, and her father's quirky humour. Max was for Max Jaffa (the name on her birth certificate was Maxine, which no one ever called her) – 'a vastly underrated artist,' daddy frequently told her, 'whose genius was never really acknowledged.'

And Antonio had been named after the world famous violinmaker, Stradivari. Or so Aunt Charlotte had insisted. Max had known nothing of this 'cousin', of virtually the same age except for a few weeks. He had suddenly appeared on the scene soon after she had come to live with her aunt, with a musical talent to equal that of Max. 'Your namesake created things of great beauty and pleasure,' Charlotte informed him, 'as you will, one day.'

She had discovered him, she said, living in a children's home, after he had been abandoned at birth. His upbringing could not have been more different from that of Max. *Her* childhood had been cosmopolitan, she had lived in the cities of Europe, and even further afield, in Africa and Australia. She hardly thought of herself as British, though her father was a native of England. Her mother's family was Austrian, but Aunt Charlotte was the only member she had kept trace of. In contrast, Antonio claimed to have known nothing but the bleak institution in the equally grim Yorkshire town from which 'Aunty' Charlotte had rescued him soon after she became Max's guardian.

Yet, in spite of their vastly different circumstances, they looked amazingly alike. They were frequently mistaken for twins, for Antonio had the same dark delicately fine frame and features, almost too close to Max's blossoming beauty to be described as a conventional male handsomeness. And not only were they close in looks but in other genetically linked ways, it seemed. Antonio was already a talented pianist when he came to Aunt Charlotte's. Under her remorselessly firm tutelage, his skill had developed until now, a mere six years later, he was as gifted in his way as Max was in hers.

The children themselves laughed many a time about their names. People expected Max to be a boy, and Antonio to be Italian. They delighted in their closeness in both looks and temperament, and loved to pass themselves off as the twins folk took them to be. For both of them, having each other was the answer to the loneliness they had endured through their isolated childhood.

It had not been easy to find things to laugh about under Aunt Charlotte's custody. Max could still recall vividly the shock of that first beating; the two youngsters side by side, bent over that long darkly gleaming dining table, held down by Davies, Aunt Charlotte's maid, a woman with the build and strength of a navvy, while the strap cut fiercely across their flinching bottoms. It was a painful degradation repeated many times over the three years that had followed, physical punishment ceasing only when they had attained their fifteenth birthday.

Her present sombre reflections reminded her. Where was Toni? Why hadn't he come here with her? She had not seen him for two whole days. She hated being separated from him, she felt so uneasy, almost incomplete, away from his presence. They had scarcely ever been apart for more than a few hours. Only during the hours of sleep and their music tuition had they been divided, and even then they had often come together, for lessons, and then later, as their talent grew so formidably, for performances before select private audiences, Toni providing the piano accompaniment for her violin.

Aunt Charlotte's regime had tried to clamp down firmly on the physical intimacy, however innocent, which the children had shared. One of her earliest beatings came when Max, clad in her pyjamas, was caught trying to sneak along the landing late one night to Toni's room. The girl was horrified at the indignity, but the degradation was soon forgotten in the onslaught that followed. The cracking blows rained upon her, and her sobbing pleas for mercy drew no quarter. Her suffering was made worse by learning that Toni had endured the same fate. His backside was as tender and bruised as hers.

Still, the strong bond of intimacy between the 'twins' could not be broken, only driven underground. They learned to conceal it, and, as they grew towards young adulthood, the severity of the regime relaxed. Charlotte felt that she had won. In some ways she had – but not in all. Just after their recent eighteenth birthdays, which had passed with only minor, private celebration, Max was taking her bath when the door opened – they were forbidden ever to lock the door of the bathroom – and Toni's grinning face appeared. 'Aunt C's out, and Davies is shopping. Freedom!'

He advanced into the room, and stood gazing down at her. 'My word! What a big girl!' he teased. 'You're actually getting boobies!'

She gave a mock pout and sat up. Critically, she hefted her small breasts, proffering them for his inspection. They were slight, but the nipples, though small and with very little areolae, appeared permanently erect, enhancing the budding conelike shape of the small swells they crested. 'Well, at least I'm not entirely flat any more. I thought they'd never come.' She glanced towards the open door. 'Hey! Why don't you hop in?'

His face mirrored her mischievous excitement. Eagerly, he stripped off his sweater, thrust down his trousers and the small underbriefs with them, dragged them clear of his feet, then peeled off his socks. She squealed and drew up her knees, parting her legs as he settled with a splash opposite her. The perfumed bubbles were thinning. She saw, as well as felt, his narrow foot as it pushed into her loins and pressed against the base of her belly. The ball of his foot pushed arousingly against the cushioned flesh of her vulva, his toes flexed against the flat dark little fleece of her pubis, and, unable to stop herself, she pushed back, the shivers of desire pulsing through her.

'Stop – you shouldn't – you're doing naughties,' she murmured, using the formula of their childhood.

He stretched out his right hand, and fondled her left breast, before tweaking the throbbing nipple quite hard. 'Not big naughties!' His voice was thick, too, with his excitement. She could see his penis, the lengthened shape of it, bobbing up above the surface. 'No one's ever done big naughties to you, have they?'

She shook her head. Now she was thrusting her belly rhythmically against him. Her mouth was open. He saw her tongue flicker round her shining lips. 'No. I wouldn't want them to. Except, maybe . . .' She now reached forward, and let her fingers lightly touch his penis. She was startled at its pulsating hardness; it reared up at her caress. Then she gasped, overwhelmed by dismay as, with a great heave that sent the water sloshing all about them, he jerked back, withdrew his foot from between her thighs, and sat with his knees drawn primly up to his chest, only their submerged feet touching now.

'Never mind all that! I've got some news. Big news. Things are going to change. We're getting out of here.'

Her physical arousal, and her disappointment at its abrupt termination, was soon forgotten. He told her of the proposed move to the home of Professor Wolfgang Labat and how the Maestro, as he was known, would take charge of their future career. 'Apparently, he knew your mummy and daddy for years. He's a great teacher and impresario. He's going to train us for the concert circuit.'

Toni was elated at the prospect of this sea change in their young lives. Max was rather less certain. Nevertheless, it would be good to escape the tyranny that had been Aunt Charlotte's rule for the past six years. Max had somehow clung to the belief that Toni would find a way to set them free. At first, he had carried the secret flame of rebellion inside, as

Max had, and she had hoped that, with his masculine boldness, he would find a way out for both of them. But lately, over the past year or so, she had felt secretly dismayed and let down by his apparent ambivalence of attitude, his seeming readiness to accept their aunt's dominance over them.

Now, as she sat listlessly in that strange room, her things still in the open cases, Max thought of the professor's disturbing behaviour. She stared down at her legs, reliving the feel of his hands, those fingers, while she strove all the time to keep on playing for him. More than ever, she longed for Toni's familiar face, so closely mirroring hers, for his comforting arms around her. Why hadn't he come? Why, at this most crucial time, had he been taken from her?

Two

'You will be gentle with her, at least for a while, Maestro?' Charlotte's husky voice trembled with emotion; an emotion rarely felt, and which only a very privileged few had been allowed to see. The professor, of course, detected it at once. She was displaying an uncharacteristic weakness, against which she was helpless. Her own powerful personality had always recognised his superior strength, from the first time she had met him, when she was a young girl and he was tutor to her younger, more talented sister.

She recalled how the girls had fought over him, this strangely magnetic young man no older than herself, but with an utterly self-confident manner that went beyond conceit. At eighteen, Anne was already strikingly beautiful. 'You're just jealous!' Anne had taunted, tossing those clouds of black hair, lying back on the bed, and parading her beauty deliberately, in her brief underwear. And she was, Charlotte was forced to admit, if only to herself.

Already in her young life, she had discovered that her sexual orientation was cloudy, to say the least. She had found her attraction towards those of her own sex far stronger than anything she had felt for males. The unclothed male form filled her mainly with contempt. Not that she had ever tried to test that contempt with any practical experiment. She had never progressed beyond several open-mouthed tongue-probing kisses, and had wriggled and fought herself free of clutching hands on her breast, and up her skirt, with nothing more disastrous than a few popped buttons and a torn bra strap. Her explorations and rapturous gratification had been with lithe and willing silk-wrapped bodies that mirrored her own.

Just what was she jealous of? she had asked herself, staring down at the lovely body of her sister, draped provocatively across the bed. Jealous because, for the past few years, she had watched that body develop like a chrysalis into a budding beauty? Or because the strangely disturbing dark eyes of that young man had pierced right through all her youthful suppositions, arousing facets of her make-up she had not hitherto dreamed of?

Anne had looked up at her, and laughed again. Those full lips had pouted invitingly and the long black lashes had flickered, brushing against the perfect cheeks as though she could read Charlotte's most secret thoughts and was mocking them. Crimson with fury, Charlotte had flung herself upon the slender form, ripping away the lacy scraps covering her enchanting breasts, stripping that tiny film of satin and lace from her loins. For just a few seconds, Anne had struggled to resist, then suddenly her body went limp beneath her aggressor.

'Feel better now?' Anne asked, and Charlotte had heaved herself up, turning away from the prone figure with a convulsive sob.

After that, Anne seemed to take a weird pleasure in driving Charlotte to the point of physical violence. It was, in a strange way, an inverted kind of dominance, that the beautiful young girl could make her lose control like that. The young tutor showed only distant politeness towards Charlotte when they met, usually in the girls' home and in the presence of their parents and friends. Just occasionally, those compelling dark eyes would fix on hers with an enigmatic smile and she would feel the colour mount hotly. It was as though he could at such times look deep inside her, and knew the conflicting passions raging within.

Once, unable to help herself in the young man's presence and under the scourge of her younger sister's odiously smug smile, she pleaded with her father to allow her, too, to have lessons with Wolfgang Labat. 'I wouldn't throw my money away, nor waste Wolfgang's valuable time, Charlotte. To be frank, it's not worth it. You don't have the talent, my love.' She had wanted to curl up and shrivel on the spot, flaming dumbly with humiliation.

The next evening, Anne was looking dazzlingly lovely, her soft hair carefully arranged to fall on her creamy bare shoulders in a daring evening gown cut low to expose the slight rise of her small breasts. 'Keep your stole on, dear,' her mother advised cautiously. Wolfgang was taking her to a concert.

Dumb with misery, Charlotte could not bear to watch them leave together. She retired to her room, excusing herself as soon as supper was over. There, her blood raging with a desire she could not ignore, she stripped naked, and stood contemplating her tall rangy figure in the long mirror. Unable to stop herself, she let her hands slide over her skin to caress the sharp pointed breasts until their nipples stood rock-hard and tingling under her arousal. Then her right hand slid down, over her belly, through the dark bush of her black pubis, the fingertips probing, seeking the enflamed core of her hunger. Eventually, exhausted, sobbing with cruel unfulfilment still, in spite of the soaring heights of passion to which she had peaked, she rolled over onto her stomach, her feet drumming, her hands clutching at the coverlet she was staining with her muffled tears.

She woke hours later, still lying naked on top of the covers. She was chilled, her head was throbbing, her eyes puffed with weeping. She heard someone in the bathroom, then the flushing of the lavatory. A glance at the clock showed it was half past twelve. She grabbed her dressing gown, pulled it on, and went down the corridor. She opened her sister's door without knocking. Anne was just removing her gown. 'You still awake?' She smiled brightly, but Charlotte detected the hidden wariness in her look, and felt a grim satisfaction beginning to stir.

Anne sat at her dressing table. She was wearing a black strapless bra and tiny pants. Charlotte glanced swiftly about her. 'No tights?' The casual tone could not hide the tautness.

Anne responded with a gurgling laugh. 'It was a bit hot. I slipped them off.'

'Whereabouts? In Wolfgang's room?'

Now, Anne tossed her hair back and half turned. The lovely face lifted, with that challenging look, inviting retribution. 'What's wrong, big sister? Jealous, are we?'

The colour rose in Charlotte's features. 'Was that all you slipped off?' Her teeth were clenched, her nostrils flared.

All the danger signs were there. Anne did not ignore them. With that wicked sense of devilment, she courted them, tormenting Charlotte beyond control. She stood and faced her, reached behind to snap open the bra fastener, and let the tiny garment fall free of her breasts to the floor. Without taking her steady eyes off her sister, she slipped her thumbs into the elastic of the briefs and pushed them down, bending to step out of them.

'You little slut!' Charlotte hissed. She stepped forward menacingly, but Anne stood her ground.

'Going to thrash me, are you? You might as well. Because the answer's yes, he's fucking me, big sister! Fucking me till my teeth rattle!' She laughed. 'Go on then!' Anne whispered. 'Now you try, eh? But believe me, you won't be as good as Wolfgang, I can promise you!'

Anne's words were more devastating than any blow. They struck through to Charlotte's heart with sickening effect. Anne could see the locked muscles go limp. Charlotte gave a shudder, and suddenly she turned away and slumped on the bed, her grief tearing through her in jagged sobs while Anne stayed motionless, making no move either to repel or comfort her.

It was Wolfgang himself who introduced Richard Audley, her future husband, to Anne, and encouraged their romance. Only then did he first take any real note of Charlotte. But if she expected him to court her, to establish the intimate gentleness he had exhibited towards Anne, she was disappointed. But then Charlotte could never make up her own mind what she really wanted. 'Don't you know?' she said tartly, when he first showed interest. 'Hasn't Anne told you? I'm a lesbian.'

He smiled with infuriating calm. 'Nonsense! You're far too pretty to confine yourself to your own sex. After all, variety is the spice of life.'

To her own disgust, his compliment set her heart beating faster. Secretly, she had indeed always considered herself good-looking, not in the softly feminine mould of her sister, but in a more distinctive and subtly intense way. She knew that certain girls found her attractive, just as she found their femininity arousing. She had never developed any relationship with a man sufficiently to learn how they viewed her. She knew that part of the thrill she could achieve with a girl was her sense of power. She could not imagine herself being able to keep that sense of power with a man. Any man who allowed her to do that would not be a true man at all, and she would despise him.

But she was totally unprepared for the shattering intensity the surrender of that power would bring with Wolfgang Labat. When he first asked her out on a proper date, she had wondered where he would take her. To a concert? Or for a meal? Confused, and untypically shy, she had asked him over the phone where they were going. 'Leave it to me,' he said abruptly.

'But what shall I wear? Do I need to dress up? A posh frock?'

He chuckled. 'We're not going to the ball, Cinders! But wear something nice and frilly! Something feminine and sexy!'

She discovered she was blushing hotly when she put down the phone. And disturbingly close to tears. He was making fun of her! She thought of Anne's dainty underwear, the passion he must have enjoyed with her. In a petty mood of defiance, she wore her smartest suit, cut very stylishly to reveal her slim figure, but severe in its elegance. To go with it, she wore a pale-blue shirt and dark silk tie, her hair expensively cut short on her neck and around her ears. Braless, her breasts were scarcely discernible under the hugging waistcoat, which matched the jacket and trousers. She looked temptingly androgynous, she felt. Not butch, yet somehow teasingly stating her sexual ambivalence.

She drew several appreciative looks from members of both sexes as they ate at the unfashionable restaurant he had chosen. In the taxi, he gave the driver his address. 'But it's only eight-thirty!' Her voice betrayed her surprise. 'Aren't we . . .?' He let her flounder. She was glad the dimness hid her blushes. 'I thought we'd be going somewhere,' she ended feebly.

His laugh was deep, and oddly, disturbingly, caressing. He patted her trousered knee, letting his hand

16

rest there for a long second. 'I've fed you. I can wine you at home if you want. Enough of the formalities!'

His flat was coldly functional. She had expected it to be more expressive of his deeply artistic personality, a place of refined comfort and taste. Though perfectly clean and adequately furnished, it was cold and impersonal, adding to her suddenly insecure mood. 'Take your jacket off.' She didn't like the way he gave orders when he spoke to her, but she found herself obeying. His smile was mocking as he stood and surveyed her, in the tight waistcoat, and the long shirtsleeves, complete with jewelled cufflinks at the folded cuffs. 'How very laddish! I guess you're making a point with this gear.' Without asking what she wanted to drink, he poured two glasses of dark wine and handed her one. 'Unless you'd rather have beer?' he said, in that taunting tone.

'No. I'm on my best behaviour tonight,' she fired back. 'I haven't even brought my pipe and baccy. Aren't I a good girl?'

'Would you rather be a good *boy*?'

'No, thank you. I'm quite happy the way I am.'

'And what way is that? Or are you not really sure? Maybe I can help you make up your mind. Shall I call you Charley? Shall I pretend you're my cute little boyfriend?'

She suddenly realised how frightened of him she was. She was trembling, and so unaccustomedly weak she could not move. She was staring at him as if hypnotised. 'Please,' she murmured feebly.

He took the drink from her nerveless fingers and put it on the sideboard. 'Come here, my little queer!' When she didn't move, he grabbed her, spun her round and pushed her down onto her knees in front of the sofa. His hand clamped brutally on the back of her neck and forced her head down into the cushions, folding her forwards. With his other hand he was ripping brutally at the fastening of her trousers, tearing open the fly and dragging them off her hips.

'Please, no! I've never – I'm a virgin!'

He stopped, genuinely amazed. 'What? Not another one!'

She was weeping, deeply ashamed, and struggled blindly to haul up her trousers, to secure her flapping shirt tails. But now he bellowed with laughter. 'That's all right. Even better!' She screamed again as he grabbed her once more. This time, he seized her legs and pulled her over onto her back on the rug. She kicked out helplessly as he pulled off her shoes, then seized the pants, still unfastened at the waist, and swiftly hauled them down off her kicking legs. Even in her fear, and her shame, she was deeply aware of the indignity, and the ridiculous spectacle, of her waving feet clad in the short navy blue socks, her fully clothed upper body in the knotted tie, the shirt and waistcoat, while he bent and roughly tugged the plain white cotton briefs from her. She stopped kicking out and instead tried to pull the shirt down to hide her sex with its cap of black hair.

She was startled at his strength, while, at the same time, she was aware of her own feebleness, her inability to fight back. It was a novel sensation. Her struggles had all but ceased, except for that rapid little movement of her feet, the scissoring thighs that intensified that melting excitement between them. The sick thought that he had also taken Anne's virginity passed through her racing mind.

But then she experienced the greatest, most fearful shock of all. As she felt that brutal column forcing and thrusting – so that all at once she yielded, feeling the ring of muscle relax, the conqueror gain entrance and sink deep – a thrill of unholy ecstasy flooded through every fibre of her being.

Three

Twenty years later, Charlotte blushed hotly as she felt again the helplessness she had experienced then in the presence of this compelling figure. She recalled even the sound of his quiet scourging laughter on that night long ago, when she had collapsed onto the floor, weeping desolately, her lower half naked, her face hidden in her folded arms.

'What's wrong, Charley? Didn't you like playing the girl after all? Would you have preferred to play the boy? Still be as pure as the driven snow for the next rampant young stallion who wants his wicked way with you?'

Unable to look at him, or to stem her tears or stop her trembling, she had made use of his tiny bathroom, hauled on her trousers, and hurried shamefully away. She had vowed never to see him again. The very idea of those deep mocking eyes gazing at her, into her, made her shiver with revulsion. She was glad the newly wed Anne was still away in Europe with Richard. She saw virtually no one, and hardly stirred from the house for days, until her parents became worried for her. Then he called for her one morning, beaming his charming smile and bearing a huge bunch of flowers. He held out his hand, and she took it, and went with him.

And he had never relinquished that power over her, in spite of the long intervals, sometimes years at a time, between their meetings; like the long gap which had followed the days of that first whirlwind possession of her, and the terrible guilt of the secret she had kept from him and from the world throughout these intervening years. It was the vivid memory of it now which made her so untypically plead with him for gentleness and restraint towards her niece. And, as she expected, his response was that deep mocking laugh. 'As gentle as you've been with her these past six years?'

She crimsoned again. 'She had to be disciplined. She was too much like her mother, too inclined to waywardness.' She felt the colour mounting. There was a look almost of desperation as she faced his gaze and she felt that inner tremble, the clutch of fear. 'And the boy. They both need discipline.'

'Ah, yes! That beautiful boy! The gorgeous and mysterious Toni!'

Her panic mounted at the mention of his name. 'It's true. I've been strict with both of them. I've taught them both to be obedient.'

'You and that dike of yours. Davies, wasn't it? You've still got her, I suppose? Well then. You'll have to play your part, my dear. I'm horny as hell already.'

His eyes bored into her and she felt utterly naked before him. She was sweetly, cruelly aware of her body, of every thrumming nerve, and of a melting hunger deep at her core. She bit her lip hard, almost moaning aloud at her need and her helplessness. She swallowed, finding herself unable to speak.

'It's been so long.' The timbre of his voice stirred her, passing through her like a caress. 'Come here!' The quietness of tone did nothing to diminish the implacable demand.

20

She found herself almost stumbling as she obeyed him. 'Wolfgang! I have to go –'

He ignored her murmured plea and chuckled again. 'I see you've even dressed like a girl for me. How touching!' He took her by the shoulders and spun her round, then his fingers quickly found the zip at the back of her neck and drew it down its full length to the swell of her buttocks.

She felt the tears stinging behind her eyelids. 'Please!' she whispered faintly. 'Someone will come. Max. Holger –'

'Surely your little girl is well-enough trained to stay where she is until she's sent for? And as for Holger – we have no secrets between us. He is my, er, Davies!' His laugh rang tauntingly. He peeled the silk dress down off her shoulders and her arms. It clung to her hips, until his firm tug sent it cascading down her limbs to lie about her feet. She hung her head, blushing, the tears ever closer, as she endured the slow sweeping survey he made of her. 'My word!' he chortled appreciatively. 'You certainly *have* dressed for me, haven't you?'

She was wearing a black body, satin-panelled and trimmed across the bosom with lace. The brief cups allowed the pale swell of her breasts freedom almost to the nipples. The rest of the garment was equally brief, disappearing into the divide of her well-rounded bottom, and cut so high at the crotch that the jut of her hip bones was fully revealed, the satin just hiding the distinct pout of her mons. A double tier of narrow lace at her loins added to the dainty provocativeness, enhanced by the long slender straps of the suspenders, which followed the full curves of her behind and bisected the white expanse of thigh leading to the tops of the darkly transparent stockings. The effect was completed by the narrow four-inch heels, making her a good deal taller than the professor.

'How divine!' He waited a long second, his finger crooked under her chin, staring into her eyes, which shone now with the tears filling them. She watched that sensual mouth approaching hers, saw the lips parting, felt them seal themselves to her with total possession. His tongue drove in deep, sucking every vestige of resistance, every iota of self-awareness from her. The room spun, she was fighting for air, her breasts pressing as though they would burst from the confines of their flimsy cover. She would have sunk to the floor if he had not held her fiercely to him.

She found herself lying face down on his desk, her head turned sideways, her cheek resting on the large blotting pad of pale-green paper framed by the engraved leather. A silver-framed photograph stood inches away, so close her vision was too distorted to make out the figures. She was standing with her feet well apart, her legs straight, knees locked. Thus her bottom was raised high for his leisurely inspection. She closed her eyes. A tear hovered on her lashes, fell to her cheek, ran down onto the paper and was soaked up.

She heard the drawer of the desk open, then shut. The blow, when it fell, with no warning except that micro-second of disturbed air pushed ahead of it like a bow wave, was a cracking flare of fire, clean as lightning, which shot through her, snatching her breath and burning her quivering flesh like the burn of ice. She tried to smother the scream in her throat, the fierce need to claw at her scorching bottom, the agony homing in now to that thick red brand, neatly horizontal, across the centre of the twin cheeks. Through the dancing tears, she saw him, his face alight with pleasure. He was holding a short thick leather tawse. 'Keep still, Charlotte.' His voice was gentle, rich with affection, his expression almost loving.

He stood there, smiling. With a sob that shook her, she once more placed her upper body across the desk. This time, he put his left hand heavily on the base of her neck, between her shoulders, before he struck again. She jerked, but she was exerting every ounce of control over her body, her muscles locked to prevent movement. The torment burnt through her again, but she managed to smother the scream in her throat. Instead, a gasp and a low groan were the only sounds after the crisp snap of the leather on her flesh.

She fought to muffle her sobbing, and wondered distractedly how many more blows she could take before all her control snapped. The pressure of his hand on her neck was brutal as the tawse cut into her for the fourth time, and she was glad, for without it she would have succumbed, would have howled and torn herself free, to caper in shocking degradation. Her buttocks were deeply marked now with the crimson bars, and rising in blisters along the edges of the parallel strokes.

Dimly, she realised that the beating had ceased, the flayed skin throbbing in a steady torment. The suspender straps at the rear had parted with the stockings at the force of the blows, and dangled loosely. The undergarment had all but disappeared in the cleft of the buttocks, and had proved no deterrent to the cracking strokes on her bared flesh.

She hung there over the desk, weeping quietly, unaware almost of her appearance or her surroundings, her mind fragmenting with the swirling sensations of throbbing torment and the savage pulses of desire that soaked the narrow strip of cloth tightly hugging her vulva. Consciousness of what was happening around her returned, and she cried out in fresh pain at the harsh touch of his fingers in the very centre of her abused flesh. They dug into that deep cleft, thrust inside the narrow band of her under-garment, dragging it clear. He had taken a small knife from the drawer wherein had lain the tawse, and now he sawed roughly through the material, severing it easily. She felt it give, her bemused mind spinning in wonder as he lifted it from her branded backside and thrust it high up her back. Her pungent sex, too, was released from its tight confinement while the sus-penders, still attached at the front, dangled limply from the sagging stockings. But the ridiculous indig-nity was forgotten as, with a whimper, she felt him prising open her scarred cheeks and felt the merciless boring of his rampant prick. 'No! Don't! Please!' she whispered, hating herself for her own desire.

His chuckle, the hot brushing of his lips against her ear as he leaned crushingly over her, were both hateful and sweet, as was the final yielding of that hard little ring of hidden muscle to his potent penetration.

It was the pressure of her bladder that finally decided Max to act. The exploration of her new bedroom had not taken long. Though perfectly comfortable, and adequately furnished, there was not much to dwell on. A bed, with a low wooden locker beside it, on which stood a small lamp; a neutral carpet in a flecked pattern, in keeping with the pale plain colour of the walls and curtains. She parted them, but could see nothing but a dim reflection of herself and the room in the blackness outside. The window was double-glazed, and securely sealed. She tried to open the narrow section at one end, but it was locked. There was no sign of a key. A dressing table with a single mirror, a chest of drawers, and a single wardrobe made up the rest of the furniture, except for a low hard-backed chair standing against the wall by the door.

It did not take her long to unpack her clothes and put them away, or to spread her modest collection of cosmetics, along with her comb and hairbrush, on the top of the dressing table. As she did so, her mind reviewed the weird scene that had taken place in the room below. 'You belong to the Maestro now.' Her aunt's words re-echoed in her brain. They disturbed her greatly, more so because of the strange excitement they aroused in her.

Again, she experienced a deep sense of longing for Toni's presence. She wished fervently for the security of lying once more in his arms, and for the oddly innocent pleasure they had known in childhood of those embraces, the slow and languorous kisses which made even their breaths a shared delight.

She felt a sudden renewed urge for the toilet, but still she hesitated for quite a while, sitting trancelike on the bed, trying to divert her mind from the need to pee. Professor Labat's rather creepy manservant, the tall saturnine figure of Holger, had told her in that gruff abrupt voice of his to wait until the professor sent for her. But this is ridiculous! she scolded herself. If she didn't go to the lavatory right now she'd wet herself. She went to the door and turned the handle. It was stuck! She jerked it several times, pushed harder and harder against it. It wouldn't yield. Shocked, she realised that she was locked in. Holger must have locked it as he'd left, without her noticing. She'd been too glad to see the back of him to observe his departure closely.

She rattled the lever up and down, feeling foolish, and suddenly tearful. She knocked on the door with her knuckle, softly at first, then, her helpless anger returning, more loudly, banging on the wooden panel with the heel of her hand. 'Somebody! Let me out, please. I need to go to the bathroom.' She stopped, pressed her ear to the door, and listened intently. Silence. Perhaps they had all gone out. The house seemed deserted.

The pressure increased, her muscles achingly tensed. She banged and shouted again, then the tears came, and she sat down on the edge of the bed, hot with the humiliation of it all. She was sitting, weeping and moaning softly to herself, rocking back and forth and with her fists jammed tightly in the apex of her thighs and belly when, at long last, she heard soft footfalls just a fraction before, with a click, the handle turned and the door was opened. 'I need the loo!' she gasped, red-faced, her cheeks glinting with tears, but no longer mindful of the spectacle. 'Where is it? Quick!'

She thrust past the grinning Holger, glaring at him wildly. He nodded towards it and she raced down the corridor, opened the door on the right, and saw a spacious bathroom with corner tub and a glassed-in shower stall – and, ahead of her, a blessed lavatory pedestal. He was standing there outside the door when she emerged, pink-faced, but with relief now. Still with that mocking grin, he tut-tutted at her, waving a finger admonishingly. 'No locked doors here, missy. Anywhere!' He nodded at the doorway through which she had just emerged.

She jerked her head expressively in the direction of her bedroom. 'You could've fooled me!' she answered angrily.

'I meant for *you*,' he said, still with that infuriating grin. 'Remember next time. You don't want to get off on the wrong foot here, do you?'

'My word! How good your English is!' Her tone was bitingly sarcastic. 'Holger, isn't it? German? You work for the Maestro, don't you? His manservant? Will you be acting as my maid as well?'

He was still smiling, but she saw the pale eyes narrow a little. 'Of course! If you need one! I can dress you – and bathe you, if that's what you want.'

'*No, thank you!*' She gave a deep exaggerated shudder. 'What a horrible thought! I can manage quite well for myself, thanks.' She turned away, but could not prevent herself from pausing and adding, 'Where's Antonio's room? When is he coming? I thought he'd be here.'

The grin broadened once more, even more unpleasantly. 'Oh, don't you worry your pretty head about him. He'll be along some time, I expect. But I think the Maestro just wants to enjoy having you all to himself for a while first.'

'Where the devil is she? Why do I have to stay here? I thought we were both going to Professor Labat's? What's happening?'

'My word! All these questions! Who's a cheeky boy then?' Davies' gruff Estuary accent seemed to give added insult to her mockery.

Toni's face flamed and he could not hide his agitation. His voice cracked, shrill with his concern. He felt doubly vulnerable and unsure now that he was alone, cut off from Max, from whom he had been inseparable for the past six years. In spite of himself he felt his inner weakness assail him, his emotion rising like a welling sob. It showed as he faltered, the catch in his breath audible. 'Where's Aunt Charlotte, Davies?' But his voice was quieter, there was an undertone of pleading, and Davies felt a deep throb of satisfaction.

'More bloody questions, is it? You're beginning to get on my tits, Master Toni, and that ain't a good idea. You should know that. Don't you worry your pretty little head about where Miss Charlotte's got to, or what old fancy-pants Max is up to. You got me to look after you, all right? I think you'd better have an early night, sweetheart, don't you? Come on now. Get undressed and have your bath, and I'll do you some supper. OK?'

'Look! I'm not a kid any more!' He glared at her, but his voice shook even more, and he could feel his heart thumping in his ribs. All at once he was vividly aware of the quiet of the old house, and their isolation. The late afternoon sunlight fell in a broad bar on the bed, its cover still rumpled and indented with his shape where he had been lying dozing and reading for the past several hours.

The strong plain face split in a mocking grin as Davies' tall muscular figure faced him mockingly. 'Is that a fact now? A big hairy-arsed man now, are we?'

The old weakness assailed him, churning his gut, making his limbs tremble, insidiously arousing. He cleared his throat. 'Don't, Davies. Please!' It came out as a scratchy, pleading whisper almost, and the deep rippling gurgle of her laugh made him shiver. The large firm hands reached out, caught his thin wrists, pulled him irresistibly forwards, then thrust him easily backwards onto the bed.

When her hands released him, he lay back, struggling to keep the tears from flowing. 'You're just a bad little boy, ain't you, Toni, my love? A wicked little feller who don't know what he wants to be. Ain't that right?' Her strong fingers were plucking remorselessly at his belt, tugging down the zip fastener of his flies, then those hands were rough as they dragged down the tight jeans, fought them off his narrow hips and down to lie like bonds across his thighs, just above the knees. The swell of his genitals filled the small black silk pouch of his briefs, and Davies chuckled deeply, pulling the shirt up to expose them fully.

'Look at that! See what I mean? Little girlie's knicks they are! Borrow them off Maxie, did you? And what you got inside? Let's see just how big a man you really are, eh, Toni?'

The fingers moved once more, peeling away his final cover. His knees jerked reflexively, an instinctive attempt at shielding, then straightened again on the bed at the slight pressure as she leaned in over him. His hands, too, which had sprung to restrain hers, fell away, and lay helpless at his sides as she took the satin slippery softness in her grip, felt its stirring throb, and savoured the whimpering sigh of his yielding to her.

Four

'What the hell's happened to *you*?'

Charlotte held up one hand, and continued her slow stiff walk over to the table, where she placed her handbag. 'Just come up and help me out of these things!' she groaned, moving painfully to mount the stairs and to head for her room. 'Where's our boy?' She spoke quietly, nodding in the direction of Toni's room.

Davies grinned. 'Poor little lamb's having an early night. Not too good. Missing his other half, I guess.'

Charlotte was too preoccupied to worry overlong at the note of mean humour and triumph in Davies' voice. Safely behind the closed door of her room, she stood at the foot of the bed. 'Get these things off me.'

Moving quickly, Davies undid the thin dress and eased it over Charlotte's head. Her eyes quickly took in the dangling suspender ribbons, the pale stockingless legs, the ruin of the black undergarment, and she recalled the cutting insolence of her earlier remark when she had helped Charlotte to dress. 'Done up like a flaming stripagram!' she had sneered. Now she gasped in shock as Charlotte gingerly lifted the ragged severed tail of the body to expose her flanks, with the livid brand of the strap marks across the full rounds, the edges raised in darkening hard blood blisters.

'You silly sick mare!'

'Shut up!' Charlotte snarled, blushing deeply in her discomfort. 'Just remember who you're talking to! Come on! Get this thing off me!'

'Yes, ma'am.' It was Davies' face now which was brick-red, but more with repressed anger than embarrassment. Quickly, she unfastened the hooks between the shoulder blades, eased the cups from the full breasts and carefully drew the strip of silk down over the hips and legs. Moaning now with tired relief, Charlotte carefully laid herself face down across the bed. She turned her head to the side, resting her cheek on her folded arms.

'He did this to you? The Maestro?'

'Don't interrogate me. Not tonight. I've had as much as I can take.' She could not keep the tone of pleading, almost of defeat, from her voice. There was no more anger.

'You're mad. You *and* him, the pair of you! To let him do this! Absolutely raving bonkers!'

'Please, Davies. Don't go on, I beg you. Not now. Run my bath, will you?'

After she had tenderly ministered to Charlotte in the fragrant foam-filled tub, and patted her dry to the accompanying gasps and flinches at the lightest touch on the abused flesh, Davies once more helped her mistress to stretch out face down on the bed. She brought a jar of cold cream, perched beside the prone figure, and gently smeared the area until Charlotte's buttocks gleamed in the subdued lamplight. 'You'll have to lie on your front tonight,' she advised. She brought a plain cotton pyjama jacket from the drawer. 'Here. Put this on. I don't suppose you'll be able to bear even the sheet over you tonight.'

Charlotte turned awkwardly and patted the bed space beside her. 'Come on. Stay with me. Just cuddle me. I'm badly in need of some TLC.'

'Oh God! What the hell am I going to do with you,

eh?' But Davies smiled with deep appreciation, and eagerly peeled off the dark jogging-suit to join her employer and enfold her in her loving embrace.

The corridor was empty, and, for a second, Max stood indecisively. Should she return to her room? She had half expected Holger to appear to tell her what to do. Then she heard music coming from downstairs. She descended quickly. The sounds were loud now, coming from the open doorway across the spacious hallway from the room where she had been introduced to Professor Labat. The rich sounds of a Mozart symphony beckoned her. The Maestro was stretched out on a long sofa in a comfortably furnished drawing room, made more welcoming by the flickering flames and the glowing logs of a realistic-looking fire with a high marble surround. He looked up with a beaming smile and flicked a remote at a cabinet in a corner, killing the music immediately.

'Ah, my dear! How timely! Come and join me for a glass of sherry. Or something soft, if you prefer.' He waved her to come to him. She approached diffidently, but he did not move his feet to make room for her, and she turned away to one of the deep armchairs across the large oriental rug in front of the fireplace. 'No, no! Here. Sit on the floor beside me. Let me look at you.' Blushing, she did as she was bidden, modestly folding her feet to her left side, but again he gestured with his hand. 'No, no, no! Don't be so repressed, Max! Cross your legs. At the ankles. Raise your knees, that's it!' More embarrassed than ever, she sat as he had dictated, like a guide round a campfire, facing him, close enough for him to reach out and stroke the side of her cheek and her dark hair. She was aware of her jutting knees, exposed as the short hem of her dress stretched tautly across her lap.

'Barefoot, I see. Taking me at my word, yes? But delightfully dressed. How charming! What a delicately lovely little creature you are!'

She blushed and glanced down at the floral pattern of her thin summer frock. She didn't like it, thinking it far too old-fashioned and childish, and wondered if the great man was poking gentle fun at her. 'I wasn't sure,' she said hesitantly, 'what to wear. Normally I wear jeans, or a jogging-suit bottom.'

'No jeans or trousers, please! Not in this house!' The firm incisiveness of tone made it a command, despite the 'please'. She started as he reached down, gripped her right ankle firmly, and raised her foot high, resting the heel in the crease of his belly and thigh. She could feel the fine material of his trousers rubbing softly against her skin. She flinched at the strange tickling sensation of his thumb tracing the high narrow arch and the instep, before his fingers seized on and explored her toes, shaking them like an adult playing with an infant. 'How cold! But how enchanting!' He chuckled and held onto her, so that she had to lean backwards and stretch her hands behind her to prevent herself from toppling over. She was also deeply aware of how high her dress had ridden, revealing the full expanse of her leg – and, no doubt, she speculated, the white V of her briefs.

Holger entered, carrying a tray with bottles and glasses on it. He smiled, and Max's thigh muscles tightened as she made to withdraw her foot. The professor's grip clamped down, stopping her from doing so, and, for an instant, she thought he was going to keep her imprisoned in the ridiculous posture. After a deliberate pause, he released her, and she sat hastily, rearranging her displaced dress as best she could.

'You will take a sherry, Max? You're grown up now, after all! It's very fine – not too dry for you, I think. Very rich.' His hand remained resting on her head all the while Holger was pouring the drinks. She felt like a cat curled up at its master's feet. Which was, she guessed, exactly how he wanted her to feel. And she sipped obediently, her head down, demure, staring into her lap, and feeling the caressing warmth of the fire on her body.

'Now, as you know, Max, your aunt has entrusted you to me. That means you are in my care, and I have full jurisdiction over you. You are my responsibility – in effect you belong to me. Do you understand?' In spite of all her mental preparation, his words shocked her, and she glanced up quickly, her eyes widening. Her heart was racing, her throat felt closed. 'Answer me, child!'

The words, though spoken quietly, resonated with his authority. She shivered. 'Yes, Maestro!' she managed, in a throaty whisper.

'Good. That means you will obey me without question, and without hesitation. Always. Do you understand *that*?'

'Yes, Maestro.'

'Good. Then, as long as you do so, we should have no trouble. You have a delicate beauty. You remind me very much of your lovely mother. And you have a rare talent, as she did. We shall make the utmost of both. Now. Come closer, Max. Kneel up. Give me your hands. That's it.'

Her knees pressed together. She could feel the upholstery of the sofa covering them. She sat back on her heels. He held her hands firmly in both of his. She was surprised at how strong and rough his fingers felt, how large as they covered hers. Now she was overwhelmed, weak and giddy with the power of him. His dark eyes bored into hers, pinning her. She could not look away. 'You must be truthful with me always, you hear? Never try to deceive me in any way. Your obedience must be absolute. Is that understood?'

His hands were squeezing hers, pulling her ever closer, his face inches from hers, filling her vision. She could feel his breath engulfing her, and she gazed back, in fear and in appeal. She nodded. 'Answer me!'

The softly spoken words throbbed through her and thundered with her racing blood. Her mouth was open, dry as sandpaper. 'Yes, Maestro!' She nodded, and, suddenly, he gave a deep booming laugh, releasing the tension, lightening his hold on her.

'Now a few questions, that's all. So that I can get to know you. Are you a virgin?'

The matter-of-fact tone made the question even weirder. She felt the flooding crimson spreading up seemingly through every part of her, and she gave a kind of sob. Again, he chuckled. 'Surely, it's not too difficult? Has a boy – or a girl – had sex with you?'

She gasped at his shocking brutality. This time she could not find words, and merely shook her head rapidly. The tears sparkled in her eyes. 'Oh, come now, Max! Why so coy? I'm sure you know all about such things. You and that pretty cousin of yours! He is some sort of relation, isn't he? He must be, surely? You look so alike. Some relative on your father's side, isn't that it?'

'A second cousin, actually. Or something like that. I'm not really sure. Aunt Charlotte doesn't like to talk about it. He was abandoned as a baby. Put into a children's home. It was awful for him.' Her eyes darkened with her compassion. 'I had no idea – mummy and daddy never mentioned anything about it. It was a complete surprise when Aunt Charlotte brought him home.' The sadness cleared magically. 'Now I can hardly remember what it was like without him. We're just like the twins everyone thinks we are!'

'To get back to my question. What about it? You and Toni – you must have talked. You must have experimented, the pair of you. Your aunt has told me how naughty you were when you were kids. Always sneaking into each other's beds, even taking baths together.'

'We never – I mean – we didn't – haven't – not proper sex!' she gasped.

'How about *improper*?' he chortled. 'Are you saying you're intact then? If I examine you, will I find your hymen barring the way?' She hung her head, and began to cry forlornly, like a little girl.

His palm, heavy and warm, lay on the nape of her neck, his fingers fanning under her dark hair. They spread, tracing the angularity of her jaw line, toying with her ear and the swell and hollow behind it, and she shivered again at the slow caresses. He nipped the small lobe hard, and with the pain she felt a frisson of excitement stir through her as the muscles of her lower belly and the vaginal passage tightened. His broad thumb was now firmly wiping the tear stains from her cheek.

'Good girl. I think you've been as honest with me as you *can* be. Once you get used to our ways here, I know you'll be very happy.' He lifted her so that she was kneeling upright again before him, and she wiped quickly with the back of her hand at the traces of wetness still on her cheeks.

He smiled fondly at her, and she felt a surge of relief and even gratitude for this evidence of his warmness towards her. 'Unfortunately, I have to go out this evening. But Holger will look after you. You'll eat in your room. Holger will see to everything. Go now.'

His last words confused and alarmed her. She rose, and stood uncertainly. As though aware of her disturbed thoughts, he added, in his deep calm voice, 'Needless to say, in my absence, Holger has my full authority over you. You will obey him as you would me. You understand that?'

In the pause that followed, she felt the terror of a trapped panic-stricken bird fluttering in an enclosed room. But she knew he was waiting implacably for her answer, and she knew what that answer must be. 'Yes, Maestro.'

She sensed, in spite of her lowered head, the mocking contempt in Holger's eyes as he held the door open for her to pass through. 'Up you go!' It was an order, and she moved with reluctant submission to the staircase. At the top, he took her arm firmly. His grip was not excessive, but it was not the respectful touch of a servant. He led her to her room. 'Get undressed. I'll bring your supper up in a while. It's an early night for you, my girl. Busy day tomorrow. We want you nice and fresh.' His grin was as infuriating as ever.

'It's far too early. I'm not a kid. I don't go to bed at this time. I'll probably watch TV for a while. I'll eat *down*stairs.'

She cried out in alarm as he suddenly reached out and seized both her arms in his strong grip. His hands squeezed the soft flesh, encircling it like manacles, and he shook her gently. 'Listen, sugar! You'd better get things straight very quickly, otherwise you're in for a very rough time. You're in our charge now. Oh yes! You heard the Maestro. Not just him, but *me*, too! You do as you're told, my girl. If you don't –' the pause was sinister, his smile even more intimidating. '– kid or not, I'll turn you over and give you a spanking that'll make you think your pretty arse is on fire! OK?' Ignoring her squeak of indignant shock, he added, 'Now get your nightie on before I'm back with your grub, otherwise I'll do it myself – after I've put you over my knee!'

When he had left her, she could no longer hold back the tears. Her lower lip trembled, then she broke down, sobbing bitterly. Where are you, Toni? she wondered desperately. She thought of her aunt going off, abandoning her here so cruelly. Of course, Aunt Charlotte had always been strict with her young charges, to the point of tyranny, one might say. But her domination, and that of the mannish Davies, had been something the children had grown up with and were used to. This new alien regime was terrifying. She felt her cheeks hot as she relived the feel of the Maestro's hands clamped about her ankle, the lifting of her leg, the shocking nature of his questioning of her. And now this brute threatening her. But the reminder of his last words forced her to drag her clothes off quickly. In spite of her alarm at his return, she was afraid it might very well be worse for her if she did not obey him. He might well carry out his threat, and there was no one left here to prevent him. She was just wriggling the loose nightshirt over her head when the door opened, and she gave a small cry as she dragged the cotton down to cover her nakedness.

He grunted, and gave a cruel laugh. 'Hardly anything there worth hiding!'

She blushed deeply. His sarcasm and his mockery of her added to her degradation. 'You've got a pretty little boy's ass!' he taunted. 'Like your pretty cousin. Maybe we'll bring a blush to *both* your backsides before too long!'

He drew back the sheets and merely nodded peremptorily at the bed, and she suffered in silence the humiliation of his contemptuous stare as she climbed in, self-consciously tugging at the short hem of the garment to try to hide her further exposure as she did so. The word 'cousin' sparked yet again the disturbing speculation. She experienced that deep surge of longing and fear, as she wondered why Toni had not entered this strange new world with her. Where was he? Why wasn't he here, at her side?

* * *

Antonio woke with a jerk. His heart pounded again with fear. He looked up, and saw the features of his aunt. 'Oh, Aunt Charlotte! What time is it? I must have overslept.'

She whipped the sheet off him and his hands flew to cover his genitals, which were swollen and throbbing with the nature of his sleeping emotions. He was even more embarrassed as he remembered the events of the previous night, and Davies' visit. He lay back weakly once more, his head down on the bed covers. But then he flinched at the light touch of her hands on his wrists. His face burnt anew at the reaction of his flesh, and his helplessness to control it.

'My word! What have you been doing, you disgusting boy?'

He began to mumble his ashamed excuses, but was startled at the venom of her interruption. 'Stop your snivelling!' Her snarl took him by surprise. 'No doubt that's what your little bitch of a cousin is doing right now – or maybe she's got past that by now. Maybe she's howling with ecstasy instead, at the feel of a real man's prick boring through her for the first time!'

Antonio gave a small cry of shock and revulsion, which drew a vengeful smile of satisfaction from Charlotte. 'Oh, don't think I don't know what you and her get up to whenever our backs are turned! Or what our sweet little Maxie would like to get up to!' She stared pointedly at his loins once more and, in spite of himself, his hands moved once more to shield them. 'Though, as far as *you're* concerned, I don't think you've got the equipment to measure up to her demands, have you? Still, she won't be worried about that any more. Not if I know the Maestro – and I do, believe me! I know him very well! And so will Max, by now, I suspect. It's not just at things musical that he's a maestro. His skill with other instruments goes just as deep. And your little cousin will be learning a few new tunes, I can tell you!'

Five

Professor Labat came towards her with a piece of black velvet in his hand. She saw that it was an eye mask, held with a strip of elasticated material, which he proceeded to fit over her head. 'Oh no, please don't!' He laughed indulgently at her whispered protest.

'You'll find it helps amazingly to concentrate you, my dear. Being deprived of sight for a while will teach you that your musical talent must be the centre of your being, the very essence of who and what you are. Nothing else can ever be as important. *Nothing*!'

The last word was delivered with the force of a whiplash, and she jerked as though he had indeed struck her. The blackness which sealed her was a refinement of all that she had so far endured on this momentous day. Soon, the velvet pad was damp with her tears, and she was reduced to a blind quivering helplessness as she waited for what might follow.

She realised how little she knew of the man who now had total control over her. Even his name gave no clue, at least to her, of his origins. He displayed no trace of accent in his English. Only the precision of his speech gave a hint that he was not a native speaker.

In that way he was unlike his odious manservant, whose guttural tones already filled her with both revulsion and dread. The professor clearly trusted him implicitly. Max's embarrassment had been as extreme as ever when, after a largely sleepless night, she had been woken in the early morning by the blankets being violently plucked off, and finding herself lying there with the nightshirt rucked around her waist. Holger stood there, watching with delight until she came to full consciousness and strove to cover herself. She jumped, and gave a small cry of alarm at the touch of his hand on her shoulder. 'Come on. Up you get!'

He waited until she had scrambled from the bed and swiftly pulled her short towelling robe around her. 'I'll run your bath. Breakfast's at seven sharp, so you'll have to hurry. And don't forget what I said about locked doors, eh?'

He was still in the bathroom when she entered. There was that hateful grin again as he paused deliberately before exiting. She moved instinctively to click home the bolt, then, ashamed and full of self-scorn for her cowardice, withdrew her hand. Seething with helpless fury, she noted that he had already added some fragrant essence to the water and whipped it up to a froth of creamy bubbles. Evidently she was not to be allowed a choice over even such personal minutiae. But she was glad of those bubbles a minute later when, having just settled herself in the tub, she heard the door open, and he was standing there, gazing boldly and chuckling as she squealed and lowered herself so that her breasts were hidden from his view. 'Just checking!' He nodded at the door. 'You're learning, I see.'

Back in her room, she found him delving in her drawers, from which he had selected a pair of white briefs, a light cotton bra and the same dress she had worn the previous night. Face aflame, she opened her mouth to make heated protest at his familiarity. Then

41

she recalled the Maestro's cheerful command. 'No trousers in this house!' She stood facing Holger, her robe firmly belted in place. 'I'm a big girl now. Would you mind leaving? I can dress myself.' She was deeply relieved when, with one last expressive glance and deep chuckle, he departed.

Breakfast was set for her alone in the modern, modestly proportioned and equipped kitchen. Holger was there to serve it – a half grapefruit already segmented, followed by a lightly boiled egg and two slices of toast. 'I see! I don't get a choice!' she said, with what she hoped was a calm iciness.

'Of course you do, your Highness!' he answered even more sarcastically. 'You can take it or leave it.'

She was glad when he left her alone to eat. She had plenty of time to reflect and to feel nervous of what lay ahead in this unfamiliar territory, for it was just before eight o'clock before he returned. 'Come! Time to start work.' Heart pounding, she followed him to the room where she had played for the Maestro the previous day. There was no one there. He withdrew, closing the door behind him. She stared around her. The room was larger even than the drawing room across the corridor, and must run almost the length of the house. There were three French windows which broke up the long wall to her right, through which she could see a narrow strip of well-tended garden, bounded by a high brick wall, over which the foliage of trees showed. Sunlight fell in bars across the polished wooden floor. The room was bare of furniture, except for two or three upright wooden chairs, and the cabinet housing the impressive music system with its tall solid speakers. There was a wide row of shelves, compartmented to house vinyl records, CDs and stacks of scores and music sheets. Dull-metal music stands were scattered about the room, and, at the far end, stood a grand piano. Her knowledgeable eye took in the detail of the walls and ceiling modified to improve the acoustics.

All at once, she jumped at the rich wave of music that swept over her. It was the Beethoven violin concerto. She knew and loved every note, yet, in these weird circumstances, she was unable to take any comfort from its beauty. It soared at full volume from the high-quality music system. She tried to lock onto the majestic combination of the sounds, their beauty, and the pathos. She and Toni had so often been able to shut out the stifling restriction of their life by losing themselves in the music that had become the core of their existence. Yet now a strange and new phenomenon occurred. Far from enabling her to escape from her physical surroundings and her condition, the music seemed to fuse with a new bodily awareness of her fear and her nervousness. Suddenly faint, she groped for a chair near the source of the music and sank down on its hard wooden seat. As the sound rose to a crescendo, she could feel it literally vibrating through her, through her feet, up through her strangely heavy limbs, through the flimsy wooden frame of the chair, to the backs of her thighs, her throbbing buttocks and, finally and most disturbingly, to the narrow fissure of her sexual cleft. Her thighs tightened and pressed harder together, the deeply hidden muscles of her vagina began to spasm, spreading that insidiously weakening desire throughout her belly. Her breasts tingled and she felt her nipples bud to an erection. Like a skilful lover, the music roused her, seducing her, so that she could scarcely breathe. Her mouth hung open to draw in ragged breaths.

She slumped there when the last note died away, trembling and ashamed. She felt as though she wanted to weep for her own body's perfidy. Her whole frame leapt at the Maestro's sudden entrance, timed to perfection at the end of the piece of music. The tide of colour mounted through her hotly, as though he could read the shocking sensations she had just experienced. 'Right, Max, my darling! The work begins!'

The hours that followed were timeless for her. He was a hard taskmaster, as she had expected, but it was something far more powerful than that, she acknowledged. His strength was irresistible, inexorable; he took her over, body and will, until all she wanted was to please him, to do better for him, to win his praise. She forgot all the rest of it, the weirdness of her new regime here, the odiousness of the dreaded Holger – everything outside the confines of this room and the 'task' was forgotten.

He began again, taking her back to the very basics of the art, the foundations of her skill. Scales, arpeggios, bow strokes, up and down, the position of her body parts. Her embarrassment flared, and then was forgotten, or sacrificed to his undoubted genius. He stood close until she was almost in his embrace. His hands were on hers, and on her wrists. He caressed her arms, his touch feather-light, his fingers tender on the flexed muscle of forearm and wrist, her dipping shoulder, the growing moistness of the cavity of her armpit as he moulded her, over and over: wrist, elbow, arm, shoulder blade. She felt his breath warm on the back of her neck, on the bareness of skin as he stood so close behind her, leaning in to follow the flow of her body, the hands moving now to press into the hollow of her back, straightening her stance, feeling the ripple of muscle, the slight clenched swell of her buttocks, and down, brushing the backs of her thighs, then parting her legs, moving, caressing her inner thighs, the satin quality of the skin as he placed her like a sculptor creating his own beauty.

She was exhausted, trembling, aware of the pungency of her wet sweat-soaked body, to which the light material of her dress now clung. There had been a brief pause when Holger came in with scented herbal tea and a few dainty sandwiches, whose tiny triangular wedges she could not believe had been fashioned by those powerful ugly thick fingers. She had sat there, drained, gulping two cupfuls of the reviving hot liquid, wolfing down the food.

She had fully expected that to be the end of her practice for the day. She had never experienced such a fiercely exhausting session. But then, when Holger had cleared away the tea things, had come the mask. She was sitting in the uncomfortable hard-backed chair, and had stared disbelievingly as he drew near, then sealed the impenetrable darkness over her eyes before he placed her instrument and its bow in her nerveless fingers once more. The fingertips of her left hand were swollen, reddened, throbbing with pain. 'Please!' she whispered.

His breath was warm, she could feel his lips brushing her ear, so close was he. 'Nothing must ever come between you and the music. You feel it, I know. It must overcome everything, little one. It will always prevail.'

He called out scales, notes, runs, commanding her, demanding more and more. He moved away, then she heard the opening notes of the accompaniment to the Paganini concerto they had been working on through the morning. 'Play!'

She remained seated this time, leaning forwards, her upper body swaying into the melody, her right leg extended, her left foot tucked under the chair. She struggled, weeping into the mask as she fought to concentrate on her playing, to lose herself in it as he wished, as she knew she must learn to do. 'Play!' The voice was close again, she could sense him, near to her, in front of her. Yet her nerves jangled at the fall of those hands, firm now, on her legs above the knees.

Her insides seemed to melt, and she wondered dazedly if she had the strength necessary to obey him. The hands were moving upwards, warm and firmly gentle, the material of her dress riding up with them, until the fingers reached the very top of her thighs and traced the edges of her pants.

'Play!' She was crying audibly now, her breasts heaving, yet somehow she managed to keep the notes flowing, imperfect and tremulous though they might have been. 'Do not stop!' The husky whisper was a thundered command. His fingers were brushing over the thin cotton of the briefs, and she could feel the swelling of her throbbing sex, the wet folds of her vaginal lips coming up under the material, darkening, like a brass rubbing of a sacred tomb.

This was it. After all her wondering, all her feverish fantasies, and her fears, and her own shameful fearful explorations, this was the moment. He was about to take her virginity. To fuck you! a cruelly mocking voice screamed inside her head. And you're hot and wet and ready for it! If music be the food of love – play on! Her childish fancies of a love that would make the act one of flesh and spirit fused, crumbled. She had always thought until now that it would be Toni who would be her first true deflowerer. She had at times been deeply confused as to how she felt about it, except that somehow it had seemed inevitable, for somewhere in the base of her she had already recognised it should be so. One day. A day she had dreamed of, hotly sometimes, alone, but a day which she had been in no hurry to make a reality. They did, after all, belong to each other.

Except that now, bewilderingly, things were very different. 'You belong to me now,' the Maestro had told her. So had her aunt. 'You belong to the Maestro now,' she had said, delivering her to him. Her head swam with the force of that feeling, the words clanged imperiously in her head. Vaguely, she realised she was still obeying him, that implacable command to 'Play!' And all at once the music was not something she was conscious of, the instrument tucked at her chin, her hands busy, sawing out the melodious notes – it was all part of this monstrously inescapable tumult flowing through her, the remorseless strokes of those fingers, the fierce hunger of the need they were arousing, until . . . until with a final shock she realised she could not bear it a second longer, her body was about to betray her; she was not finally worthy of that – honour? – of her sacrifice, and she convulsed, her knees jerked up as her limbs writhed in the storm of the orgasm that swept her. The delicate instrument fell from her as she lurched forward, toppling from the chair, crying out harshly at the force still tearing at her, feeling her collision against the figure kneeling before her who pulled away suddenly, leaving her to sprawl, weeping and shuddering on the cold floor.

Engulfed in her despair, she did not hear him leave, and only gradually became aware of his absence. Still she did not think of removing the soaking mask or moving from the sprawled abandon of her pose on the floor. In fact, she thought of nothing for a long while, and, when the faculty of her reason returned, it brought only deep pain. She already knew from her aunt's graphic descriptions that her mother and Professor Labat had been lovers, even after Anne's marriage. He had told Max that she had the same beauty. Yet now she felt he had cast her aside, after the ease with which he had roused her and brought her to such a precipitate climax, like the youthful she-animal he so clearly considered her.

All these fragmented thoughts whirled crazily through her mind as she lay there in the silent room. The opening of a door caused her to scramble up in sudden horrified haste. She clawed at the mask, dragged it from around her eyes, and saw Holger's bulky frame grinning insufferably at her. 'Practice is over until this evening. You're to go to your room. Stay there and rest. Dinner will be early, at six.' He chuckled, staring at her so keenly that she could not meet his gaze despite her best effort to do so. 'You might like to take a shower. You look as though you've been working up a sweat!'

She thought wearily that there was little else that could make her feel more miserable or shock her after the past eventful hours. But she discovered she was wrong when she returned to her room after the much needed, reviving shower. There, in the centre of her neatly made bed, lay a package wrapped in bright gift paper. Intrigued, she read the small tag attached to it:

May you find many hours of pleasure with this instrument, in preparation for the greater pleasures yet to come.

Impatiently she stripped away the wrapping to reveal a narrow box of simulated leather, with delicate twin catches of gold-coloured metal. She snapped them open then gave a small squeal of amazement and dropped the box on the bed beside her. Nestling in folds of silk lay a most realistic flesh-coloured replica of a male penis, complete with fully engorged helm, and an erectile shaft roped with swollen veins writhing vinelike down its huge length, which must have been all of nine inches or more.

She gazed at it breathlessly – shocked, horrified, her cheeks hot then blanching, but chagrined at the immediate telltale throbbing response of her sexual orifice. There was a folded sheet of glossy paper over the instrument, which had fallen from the box as she dropped it. Fingers shaking, she opened it. With growing amazement, her eyes took in the explicit colour photographs, then turned to the text.

WELCOME TO THE WONDERFUL WORLD OF NIGHT RIDER!

Your instrument of pure pleasure has been designed to give you maximum thrill, wherever you want it. Just touch it to see it's realer than real! No more lonely nights! Those nights alone will now be the most magically satisfying you could ever dream of. Feel it, take it, taste it (see fig.3). It will give you all the thrills you could ever want, and more. What every woman longs for, nine throbbing inches of pure bliss, there for the taking, again and again and again. Night Rider will NEVER let you down. May your ride be the first of many! (Batteries supplied.)

As though it were an explosive device, she lifted it from its box. Immediately she shivered, her skin becoming covered with goose-bumps. The material, some kind of latex, actually felt like living tissue. Gently, her thumb pressed the great dome of the helm, and felt it give spongily, in contrast to the hardness of the shaft beneath those realistic veins. She discovered the concealed button in its base, pressed it, and almost dropped the instrument again at the thrilling deep hum of its vibration under her hand. Helpless to prevent herself, she lifted it, touched the tip of that giant helm to her right breast, to the pale tip of her nipple. She gasped at the powerful pulse that ran through her soft round, to disperse like ripples in a pool through her flesh. The little teat tingled, rock-hard, the electrical impulses transmitting through the sensitive tissue.

Utterly possessed with her magically revitalised and urgent need, she threw off her robe. In an agony of indecision, she glanced towards the door, vividly aware of the prohibition against locked doors so vigorously laid down by Holger. There was no key visible, and no inner bolt. Whimpering with fear and with the fire of her hunger, she slipped into bed, pulled the covers high around her shoulders, and turned on her side, away from the door. She drew up her knees, splaying wide her thighs, and touched the tip of the phallus lightly to the upper folds of her vulva, then stroked it the length of her labia. 'Sweet Jesus!' Again, she followed the line of her cleft, her belly jerking at its flowering response as it opened, and she felt her juice lubricating the dome of this tool of divine torture. Still helpless, she thrust into the tightness of her orifice, whose lips parted eagerly to embrace the invader.

Max's teeth bit painfully down on her lower lip as those other lips yielded reluctantly. For the first time, she felt the pain of that mighty intruder stretching her, thrusting its girth into her virginal tightness. She gave a small cry of discomfort, yet her shaking hands could not stop assisting this throbbing monster in its penetration. The dark head flew wildly from side to side, the knees were drawn lewdly up almost to her ears, and she yelped shrilly at the surging orgasm which tore through her for the second time that eventful day as she plunged the instrument fully home.

Six

'Wake up, my little debauchee! Don't tell me you've worn yourself out completely with your new gift!'

Max, jerked from sleep by the professor's hearty voice, blinked blearily up at him from the dishevelled bed. He towered over her, beaming. He was wearing a patterned dressing gown of dark silk, but was freshly and fragrantly shaved and groomed. All at once, she became aware that she was displaying her nude body almost to the base of her belly. With a gasp, she clawed at the sheet, dragging it up over her breasts.

'I can see you have made yourself well acquainted with it,' Labat chuckled, and Max burned with shame. Her eyes puffed up, the lines of tiredness stamped on her youthful features, Max felt every bit as decadent as the image she was surely projecting. She did not need the dull throbbing soreness from her concealed genitals, nor the stale aromas of her perfumed body, to remind her of the hectic night hours she had passed before falling into an exhausted slumber. Nor the scourge of the Maestro's mocking grin, as he delicately picked up the object he had retrieved from her bedside. 'I'm afraid the first man who fucks you will be a sad disappointment after this magnificent implement!'

She was still coming fully awake, and wondered why she should be feeling both shocked at the direct crudity of his language and relieved, despite her shame, that it was the Maestro who had woken her – he was, after all, the donor of the unusual gift – and not, as she had half feared, his man, Holger, whom she noticed for the first time standing a little behind his master. 'A new regimen, my child. Up with you. *Mens sana*, as they say. Your aunt tells me you and your cousin are both lazybones. That must change. Holger will take over in that department. A run before breakfast – and before our day begins.'

She scarcely had time to blush at her nakedness as she scrambled up from the bed, and grabbed at the new red tracksuit Holger passed to her. Hastily she struggled into the loose pants and top before she realised she was wearing nothing underneath. He also held out a pair of short white ankle socks and blue trainers of the right size. 'I'll see you after your breakfast. Enjoy your jog!'

Professor Labat's cheerful tones set them on their way. 'My aunt's right,' Max muttered defensively. 'I'm not exactly a keep-fit fanatic, so don't expect me to be a Paula Radcliffe.'

'Oh, you'll keep up, I'm sure,' Holger chuckled, and she gasped in amazement at what followed. In the narrow garden, by a rather shabby-looking door in the wall that led to the outside world, he produced what looked like a short length of rope, at either end of which was a metal circlet, like the expanding strap of a wrist watch. The material joining them was not rope but some sort of elastic fibre, which stretched easily. He fitted one metal band to her slim wrist, the other to his more substantial joint. Thus linked, they passed through the door into a lane, wet and leaf-strewn. The cars parked along its length were beaded with raindrops, their windows misted with condensation in the chilly September morning air. The day was overcast.

The bond between them stretched, then tugged her inexorably in his wake, as he set off at a steady pace, his feet thumping solidly in the wetness. She was towed helplessly along, her right arm outstretched towards him. They came to a busy road, where the traffic was steady in spite of the early hour, but after a hundred yards or so, they turned into the parkland of the common and a narrow tarmac footpath surrounded by dripping trees and dull sloping stretches of grass. Soon Max was wheezing, dragging behind, her face hot and crimson, saliva flecking her lips, tears and sweat mingling. 'Wuh– wait!' she panted. 'I cuh– can't – I'm knackered.'

'Language!' he admonished, smiling round at her. 'Keep going, baby, or I'll pull you along on your belly!'

She wailed, spluttering breathlessly, each breath a fiery agony now, lungs working like bellows as she threshed along, tethered to him like a beast. A few hundred yards more and she could go no further. She doubled over, coughing and hawking, spitting inelegantly, the saliva hanging in silver threads from her gaping mouth as she stared down at the wet ground and her darkly spattered, besmirched new finery. 'Oh God! Oh God! I can't – I'm dying! I'll collapse!'

She had just enough breath left to squeal in renewed shock when he gathered her roughly onto his shoulder in a fireman's lift and easily bore her over the wet grass to a clump of trees and set her down with her back against the rough bark of a tall beech, some distance away and partially hidden from the path. 'Better cool off, yes?' Before she was aware of what he was doing, he had hauled the top of her suit up and over her head, and pulled it down her arms so that it hung like a red flag from the short rope that still joined them.

It flapped as she swept her arms up to cover her bared breasts. 'Someone will see!' she gasped, glancing at the path they had left. There were several runners like themselves, and muffled dog walkers out in the greyness of the new day. He moved in so close that he hid her from view with his own bulk. His arms encircled her waist and drew her in so that the roughness of his top pressed against her bare torso, on which the sweat sheen was already drying coldly. Her nipples were rubbery, erect and tingling at the touch of his clothing. The bark of the trunk grated painfully on her back as she tried to hold him off, without success. His large red hands, those thick fingers, came up to cup the slight rounds, the pads brushing against the small sensitised area of the areolae and their tips. All at once, she went limp, gave up her resistance and let her hands fall lightly on his stooping shoulders. She saw his reddened face descending, and she raised her own, her mouth opening to meet the force of passion with which he kissed her. She felt his tongue slide into her warm wetness, her own yielding, responding, while the excitement pounded and flared through her half-bared body.

'What is this? That toy of yours whetted your appetite for the real thing?' He was smiling, his big face only inches away from her, his warm breath fanning over her face. She met his gaze with a new boldness. She was unsure of the crazy whirl of emotions running through her – except for the effect of his embrace, his hands on her throbbing breasts.

'I've never had the real thing!' Her voice was a throaty whisper, her eyes wide, fixed intently on his.

Did she really want him to be the first? The question reverberated in her brain, and she realised she was not sure of the answer. Not at this intensely seminal moment.

'What?' he growled, with that mocking rumble of laughter. 'You really mean to tell me that pretty boy cousin of yours hasn't dipped his wick in you, after all this time? It's true, then? He's a nancy boy, yes?'

Her eyes flashed defiantly. In the midst of her arousal she felt a fierce hate for his contemptuous insult to Toni. '*You* want to do it, though, don't you?' It was flung at him like a challenge.

He laughed louder. 'Right here? Up against a tree trunk in the park, during the rush hour? Of course!' He stepped back, releasing her, and hooked the forefinger of his right hand in the thick elasticated waistband of her tracksuit. He pulled it, stretching it widely towards him, until she felt it digging into her back. He stared down through the gap, at the curve of her pale belly and the tuft of dark hair at its base, between her thin thighs. He let it go, and it twanged back into place, making her yelp at the sharp sting on her midriff. His hands moved, quickly slipping the discarded top back over her head and shoulders. He pulled her round, away from the tree, and gave her a playful hefty slap on her bottom before once more tugging her after him. 'Plenty of time, princess! You've waited much longer than most girls do – if you're telling the truth! A few more days won't make any difference. Now let's get you steamed up in a different way!'

After a hot shower and a simple breakfast of cereal and toast, she returned to her room to find a burgundy-coloured full-length gown laid across her bed. There were no other articles of clothing with the dress and she was staring indecisively towards the

55

drawers which contained her underclothes when the door opened and the German's grinning head came round it. 'Just the dress, my princess!' She stood pointedly clutching her towelling robe to her, but he advanced, his smile broadening. 'Come on, baby. Whatever you do, don't keep the Maestro waiting. You wouldn't want to see him angry, believe me!'

Oh well! she thought, striving to appear unconcerned. This oaf had already glimpsed her naked that morning. She slipped off her robe, conscious of his devouring gaze, and stood while he approached and carefully eased the weighty gown over her head and shoulders. It fell with a comforting heaviness down over her body, to her very feet. It was lined with satin that caressed her coldly, especially about the fitted bodice, which was just a little large for her slight breasts. From the waist the long skirt flared slightly, but Max discovered that it was slit on the right side, almost to the hip. When she walked or moved, it gave enchanting swift glimpses of her pale limbs.

'Shoes?' she asked.

Holger shook his head. 'Little Polly Flinders!' he sang mockingly, and she found time to acknowledge the amazing depth of his familiarity with the English language. 'Hurry!' he snapped, the smile disappearing. 'The music room. Quick!' He clapped his hands, and, despite her flash of resentment, she scampered out and down the stairs to where the Maestro was already awaiting her.

She had hoped he might pay her a compliment on her appearance in the elegant gown, but he hardly seemed to notice. 'You're a little late. We must begin.'

It was a long and gruelling session, though this time he allowed her to sit for most of it. It rested her legs, whose muscles were already beginning to ache from the unaccustomed running, but her shoulders and back, her arms and wrists were aching, too, by the end of the long morning practice, from the constant sawing and dipping and swaying to the music. The Maestro again paid meticulous attention to her physical movements. His warm dry hands continued to mould her and his voice became hypnotic, urging her to extract the utmost feeling as well as technical excellence from the difficult study pieces, which culminated in a painstaking working through of the Brahms *Sonata in G minor*. The Maestro's exhortations and bellowed interruptions seemed endless until, finally, she was utterly limp and her body soaked in sweat under the heavy material. From where he hung over her shoulder, behind her chair, she guessed he could see the entire pale slopes of her breasts, while the skirts of her dress had parted through her vigorous efforts up to the very top of her thigh. And good luck to him! she thought wearily, feeling the prick of tears not far away now through her nervous exhaustion.

At last came the blessed relief of Holger's appearance with the tea things and the sandwiches. 'I never thought I'd be so glad to see *you*!' she greeted him daringly.

'Cheeky madam!' Holger returned, while the Maestro beamed at them like a benevolent uncle.

'I'm absolutely exhausted!' she said hopefully, after the half-hour pause to eat. 'The run this morning . . .' she added, hoping to charm him with her winsome pleading, but to no avail.

However, when she saw him approach once more with that black eye mask, her heart began to pound as she remembered what had happened the previous afternoon. But I'm not wearing any knickers today! she thought, with both trepidation and excitement.

She stood as before, blindfolded, while he positioned her, then began to call the series of exercises for her to practise. She had to force herself to concentrate fiercely on her task. All the while, her body trembled and beat with a fearful eagerness and anticipation. 'Keep playing!' the hypnotic voice commanded. 'Go through the Brahms' opening movement once more. Do not stop!'

She felt the coolness of the air on her limbs as he parted the divided skirt of the gown, and his hands, warm and steady, not at all hesitant or furtive, on her, tracing up from the ankles and calves, over the knees to the thighs, whose long muscles clenched and hardened at the invasive touch. In her darkness, she felt his lips tickle her ear, the warm breath caressing as he whispered, 'Never stop the music, my dear. Never! Let it make love to you. Feel it, deep inside you.'

His fingers moved across the crease of her thighs and belly, brushed the wiry pubis, and pressed on, to find those dampening folds of hidden tissue, to tease and caress them until she could feel their swell and bud, their unfurling, the release of their pungent nectar to make his caresses even easier, smoother. Her brain raced frantically, she became aware of her frantic prayer, like a mantra: 'Oh God! Don't make me come, not yet! Not yet!' She was wet now, and his fingers were playing like lightning, exquisite torment, along the divide of her sex lips, and she wanted him to go on, she wanted more, so much more ... and suddenly she gave a helpless cry, a groan of torment at the sudden withdrawal of those hands, the feel of the heavy skirt swinging in to conceal her, the utter deprivation of that throbbing narrow passage, the funnel of her desperate need.

She realised she was emitting long rending sobs. She stood there, her upper body bent; felt him take the violin and bow from her hands; and she quietened, while the tears dripped and soaked into the velvet of the mask. But then his fingers were at the back of her neck, seeking out the tag of the zip, drawing it down, slowly. She felt the cloth parting, the cooler air on her back, the satin falling away from her bosom. He drew the zip fully down to the base of her spine, and she held her arms down stiffly in front of her, gave just the slightest of shivering motions to assist the gown as it fell from her, folding softly in a cascade about her ankles. His arm round her waist guided her, helping her to step out of the pool of material, until she stood there, fully naked in his embrace.

He was behind her, so close she could feel his clothing on her, the brush of it on her back and her buttocks. His chin rested on her right shoulder and his mouth again caressed her ear. 'You can feel what it's like to be an instrument of beauty, Max. See how you are caressed. You are my instrument of pleasure, my darling.' The accompanying music to the sonata was playing in the background while his deep tuneful voice hummed the violin's melody in her ear. Then she gasped at the sudden sharply rousing touch of the horsehair on her right nipple while his hand moved, hot and heavy now, round her slim neck, transforming it into the scroll of the instrument, and his finger pads pressed hard on the top of her breastbone as they would on the strings. There was an ecstatic blend of joy and pain – a unique sensation as the bow sawed like a fine knife across her right nipple, then found and stroked its fiery caress across its companion.

The sensitive little teats burnt and tingled, but then the bow was withdrawn. The Maestro's hand dropped suddenly from her throat to slide onto her bosom, whose contours he traced and cupped, his fingers playing with her throbbing points until she moaned with painful pleasure. Meanwhile, the thin bow had slid down around her hip, across the base of her belly, knifing its way across the patch of dark hair, pressing on the cushiony swell of her mons. The muscles of her thighs and buttocks clenched to stop her instinctive move to pull away from its novel caress.

Worse, and better, were to follow. She felt the cold bone of the bow's tip between her thighs, then the slender instrument was used like a rod to flick at her inner thighs, to part them, and the Maestro hugged her, his left arm clamped around her midriff so that she could feel the length of him pressing intimately into her from behind. The right hand manoeuvred the bow until it pointed vertically, and found the tight fold of her labial cleft. Once more that fine fire burnt at her most sensitive flesh, as the horsehair was slowly drawn along the length of her sex, concentrating on the folded upper tip, teasing it open, stroking the wetness where beat the hooded centre of her arousal. She shivered convulsively, could not keep still any longer, as her hips twisted, her belly thrust out to meet the tormenting caress of the bow, and her thighs jerked violently.

'Please!' She cried out desperately, fell on her hands and knees, blind and helpless, begging – for what, she hardly knew.

'Keep still!' His hand was on her neck again, but at the back, and his grip was rough, imprisoning. There was a swish of air and a soft thud as the thin instrument delivered a cut across her proffered buttocks. The pain was a fine blazing line across her taut flesh, and another two cuts followed in rapid succession, their burn throbbing as she knelt there and let her head sink down to the floor to rest on her folded arms, her backside thrust upwards, presenting itself for the punishment. But the pain was a steady throb now, there were no more blows to follow.

She crouched there, desolate and sobbing violently, for a long time before she moved from her ridiculous posture. She sat and pulled the soaking mask from her tear-soaked face, to find the room empty. The sobs tore through her. She gave way to her grief with an abandon that was almost a physical pleasure, like the sensations he had so mercilessly roused in her. Her face felt swollen when the weeping fit finally passed, and her whole body was a mass of weary pain. She dragged herself up, picked up the dress and flung it over her shoulder. She stepped into the deserted hallway, completely careless of who might see her as she crossed, and climbed the stairs again to her room.

She bathed her face and examined herself, turning to look over her shoulder at her reflection in the dressing-table mirror, surprised to find there was merely the faintest trace of a line where he had struck her with the bow. She had slipped on her robe and was standing, uncertain of what to do next, whether to go downstairs again or not, when the door opened and Professor Labat entered. She gazed at him helplessly. His voice was deep and richly soothing, warm with an affectionate chiding. 'Max! Don't pretend you're shocked at my touching you. I'm sure you're no stranger to such things, even though you *are* still a virgin. I know all about you, my dear. I know you like to play with yourself. Have you forgotten? And I know how you and that pretty cousin of yours like to amuse yourselves when you're alone together. There must be no secrets between us, Max. You understand, don't you?'

'Will you – are you going to be the first – to – to do it to me?'

His deep laugh was like a blow to her. 'Who knows? Perhaps. But not yet, little one. It's a pleasure you must wait a little longer for. Meanwhile, you have your own instrument to play with. I want you to appreciate fully what's in store for you, Max. When the time is right!'

She began to cry, hopelessly, for her hunger, and for her humiliation.

'Now, let's have a proper look at you. Keep still.'

He untied the robe, pushed it back off her shoulders, and it fell. She stood entirely revealed to his gaze for the third time that eventful day. She suppressed her instinctive movement to hide herself with her arms, or to cross her legs. She was startled to find herself fiercely wishing for the sealing blackness of the mask to be in place once more.

'Hm! Some would say you're a little on the skinny side, but then, I rather like that hint of immaturity in your figure – the narrow hips, the small tits. It adds to that gamine quality I find appealing. Your mama was very similar – perhaps a little fuller on top.' He stretched out one hand and cupped her right breast, exploring its contours, brushing his thumb pad over the tingling nipple. He chuckled reminiscently, keeping his hold on the soft warm round. 'Though she certainly filled out when she had you! Poor Anne! She was so embarrassed! But I was fascinated by the great swell of her when she was carrying you. I used to make her strip as soon as she arrived for her lesson, make her stay naked for hours when she was with me. Right up to the end, just a day or two before she went into labour.'

'But what about – I mean – was daddy . . .?'

'Your father was a lovely boy, Max. A thorough gentleman. Of course he knew how special Anne was to me. Just as *he* was. I loved them both. Just as I am now going to love *you* both! You and that sweet cousin of yours.'

He gave another playful tweak to her breast before releasing it. 'Now make yourself pretty, my dear, then come down to supper.'

But his mention of Antonio had brought to the forefront of her mind once more a major cause of her anxiety. 'When will he be here – Antonio?' she asked pleadingly.

The Maestro grinned so knowingly that she felt herself going crimson under his piercing gaze. 'You're missing him, are you? Well, all in good time, my dear. We must get along without him for the moment. Perhaps your aunt can't bear to part with both of you so quickly. Now, get dressed, quickly. I'm hungry.'

She glanced around. 'Is there – I mean, should I wear anything special? I have –'

'I think you're quite charming as you are!' he beamed. 'But put something on that will please me. I leave it to you.' He took her by the arm and patted her hand approvingly. 'But I'm very glad you asked, Max. That's a good girl. It shows you're learning fast.'

Seven

'My God! You look like something the cat dragged in!'

Antonio glared back at Davies, who was standing at the worktops, filling a bowl with cereal. 'That's hardly surprising, is it? I could hardly get a wink of sleep. What's happening? Why aren't I going to Professor Labat?' Dressed in a silk robe whose short hem reached only to mid-thigh, he moved over to her and took the proffered bowl.

'Not quite so cocky now, are we? You're missing that little slut, eh? Wishing she was here to kiss you better, diddums?'

'Fuck off, dike!' But his eyes widened warily, and he tensed for some violent retaliation.

'Don't be so crudely unpleasant, dear!' was all she said, in untypically mild reproach. 'Come and sit down and eat your breakfast.'

She reached out for his arm, and he made a token gesture of resistance, but then gave a gasp as she tugged at the sash of his robe and peeled it from him. He stood there naked, the morning light bathing the pale slimness of his body, which turned in instinctive submission at the firm hand on his shoulder. Davies grunted derisively. 'I don't know what you're moaning about, anyway. You've got us all to yourself for a while. I should think you'd be glad of a rest from that randy little bitch!' She burst into fresh laughter, her pleasure intensified at his obvious discomfort.

'Sorry to disappoint you, but *I'm* not gay, thank you very much.' He stopped as he saw the gleam in the grey-green eyes. Shamefully, he acknowledged the little frisson of excitement that quivered inside him, the undeniable thrill he got from her domination.

'Your imminent departure has made you rather bold,' Charlotte's voice said suddenly behind him. 'Don't you think so, Davies? Getting way above yourself, aren't you, my little manikin?'

He cupped his hands over his squat penis, then crimsoned at the simultaneous grins his action drew from both onlookers.

'I should say so, bleeding cheeky little poofter!' Davies' hearty tone was as jovial as her mistress's. 'I think it's time we played our old game again, don't you? It's a long time since we played whacko! And he's dressed for it, ain't he?'

Eagerly, the two women grabbed black plastic spatulas from the round jar which held the kitchen implements. It was a 'game' they had indulged in many times in the past, comparatively harmless compared with the more serious beatings he had received over the years, but enough to make him squeal, with pain as well as humiliation, at the vigour with which they played it. The sharp splats of the plastic instruments on his clenching bottom and the tops of his thighs made him yelp and squirm as he skipped high, dancing around the old wooden table while they pursued him, hooting with the pleasure of the chase. Perversely, the stinging pain and his very movements to escape it made his prick throb in hardened arousal, while his hands, too busy protecting his flanks and massaging the glowing flesh, could not shield the embarrassing evidence of his excitement – an excitement he was helpless to fight against, as pain and pleasure fused in that maddening soaring way. Strategically stationed, they struck in turn, either side of him, Davies on his left, Charlotte on his right, and he writhed more and more frantically as the stinging torment mounted, and his beating prick stiffened until he stumbled and fell on his back across the table, begging them shrilly to stop. He gave one last shriek of unadulterated agony, as Charlotte with sudden viciousness swiped the flat plastic across his groin and glared at him with transformed anger. 'Cover that up, you disgusting little pervert!'

Max tried to keep still as she stood by the side of the Maestro's elegant black leather swivel chair. It was not easy. The fingers of his left hand were toying lightly with the folds of her labia, whose inner surfaces were already slick with the emissions his caresses were causing. Her legs were still together, in the pose of parodied demureness he had insisted upon, so that she could feel his large hand rubbing softly at both her inner thighs. But his next words, spoken into the phone he held in his right hand, succeeded, at least momentarily, in diverting her from her rapidly mounting excitement.

'I'd like to take delivery of Antonio by this weekend. I've got something rather special lined up for the pair of them in two weeks, and I may need to break him in a little before then. From what you were saying, he has a little more rebellious spirit in him than his cousin. But that's how it should be. There must be a modicum of testosterone in those cute little balls of his, after all!'

Max heard the faint buzz of her aunt's tinnily distorted voice, then the Maestro laughed deeply.

'Oh, you cruel thing! Max? Oh, she's coming along fine. Matters are well in hand now.' Max jumped, and stifled a small cry as his fingers suddenly thrust upwards, penetrating through the slippery outer tissue to the narrow funnel of her vagina. She opened her thighs a little to allow easier passage, and to lessen the pain on her tender flesh. 'I've been teaching her some new bow techniques. She's with me now. We're just about to start another session. Here. Have a word with her yourself.'

He handed over the small instrument to Max, who bent forwards slightly as she put it to her ear. 'Hello, Aunt Charlotte,' she murmured, surprised at the sudden rush of emotion which clogged her throat and made her eyes smart with unshed tears. All at once, she had a childish desire for the familiar cocoon of even Charlotte's harsh routine, and, above all, the saving grace of her beloved Toni's presence.

'Are you being a good girl? Obedient? Like I told you?'

'Yes, Aunt, I – oh-h-h!' The professor had inserted one finger deep within her orifice, turning it, worming it, to cause a powerfully melting sensation to pass through her naked frame. She sighed and gasped, her words dying, her mind spinning off helplessly.

He captured the phone from her. 'I'm sorry, Charlotte,' he chuckled. 'She's so excited about our session that she can't concentrate on anything else. I'll call later, to arrange picking up Antonio. Bye.' For just a few thrilling seconds longer, he kept his finger inside her, and she stood trembling, legs splayed now, on the spit of her approaching climax, until, with typical cruelty, he brutally withdrew, leaving her gasping with unfulfilled need, bending forwards, her hands resting on his desk as she shuddered with emotion.

Ostentatiously cleaning his hand on an immaculate white handkerchief, he moved to the door of his office. 'Holger! We're starting in the music room. Lunch at 12.30. No disturbance until then.'

'Yes, sir.' Holger's grinning face appeared round the door. 'Is she all right as she is?' He nodded at Max's nude form, standing silent and submissive at the Maestro's side. Max was already becoming familiar with this preliminary routine. Part of her loathed herself for her subservience, even as she acknowledged the thrill it gave her, to add to the turmoil of her arousal.

She was used to the Maestro's mercurial changes of mood, from the uncle-like teasing, to the cold scathing contempt, the crude bluntness of obscenity, and, worst of all because it was so rare, the bellowing fury of rage. She took them as she knew she must, bowed, tearful, subservient, and always, always obedient, no matter how much hurt and resentment smouldered within.

She remembered his comments about Toni on the telephone, and acknowledged their truth. He had always been the more daring, the one who would nurture a spirit of resistance, hopeless though it was. She felt a quickening of hope now, at the thought that at last they would be reunited, that the uncertainties of the future in this strange household would be lightened at being together again. But further diversions awaited her, which helped to take her mind off her longing to have her cousin with her once more.

Although it had only been a matter of days, it already seemed almost a lifetime during which she had endured the long exhausting music lessons in a state of semi- or total nudity. The velvet burgundy gown had long gone. If she wore any clothing at all, it would be only the flimsiest of underwear – bras whose cups were of misty see-through material edged with lace, tiny silk G-string briefs or fancily embroidered French knickers, tiny ribboned suspender belts hooked to sheer stockings of dark nylon, her feet encased in the most delicate of shoes with high stiletto heels. She felt exquisitely whorelike, ashamed of her fierce bodily reaction to these scraps of finery with their blatant proclamation of her wanton sexuality. No matter how many times she tried to tell herself that she was simply the helpless innocent victim of the Maestro's weird desires, her physical response to this strange ritualistic existence declared mercilessly her complicity in it.

She made no effort to escape, or even to protest. She ran daily through the park with Holger, tied to him like a dog, while they frequently passed within a couple of feet of other joggers or walkers. All you have to do is cry out, throw yourself in their path, cry out for help, she would urge herself. She never did. And when the Maestro's hands, his wickedly possessing and arousing fingers, claimed her, peeling away the few scraps of silk, her crotch was already wet with the pungent evidence of her need and his touch all too swiftly brought on the consuming rush and explosion of her orgasm – the shattering conclusion which, each time it approached, her body longed for anew with every atom of her being.

She longed for him to take her properly, to possess her fully. Each day she hoped this would be the day – each night she wept in bed before she took the facsimile he had given her, to replay her own lonely fantasy of what it might be like. She was obsessed with it. She began to fear that, after all, he did not want her, that it would not happen with him; he would not be the first to whom she would belong.

And each time she found herself sprawled on the floor, exhausted after his amusement with her, she wanted to beg, to sob and plead with him to make her life complete, to make her his in body as well as spirit. But fear held her back from this final public acknowledgement of her subservience.

But today there was to be yet another variation in the strange routine. In spite of the keen anticipation he had aroused in her when she had attended him in his study, once in the music room, he did not lay a finger on her. She stood naked, in the stance he had insisted on, her feet slightly parted, perfectly balanced, her slim form dipping and swaying to the movements of the music, and he did not come within three feet of her while she played, not even when, after the long and strenuous exercises, he placed the eye mask over her head. Every muscle was tensed, and her sex palpitated with the anticipation of his stirring fingers, whose absence made the quality of her playing uncertain enough to earn his frequent cutting abuse. 'No, no, you stupid little girl! Go back! Again – from the beginning!' She could feel the tears soaking the velvet pad, and she struggled to suppress the sobs she could feel rising within.

They took their usual light lunch not in their place of work but in the splendour of the dining room, though only the Maestro and herself shared the meal, served by Holger. Max felt newly self-conscious of her nakedness in these unusual surroundings. Her skin was sensitive to the scratch of the stiff upholstery of the chair, her limbs were pocked with goose-bumps at the comparative coldness of the room in the autumnal chill. Her nipples peaked embarrassingly, and, of course, their erection did not escape Holger's leering notice. 'Don't get excited, Princess. It's only strawberry yoghurt for dessert.'

The meal was quickly finished and, to her further surprise, the Maestro ordered her to go to her room. 'Have a little rest for an hour or so. Maybe a nap. Or perhaps you might like to play with your new toy?' She blushed fiercely at his taunting laugh.

She should have been relieved at this break from the established pattern, for she had fully expected another gruelling session of at least three more hours through the afternoon. As she made her way obediently up the stairs, she vowed she would not touch the vibrator lying in its narrow box in the drawer of her bedside table. She was well aware already how addictive the solitary pleasures of masturbation could be, how difficult it could be sometimes to ignore the throbbing demands her body made on her, especially now, in this novel routine. She was even more aware of her physical needs, because of this state of nakedness or near-nakedness she had been kept in over the past days. Already it seemed an age since she had worn any clothing.

At least Aunt Charlotte had always insisted she should be decently clothed during the day – which had been just as well, Max reflected, recalling the disturbing glint in the odious Davies' eyes whenever she *did* see her naked. The butch dike could still make her uncomfortably nervous, in spite of being a familiar of her aunt and therefore a presence from Max's earliest days living there. Now, almost equally disturbingly, Max's feelings were somewhat ambivalent concerning her condition. She could not, or, rather, preferred not to, analyse her emotions too closely. Yet she could not deny that being constantly unclothed in the presence of the two men was arousing, however ashamed she might be. In particular, the way the Maestro stared at her, those compelling dark eyes caressing her like his hands, his obvious

71

appreciation of her young flesh, made her fearfully excited in a way she had never known before. Part of her, her shocked mind acknowledged, longed for him to possess her physically, longed to know the feeling of being taken, of being fucked by him. After all, she *did* belong to him, she was virtually his prisoner here. He dominated her entirely. Why wouldn't he acknowledge it by taking her body? She was even more shocked to admit that part of her, a very powerful part, wanted him to do so, and clung to the fact that he had promised that it would happen some time. She had to acknowledge also, with bitter tears, the fact that his refusal, his cruelty in keeping her waiting with her nerves stretched to a frenzy of anticipation, merely served to demonstrate further his hold over her.

With such a riot of conflicting emotions running through her, it was no surprise that, after a tearful struggle with herself, she found herself reaching out, taking the phallus out of its hiding place, and slipping beneath the bed covers, which served to hide her activity from any prying eyes, and also to muffle the sound of its discreet purring as she put it to use. Her climax came quickly – too quickly – and, after the swift burst of weeping that accompanied it, she fell into a troubled sleep.

'Ah! Here she is! Sleeping beauty! What have you been doing to yourself, you naughty girl? I thought so!'

Rudely awakened, Max gave a little scream at the abrupt removal of the covers. The Maestro was beaming down at her. The rumpled sheet, the stale scent of her heated body, and, most glaring of all, the huge flesh-coloured instrument lying against her left thigh, were clear enough indications of what she had been doing before falling asleep. But her shame intensified into a blaze of mortification as she observed the slight figure standing at the professor's side.

A beautiful girl was grinning at her. She was short and slim. Her gleaming black hair, fringed across her brow, hung in straight luscious locks either side of her exquisite face to just below her ears. Her skin tone was light brown, the complexion flawless. The features were fine and perfectly formed, with just a hint of oriental origins, the dark almond-shaped eyes huge and luminous. The lips were full, cupid-bowed, framing the dazzling white, even teeth. There was every sign that the lovely stranger also appreciated the frank and unrestricted view she was being afforded. Max gasped and made a belated effort to draw the bedclothes over herself once more, but was prevented by the Maestro's hand on her wrist.

'This is Meena. She's come to do a very special job for me. And for you. You'll love it. Say hello.'

Seconds later, a still-bleary Max was being tugged forcefully up from her bed and led from the room. 'Please – I need the bathroom – a wash –' she pleaded.

'Very well. But hurry. Maybe you'd better go with her, Meena. Make sure she does a proper job.' The Maestro left them at the door of the bathroom.

Alarmed at his words, Max forgot about the embarrassment of her nakedness in front of the girl, who in turn seemed sunnily unperturbed. 'What does he mean?' Max asked.

The white-coated figure beamed at her. 'I'm here to do a beauty treatment for you. Full Hollywood, the professor tells me.' At Max's blank look, the girl sniggered, and gestured towards the small dark triangle of Max's pubes. 'He wants everything off. Make you completely bare.'

Ten minutes later, freshly showered, the apprehensive Max allowed herself to be led by Meena down the stairs and in through the door of the music room. A narrow trestle-table had been set up in the centre of the floor and draped with a dazzling white cloth. Like an altar, Max thought, her heart bumping unpleasantly. At one end was a small deep-blue velvet cushion. Meena now drew her towards the table and helped her to stretch out on her back along its length, her head on the cushion. The dull light of the late afternoon, slanting through the long windows onto her body, was enhanced by an Anglepoise lamp which had been placed so that it threw its white brilliance full on to her mid-region. In spite of the warmth of the heated room, she was shivering noticeably.

'We're going to display that divine cunt of yours in all its virginal glory, my dear,' the Maestro declared, moving forwards to her side. 'Meena here is an expert beautician. She won't hurt you.' He chuckled deeply. 'Well, maybe just the teensiest bit. But it will be well worth it. Pain so often is, as you know, Max.'

Meanwhile, Meena was wheeling a small trolley full of equipment to the other side of the table. Max eyed it with growing alarm, then her fear was diverted to an intense shame at the entrance of Holger. 'No!' she murmured involuntarily, and the manservant's grin widened.

'I'm afraid Meena will need both of us to assist,' the Maestro said. 'Don't worry. We *do* know what little girls are made of. Especially *this* little girl, eh, Holger?' Both men laughed, and Max blinked back her tears. 'Meena, my love,' he went on urbanely, 'why not make yourself more comfortable, my sweet? We don't stand on ceremony here. No need for such formality.'

At once, Meena began to unbutton her overall, which she handed to Holger. Max gaped. The girl wore nothing beneath, except a minute white thong of thin cotton through which showed the pert outline, and misty shadow, of her sex cleft, as denuded of hair as Max's was soon destined to be.

'First, the glue,' Meena announced serenely, while Max stared at her superb breasts, not much larger than her own, crowned with nipples and areolae of a rich, dark red against the creamy café-au-lait skin. 'Gentlemen?'

Max felt her ankles seized and lifted, her captors positioned one on each side of the table. They parted her legs wide, and Max felt an icy liquid being swiftly and comprehensively smeared over the whole area of her pubic hair and down the outer soft surface of her labial cleft. Meena turned away to the trolley, treating Max and the two men to a comprehensive view of her splendidly curved bottom, which was quite bare. Only a thin strap ran across the base of her spine and her hips, the rest of the tiny garment being entirely hidden within the deep divide of the magnificent rounds.

'OK. Hold tight, gentlemen.' Quickly, her nimble fingers, in gossamer-thin surgical gloves, pasted strips of damp material over Max's genitals. She bent towards Max, the pointed breasts only inches from the prostrate figure's frightened face. 'This might sting just a little.' Her fingers picked at one corner, then ripped the strip away from the skin. Max shrieked, her belly lifted, and the men held tightly to her spreadeagled legs as the process was repeated again and again.

Eight

Max stared at her reflection in the dressing-table mirror. Gingerly, she placed her fingers either side of her vulva and peeled back the labia a little. 'God! It's sore!' she murmured. 'Look! It looks a bit puffed up – enflamed, don't you think?'

Meena gazed over Max's shoulder. 'It's fine. I've got some cream in my bag. I'll leave a jar. Use it tonight, and in the morning, if it's still a bit tender. Should be all right by tomorrow. It looks absolutely great!' the Eurasian girl enthused. 'Much better than all that hair, eh?' Quickly, she unbuttoned the front of her white overall, slipped her thumbs in the tiny thong, and pulled it down to expose her own smooth and hairless sex. 'Snap!' Their eyes met in the mirror and they exchanged conspiratorial smiles. Meena did not bother to fasten her overall again. 'Hey! Was the Maestro serious? Are you *really* a virgin?' Her tone betrayed her disbelief.

Blushing, Max nodded.

'How old are you?' Meena pursued.

'Eighteen.'

'Jesus!' She gestured at Max's nude body. 'You mean – they keep you like this, all the time?' Again a nod. 'And neither of those guys has screwed you? I can't believe it! I know what a randy old goat the

Maestro is! And that Kraut of his will shag anything in sight if he gets half the chance!'

'How do you know?'

'Believe me, I know! I work for Titty. I know all about Professor Labat and his henchman!'

'Titty?' Max repeated the ludicrous word with incredulous curiosity.

'Christ! Where've you been hiding? No wonder you've still got your cherry! You haven't heard of the gorgeous Lady Letitia Laycorn and her Pleasure Dome? You will, sweetie, you will!' Intrigued, Max was about to press for more details, when Meena suddenly gave an impish grin and nodded towards the still-dishevelled bed. 'Mind you, if you've been using that enormous dildo there, you're not exactly intact, are you? That means there's no fear of me busting anything, right?'

Max gazed at her uncomprehendingly, her eyes wide as the girl discarded her overall and swiftly peeled off the tiny undergarment beneath. 'So! Let's make the most of it, sugar!' Meena advanced on her and, slipping her arms around Max's waist, pulled the naked figure close to her. Too surprised to resist, Max felt those full sweet lips close over her own in a blatantly sexual kiss, which left her breathless, and struggling to escape.

'Wha– what are you doing? Please –'

'Don't tell me you've never –' Meena gestured at their still entwined bodies. 'Surely the only reason you're still unfucked at eighteen is because you're gay?'

'No – I've never – not with anybody ...' Max allowed herself to be manoeuvred towards the bed and thrust bodily down upon it. Her heart was racing again, but with excitement rather than fear.

'You're going to love this, sister!' Meena promised. She turned away, rummaged in her large grip. 'Now!

Where's that cream? As good a way as any to get started!'

'But – what about ... someone might come ... I can't even lock the door ...'

'Why do you think the Maestro sent us up here? To play tiddlywinks? Lie back and enjoy, lover!'

Max sighed. Her thighs stirred, her knees lifted, and a glow of colour rose from her neck to flood her features. 'Oh God!' she whispered thickly. Meena's fingers moved, and Max's sex beat strongly, flowering open to the caressive invader. A lost and blissful interlude followed, in which she was showered with a lover's devouring kisses, it seemed over her entire frame, from curling toes to twisting head, until Max screamed, her body arched like a spring up from the bed, consumed in the orgasm running explosively through every bit of her. How often she came, or whether it was one surging endless climax, Max had no idea; she bucked and howled and sobbed, clinging to her divine aggressor, her fingers dug deep in that glossy thick hair now falling like a feathery cloak over her lifting thighs and belly.

The private lost world exploded, this time in a nightmare roar. 'What do you think you two are doing, you depraved little sluts?'

A shattered Max felt her partner torn bodily from her. Sobbing hysterically, she felt herself plucked up from the bed, and realised Holger had grabbed her and was throwing her face down across the crumpled sheets. His master was meting out similar brutal treatment to the wailing Meena, so that they lay side by side, their hips bumping, their backs and buttocks revealed in full and vulnerable splendour to their grinning persecutors.

'What do you suggest, Maestro?' Holger asked, his thick voice displaying his delight.

78

'Oh, the whip. The cat, I think.'

It was a short-handled instrument, with a number of tails of thin supple leather, and was already to hand. Holger watched while the Maestro wielded it. Labat struck expertly, with a flick of the wrist, in a practised economy of effort. The tails fell first on Max's quivering behind. It felt as though myriad hornets had stung her all at once. Her head swung wildly, she shrieked and bucked, but at his snarled order to 'Keep still!' she found herself fighting against the torment in order to obey him, and somehow managed to do so, except for the involuntary clenching of her muscles and the drumming of her legs against the bed beneath her, proffering her scorched backside for the next swingeing blow. She had to wait for it, until he had struck at Meena's fuller browner globes rising enchantingly for his punishment. The thin tails hissed, and cracked their fiery trails over the clenching rounds, and Meena howled. The girls' pleas and sobs and yelps of torment blended, the bed shook, and their hips bumped in the intimately shared ordeal. Both sets of buttocks bore ample traces of the chastisement when the Maestro stepped back, breathing somewhat heavily, but smiling with satisfaction. 'There now. I hope this is another valuable lesson you've learnt, Max. Thank you, Holger. That will be all.'

Holger grunted. He turned to leave, though, even in her preoccupation with her own situation, Max sensed that the German would have been happier to remain.

The two naked figures stood sniffling, massaging their throbbing behinds. Max surmised that her late lover and erstwhile partner in distress was fulfilling a well-rehearsed and profitable role, a suspicion that was reinforced by her earlier words and the Maestro's next instruction.

'Watch closely, my dear, and see what you continue to miss.'

Max was thrust down on the bed, where she sat, her attention distracted from her own suffering by the arresting spectacle of the Maestro undressing with unhurried aplomb. She stared with accelerated heartbeat as he divested himself of his clothes.

His figure was far from graceful. His limbs were thick, and a discernible belly curved from beneath his ribcage. Yet his form suggested a compact strength. The most striking feature was his hirsute quality. Both sets of limbs were covered by long black hair. It clung to his chest so thickly that it almost hid his paps, it clustered at the back of his shoulders. In the front, it spread across his thrusting belly, leading down to the even thicker black mass of his pubis. And then Max reassessed her original assumption that his hairiness was the most notable feature about him – for there, jutting from the tangled nest of body hair, stretched a penis of inspiring proportions, proudly erect, the great helm fully exposed, shining red, agleam with evidence of his arousal, the long thick shaft brown and wreathed in potent veins standing up against the column whose length made her catch her breath. Unbidden, a picture flashed into her mind of Toni's comparatively tiny squat prick, scarcely a quarter of this monster's size.

He summoned Meena towards him, and she moved instantly. She dropped, kneeling at his feet, and, taking the rampant weapon in her hands, began to lick and nuzzle at it with evident skill and equal enthusiasm. Eventually, her jaws stretched wide, she fitted those delightful lips around the massive head, which slid inside her mouth. Her cheeks pouching and hollowing, her lovely neck straining, she began to suck, working her stretched mouth down the pulsing column until the helm and half the rearing shaft had disappeared inside her.

Max remembered the feel of that consuming mouth on her most intimate parts, and the excitement swept with renewed force through her. She felt the wet flow of desire shuddering through her once more. Her thighs clenched, squeezed madly together, she pressed herself against the folds of the sheet beneath her. In all the wildness of her drumming blood, she realised her bitter tearful disappointment that it was not *her* taking in that resplendent penis.

With a grunt, the Maestro seized the transformed girl by her dark glossy hair and plucked her away from his cock, which gleamed now with her lavish attentions. He turned and sat down on the hard wooden chair near the door. It was directly opposite Max, who gazed enraptured, the tears streaming unnoticed as she watched the lithe brown body of Meena straddle him, one little hand reaching down to seize the mighty girth of his prick, and guide it in the direction of her loins as she lowered herself slowly towards it. The brown thighs were splayed wide, their muscles standing out, demonstrating her fitness and her control. The head of his prick nuzzled between her narrow sex lips, parted them, and slid remorselessly into her. The long shaft seemed to take an age; Max could see the brown powerful balls hanging on the edge of the chair, and observed each centimetre of his prick's entry, until, at last, it was buried to the hilt, and Meena's flayed buttocks sank onto his thighs. She rode him frantically, her shrill yelping cries a counterpoint to his deep grunts. He held her shoulders and slowed her down for a while, much to her dismay, it seemed. But soon the pace quickened once more and redoubled its frenzy, both of them crying out. She bounced, faster and faster, on his knee. Max could see those fecund testicles jouncing on the chair, Meena's bottom dipping and lifting, until flashes of the glistening column of his flesh kept appearing. How long the coupling lasted Max had no idea. Meena gave a strangled cry, impaled herself furiously on him and against him, and he half rose, lifting her with him. Meena's piercing cry echoed, then died, and her whole frame shuddered before she collapsed limply, clinging to him, leaning into his chest and sobbing with abandon. Those great hair-covered hands cradled the slim bent back, whose ridged spine stood out beneath the honey skin, and rocked her gently in his arms like a loving parent soothing his child.

Polly Smythe reached across the tumbled bed for a tissue from the box at her bedside cabinet. She dabbed at the sticky traces of the tears gumming her eyelids and her cheeks, then blew her nose noisily. Propping herself on her elbows, she gazed down at her sprawled naked body with deep revulsion. The action threatened to bring on another fit of weeping and, muttering angrily, she heaved herself off the bed. At once, she caught sight of her slim frame again in the dark smokiness of the long mirror fixed to the door of the towering old-fashioned wardrobe.

'You filthy evil little slut!' she muttered aloud to her reflection. To punish herself, she gave a vicious tug at the tangled brown curls of her pubis, until the white skin beneath lifted painfully. Inspired by this, she grabbed the hairbrush from the dressing table and half turned, presenting the image of her almost-flat bottom, and struck hard at the left cheek, smothering a cry at the stinging pain. Rapidly, she delivered a blow to its twin, then two more on top of the first two, the sharp slap of the blows cracking like miniature rifle shots in the afternoon silence of the shabby flat.

The noise of the fusillade triggered her alarm that someone might hear and identify it, and she halted the self-spanking. She could see the red imprints of the brush darkening her skin. She rubbed at her throbbing behind. All at once, she lost the fight to hold back the tears, and she fell forwards across the tangled sheets, her face buried in them, her feet beating a rapid tattoo in the air as she sobbed forlornly. 'Oh God!' she croaked. She felt the wicked desire stirring throughout her once more, the burn of her bum contributing to her resurgent excitement. She pushed herself upright again and seized the obscenely glittering gold vibrator, ran with it through to the tiny gloomy bathroom, and flung it into the washbasin.

Her conscience goaded her with the memory of her struggle with her shame and fear, after she had plucked up the courage to send away for it; her dread that the postman, or any other inhabitant of the dilapidated old house, might recognise the parcel for what it was. But she was helpless against the seemingly insatiable demands of her body. No matter how hard she prayed, how many times she went penitently to church, involved herself in 'good works', returned dutifully to her parents' home in the far north at least once a month to endure the scathing contempt of her tyrannical father and her mother's cowed resignation, she could not leave her wicked body alone for more than a few tormented days while she fought hopelessly against the carnality raging within.

Thirty-one years old, living alone in a one-bedroom flat just one remove from a bedsit, eking out a pitiful living as a peripatetic music teacher for the local authority and making a few extra pounds by giving private music lessons, for which she had to tout among her school students, scarcely better than those girls who put the cards in telephone kiosks and advertised in the sex magazines. Like the one, she bitterly reminded herself, where she had seen the glossy advert for the Golden Glory, the instrument that had taken over her private life to such a degrading extent. At least it was discreet, and reasonably sized – not like those enormous terrifying sex toys on the other pages – blatant reproductions of a phallus, flesh-coloured and complete with realistic balls, which could be filled with cream to simulate the male ejaculation! Perhaps that would be the next shocking phase in her degeneration.

The sad thing was that she had no emotional or sexual outlet other than the masturbatory fantasies which occupied more and more of her solitary existence. Like the waking dream in which she had just indulged with the nubile Miss Kerri Dawson, the pupil to whose affluent home she would be going at five this evening to give her her weekly piano lesson. The reality would not live up to her fantasy world where, in a sun-dappled room after her lesson, Kerri had tearfully confessed her passion for her teacher, before being led to the elegant sofa and stripped of both her modesty and her clothing by Polly's warm hands and devouring tongue.

The vivid images pursued Polly throughout her hasty bath and her dressing afterwards. She herself was revolted by the pathetic spectacle of frustration she could see as she transformed herself into the dowdy prissy persona of the cardiganed bespectacled music mistress – who had never had a man, and was never likely to! So why now should her body be consumed by this secret lust? She fought to divert her thoughts from the answer that loomed always at the back of her mind. The truth was too painful to contemplate; the day when her safe dull world had been shattered by her meeting with those enchanting creatures, the Heavenly Twins as she thought of them, Max and Antonio Audley.

Striving to suppress her gloomy thoughts and her painful regret, she grabbed at her briefcase, hurried down the stairs, along the dim hallway, and out into the mellow daylight. Then she gave a small scream and wondered briefly if she were going mad, or if she were still living in her solitary world of fantasy, as she came literally face to face with that breathtaking beauty, her jaw dropping.

Antonio Audley turned the full power of his dark-eyed gaze pleadingly upon her. 'Miss Smythe. Thank God I've found you. You've got to help me. Please!'

Nine

Antonio had never been certain of anything much during the first twelve years of his life, including even his names, both given and surname. There were no relatives that he was aware of with the name Audley – at least none who wanted to acknowledge him as such. He was a waif, and definitely a stray, abandoned at birth by a mother, perhaps herself no more than a child, for whom he was clearly a mistake to be tossed out with the bath water. That was evidently his history, and no one at the orphanage or the later children's homes was prepared to dispute it. As for his exotic first name, he had clung to the romantic belief that his father must have been an Italian, in spite of the Anglo-sounding 'Audley', and he was proud to use the diminutive with *i* at the end rather than the *y*, even though it earned him many a mocking hoot of laughter, and worse, in his rough-and-tumble world.

He made up outrageous stories of glamorous film-star mothers, of sporting-legend fathers from Lazio, or Juventus, or Roma. 'Oh yeah!' his fellow inmates sneered. 'That's why you're so shit hot at games, is it?' For in truth he hated sport of any kind, on track or field or water, indoors or out, and would do virtually anything to avoid it. When he *did*, early on in that unfriendly world, discover his real talent for music, he switched his familial ancestry to that of stage and screen and opera house. He could at least be grateful that his talent was recognised and encouraged, even in those unsympathetic surroundings.

During those days he had no knowledge of 'Aunt' Charlotte's existence, let alone her secret interest and hand in his progress. When she did finally reveal herself to the boy as a genuine if somewhat vague connection, through the cloudy and tenebrous roots of her sister's husband, he was too dazedly thankful at this stunning change in his fortune to puzzle it out or even to query it. 'Yes please, Auntie Charlotte!' he sobbed with joy when she told him he should come and live with her. Even the way she turned crimson and held him at arm's length as he strove to embrace her didn't put him off.

'Get a grip, boy!' she hissed. 'I need you as a companion for my niece, Max. I've just inherited her. She's the same age as you. My sister and her husband got themselves killed in a car crash.'

'Niece? Max?' he said, his face screwed up in puzzlement. 'Max is a boy's name.'

'And Toni with an *i* is a girl's name!' she answered crisply. 'You should get on well together!'

If it had not been for Max, the change in his circumstances would have been far removed from the miracle he had believed it was going to be. But she made all the vital difference to his existence. He could scarcely believe how close they were, in every way, especially looks. In their talent, though Toni was always ready to accept that it was Max who was the genius and that his role of accompanist to her brilliance was a predestined one, there were some discerning souls, Max among them, who affirmed that his skill on the piano was in no way inferior to hers with the violin. And, most important of all, in temperament and ways of thinking, which, in reality was least amazing of all. The life they led as Charlotte's wards was both insulated and isolated. They were constantly together, and mixed very little, other than with those who were there to further their gift of music.

They knew little of the lifestyle of their more liberated contemporaries. Charlotte used the considerable family inheritance, greatly augmented by the money that came to her and in trust for Max after the deaths of Anne and Richard, to ensure that isolation. Tutors were hired and she built a carefully nurtured bubble around them to keep them free of taint. Some, who observed it from the outside, thought it a very privileged upbringing. They knew nothing of Charlotte's ruthless autocracy. 'You must live for your music!' It was the eleventh if not the first commandment.

The world outside the comfortable but far from luxurious house would have been horrified in this libertarian age to witness how harsh her discipline was. Slipper, hairbrush, strap, rod: all were frequently and vigorously applied to ensure obedience. It was harder at first for Max to endure, after the casual-to-the-point-of-negligent attitude of her parents. Though she had spent so much of her early life absent from them as they toured the world, it was possibly the shock of their sudden permanent loss that helped to make the drastic severity of the new regime less painful than it might otherwise have been. And, of course, everything was made so much better by her new soul mate, her mirror, with whom she could share everything – a wonderful sensation she had never in her life known before.

One of the few who penetrated that bubble of isolation their home had become for the two youngsters was Miss Polly Smythe, music teacher and timid young spinster, whom Aunt Charlotte decided was just the right unprepossessing type to be admitted to teach her charges some of the dreary mechanics of notation and theory, to enable them to obtain necessary qualifications to advance them in their academic career.

Polly was vetted carefully – so carefully that she was more than a little confused, as well as becoming ever more apprehensive of her assignment. If the monetary reward had not been so outstandingly high for one of her modest accomplishments, she would have backed out. One interview in particular had been positively alarming, conducted by a woman who introduced herself simply as Davies. Her features were not so much ugly as plain. The haircut was short and mannish, her build solid and muscular. Her clothes – jeans, black lace-up boots and a polo shirt outlining her broad shoulders and showing virtually no sign of feminine curves at its bosom – were in keeping with her looks.

In theory, butch women fascinated Polly. They figured frequently in her solitary fantasies. Close to and all too real, this 'Davies' frightened her. The questions were far too personal, touching on her private life, which, she thought indignantly, had nothing whatsoever to do with her suitability for the job – simply a few hours' tutoring per week for a couple of teenagers. 'Do you live with anyone? Are you in a relationship? Have you any children? Are you *gay?*'

For God's sake! She blushed hotly, staring down at her hands twisting sweatily in her lap, and pressed her knees tightly together beneath her sensible skirt. She wanted to protest, to burst forth, outraged at her interrogator's rudeness, but she was tongue-tied. She glanced up helplessly, in shy appeal, and saw the broad and mocking smile, the suggestive gleam in the grey-green eyes. The tip of a pink tongue protruded briefly, like the flick of a snake, over the thin lips, and now Polly's blushes burned, and she felt her face glowing like a lamp. Her breath caught in an audible little sob as she shook her dark brown head.

'I reckon you'll do nicely, sweetheart!' Davies announced heartily. She reached out a large red hand and clamped it over Polly's knee. She winked outrageously, and Polly could only stare in wide-eyed acknowledgement as she stammered out her thanks.

Her subsequent encounters with Miss Behr's assistant were generally mercifully brief ordeals for Polly, and were more than made up for by her sessions closeted with her Heavenly Twins. Swiftly, she fell in love with them, both of them, much to her private dismay and confusion. There was an androgynous quality about them – each seemed to possess the same delightful mixture of qualities and traits that transcended the bounds and differences of their sexuality. Poor Polly was in a riot of conflicting emotions. Her wild private imaginings had her romping with Max, with Toni, and, in an agony of sweet sinfulness, both of them together, smothered and smothering in these fanciful permutations of sweet flesh.

She was unsure whether to feel disappointment or extra pleasure when, after only a matter of three months or so, her visits to the house for the lessons came to an abrupt termination. Instead, she was assigned to attend Toni at the North London Academy, a venue where he taught a number of other pupils, to help him study for a whole series of theoretical and practical courses to further his progress as an accompanist.

'Oh! But what about Max? Er – Miss Audley?' she

found the courage to ask when Charlotte broke the news in her usual terse manner. 'I thought –'

'I don't think there's very much you can offer her now, do you?' Charlotte asked, even more brutally, and the vulnerable brown eyes blinked behind Polly's dark-framed spectacles. 'I'd say she's moving out of your league now, wouldn't you?'

Polly's mouth opened, then closed again without protest. Davies saw her out. On the steps outside, Polly stiffened as she felt Davies' hand on her arm, restraining her, then jumped at the swift but unmistakable nip at her right buttock. 'Shame you won't be coming here no more, eh? Miss your darling little Maxie, will you?' The hot flush, which was never far away in Davies' presence, suffused Polly's startled features. 'Still, never mind. Dare say we'll bump into each other at the music school. No doubt I'll have to take Master Toni to and fro. The young tosser couldn't find his way into his own drawers without someone to show him!'

She gave a raucous bark of laughter, while Polly inwardly fumed and longed for the courage to make the cutting remark that sprang so readily to her mind. The gruff tones continued.

'Maybe we could meet for a jar some time? Just you and me. I don't think under that neat little blouse of yours you're as prim and proper as you make out, little Miss Polly!' The hand fell this time on Polly's shoulder, but its touch was every bit as disconcerting as when it had pinched her bottom. She felt those strong fingers curl around the fragility of her shoulder bone, the pads pressing hard into the hollow of her frame. 'My name's Bron, by the way. Not a lot of people know that!' Another chuckle. 'Welsh, my folks were. Chapel, the lot! Never think it from my dulcet tones, would you? Nor from the way I go on, neither!

I reckon I could show you a good time, sweetie, and not *before* time! What do you say?'

Staring like a hypnotised mouse before a snake, Polly murmured some faint polite nonsense, and retreated, trying not to break into a trot as she fled.

She made up lies about having another pupil following on from her sessions with Toni to avoid any further contact with the terrifying Davies, and, after several weeks, to her great relief, Toni was allowed to travel to and from the academy on his own. They got into the habit of going down to the canteen in the basement after the lessons, and spending a half hour or so chatting over coffee. It was a half hour that grew more and more precious to Polly, as the perceptive boy soon realised. She always began by asking after Max, and listened avidly to Toni's accounts. 'She sends her love.' 'She always asks after you,' he lied, and watched the pink glow spread up through Polly's neck to cover her face. The eyes were lowered beneath those studious spectacles, and Toni thought how her shy confusion made her look almost pretty.

She wasn't at all bad, he thought. He had learnt enough during his formative years in the children's homes to know how to flatter, and how to tell people what they wanted to hear. He knew how to charm. Then, at not quite seventeen, he could tell how lonely and repressed this woman nearly twice his age felt. He knew more about the female mind than the male. And for the best part of five years he had been ruled over by Aunt Charlotte and her fearsome delegate, while he had shared practically every minute with Max, whom he thought of now almost as his alter ego. He knew her mind and soul. He was as intimate with her nature, even with her body, as she was with his.

He felt a quickening thrill as he suddenly realised that, for the first time, he could wield a measure of power over the quiet diffident young woman sitting opposite. Aware of his trembling excitement, he let his hand move over the sticky surface of the table top to rest lightly on the thin ringless hand on the other side, no more than inches away. He felt its instinctive movement to withdraw, and his fingers tightened to hold it against its dragging reluctance. Under the table, his knees pressed against his companion's. Polly sat rigid, her myopic brown eyes, wide and helpless, stared at him, reflecting her sensation of entrapment.

'Please, Toni,' she whispered. 'Don't.' But she was making no further efforts to free herself, or to break the contact of their hidden lower limbs. 'You're ... I'm ... your teacher!' she went on, in a small breathless voice. 'You mustn't –'

'You're lovely!' he answered fervently, fixing her with the full blaze of adoration, and saw her crimsoning response to it.

'You're just a child! You can't ... I'm so much older.'

'I dream about you! Not childish dreams – proper men's dreams. Hot dreams!'

She quivered, and he saw the shudder pass through her thin frame and felt the shivery movement of her legs against his under the table.

That evening, just before their lights-out hour of ten, he snatched the chance of a brief interlude alone with Max to tell her of his exchange with Miss Smythe. Max was huge-eyed with disbelief, then with shocked delight. They were on the landing, both in pyjamas and dressing gowns, with towels and wash bags to hand. They glanced warily down through the banisters at the lighted hallway. They could hear the

TV from the sitting room, where Aunt Charlotte and Davies sat together on the sofa, viewing. But, any minute now, one of them would be up to see that their young charges were safely and separately bedded.

'She was practically coming in her knickers!' Toni stated proudly. 'Next time I'm going to make a proper move. Snog her – or something!' he added suggestively.

Max was angered by the strong pulsing beat she felt from her own sex at his dramatic revelation. She threw another anxious glance down through the rails of the landing, then flung herself violently forwards, clutching him to her. Her mouth, sweet with the powerful smell of toothpaste, was wide open, covering his lips and thrusting her narrow tongue into his warm wetness. The force of the kiss bore him back, then he was straining against her, returning the feverish passion of the embrace, their bodies pressed close through the layers of their clothing.

They were both gasping for breath when the kiss ended. 'You little beast!' Max panted. 'You're mine, don't forget! If you're going to fuck anyone, it's going to be *me!* Understand?' The very use of the indelicate verb for sexual congress sent another fierce pulse of desire through the damply clamorous region between her legs.

Both Max and Toni would have been even more thrilled if they had known the positive riot of emotion Toni's provocative action and words had aroused in their music mistress. Polly was all aflutter. All the way home on the tube, her face hot and pink, her imagination ran riot as she stood primly among the jostling swaying crowds. She slipped her key into the front door of her humble little flat with fingers that still shook. Once inside, she found herself helplessly stripping off her clothes until she left a trail from the gloomy little cubbyhole of the vestibule through to the living room, where the threadbare upholstery of the settee received the discarded bra and workaday tights before the first fever eased sufficiently for her to pause, and to give a small cry of helpless resentment at her shameful display.

Red-faced, she picked up the scraps of clothing, and retrieved shoes and skirt, blouse and cardigan from the hallway, and carried them through to the bedroom. She dropped them on the bed, then stared at her reflection in the long smoky glass of the single mirror in the centre of her second-hand dressing table. She saw the thin figure, dressed in the high-waisted white briefs, gazing waiflike back at her. What would Toni think of you now? In these? In a sudden fury once more, she thrust the knickers down, kicked them free of her feet and scrabbled furiously in her undies drawer.

She pulled out a tiny garment of satin crusted with lace, no bigger than one of her tiniest hankies. With daintily pointed feet, she drew it on and eased it up her limbs, trying not to watch her awkward movements as she adjusted it. It was a thong, of orange flame-coloured silk with an edging of black lace around the tiny triangle, which snugly fitted over her pudenda. The thin strap rested across her hips, while the other nestled deep and invisible into the crack of her behind, until it emerged at her coccyx and joined its horizontal partner by means of a dainty silvered metal clasp in the shape of a miniature heart. The dark shadow of her pubis showed mistily through the diaphanous material of what was no more than a cache-sex. Several stray wiry curls peeked over the upper lace-adorned edge of the pouch where it dipped low at her belly.

She realised suddenly that tears were trickling down her cheeks, but she smiled tremulously at herself through them. 'There now, Antonio, my love! What do you think of your precious Miss Mousy Music Teacher now? I bet this would make that darling pecker of yours sit up and take notice, wouldn't it?' She spoke the words aloud, and, as she did so, her thoughts narrowed into her vision of that wonderful, pale slim Boy-David figure and the wonderful erect symbol of his young manhood. With what was almost a howl of anguish and rage, she dived into the drawer once more and pulled out her Golden Glory, the sleek and discreet purring instrument that brought such passion and, hopefully, eventual ease to her tormented flesh and blood. She fell back on the creaking bed, knees splayed inelegantly, and ministered to her imperious physical needs, to which that infinitesimal cover of silk proved no obstacle at all.

Of the two youngsters, Toni had always been the more adept at making himself unheard and invisible, and thus ferreting out secrets often not meant for their delicate ears. Perhaps his were more finely attuned than his elders gave him credit for. Thus it was that, several lonely weeks after Max had been taken away to Professor Labat's, and while Toni was still waiting with impatient hopefulness for his summons to join her, he overheard a snatch of conversation which he should definitely not have been a party to.

He was passing the sitting room door with his usual light tread when he heard Charlotte say, 'So you see, it's essential we get the boy to the Maestro's this weekend at the latest. He has to have the two of them together. And there won't be time to prime Antonio. Lady Titty's got them coming over in the next week or so. Sheikh Hamad is impatient. Not to mention that Yank, Willard Koln. They've all seen these photos of her.' His aunt's voice thickened, and he heard the deep grunt of Davies' acquiescence. 'I must say, she *is* rather gorgeous, isn't she? Enough to start you creaming your pants, yes, Butch?'

'Don't be so fucking cheeky, slag! You can talk!' Davies growled affectionately. 'But you're right! She's hot! Just look at her in this one! And when they see our cute little cockteaser Toni alongside her, those moneybags'll be selling their yachts to get a hold of them!'

Alarm bells didn't ring, they thundered, in Toni's mind as he hastened away from his eavesdropping post. Something was terribly awry, even for this sick set-up, and he had to find out what it was before it was too late.

Perhaps overfamiliarity had made the two keepers careless. Or maybe it was, as Toni liked to think, just that Charlotte and Davies had always underestimated him. Anyway, he was able to sneak down to the sitting room in the early hours, and to retrieve the hidden key. (He had long known its whereabouts but had never had the courage, or perhaps the incentive, to use it until now.) He opened the locked drawer and quickly picked out the folder with the glossy photographs, in colour and in black and white, each nine inches by seven, of his beloved Max. There must have been at least a dozen, the majority of them showing her in different attitudes of playing her instrument, both seated and standing. All of them captured her fine beauty, and that absorbed, totally involved air of being lost in the performance. Which was, Toni acknowledged reluctantly, a great tribute to the photographer, for what was really stunning was the fact that she was dressed in a variety of clothing, from a deep burgundy décolleté gown, with a side split that showed every inch of her bare leg, to saucy scraps of lacy underwear and stockings which would do justice to any peepshow stripper, and finally to one or two completely nude studies which hid nothing of her slender beauty, including, the stunned Toni noted, the tight virginal cleft of her sex totally denuded of its sweet little triangle of dark body hair.

Sickly, he realised there was something sinisterly threatening in these poses. Not just the pornographic delectation of an elderly musically gifted roué like the Maestro. Vividly, Toni recalled the briefly overheard conversation, the mention of the Sheikh, and of some American tycoon. And of the imminent necessity of adding himself as a figure in this debauchery. It boded anything but good, and all at once he was seized with a desperate need to escape before the trap should close around him as it had around Max. He felt his heart smitten, with both dismay and with deep disappointment. How had she allowed it to happen? For that absorbed countenance, that look of total concentration, lost to her artistic genius, which he knew so well, was there in every obscene and beautiful pose. How had she let herself be part of this? But it would not happen to him! He knew he had to escape, to flee now. He was able to think, to plan, in spite of his panic. Where to go? He remembered Polly Smythe, how close he had got to her during those days of his lessons with her. It was well over a year since he had last seen her, but he was certain she would not have forgotten him. If she was still around, she would help him, surely? He had to find out. Find her. He was pinning his hopes on her.

Ten

'Oh, I say! I *do* like her bald little minge! That'll drive 'em wild!'

The photographer's camp nasal tones and Estuary accent grated harshly, even on Max's ears. His hands, though impersonal, were still unpleasant; the rings which adorned almost every finger were hard and cold as he positioned her naked body, intimately moving her hips, and touching one thigh to part her legs a little further to make the furrow of her narrow sex groove more apparent. She could feel the bathing heat of the floodlights on her skin, which was perspiring slightly, despite the liberal coat of powder with which she had been dusted. The caked make-up of her face, and shadowed eyes, with their heavily mascara-ed lashes, sealed her like a mask. Obeying the photographer's instructions, she kept her brilliantly glossed lips apart, her jaw aching with the effort of maintaining that simpering idiot-grin at the camera. She was accustomed to these sessions by now, yet she was still unable to prevent that inner feeling of shock at her sexuality being so blatantly highlighted. Nor the ambivalent emotions they roused in her, of shame and of beating excitement.

The Maestro refused to explain anything to her. Not that she had summoned up enough courage to insist on a proper explanation. Were the photos simply for his private delight or amusement? But he had hinted that there would be others, connoisseurs of beauty and art like himself, who would appreciate them. Again, there were the conflicting sensations of shame and thrill at the thought of those strangers gazing on her in such abandonment. Yes, she was shocked. But she had to admit that since her incarceration in this strange place, her whole personality had undergone a deep change. 'You belong to me now.' The Maestro had told her this, over and over, and, in some strange way, her mind seemed to accept this as the truth.

Perhaps she had been too well-schooled in subservience by her years with Aunt Charlotte and the formidable Davies. From the age of twelve, her life had been regulated in the extreme: what she wore, how she looked, how every minute of her time was filled. She was dedicated to her talent. Aunt Charlotte had drummed this into her every day, and she had never thought to question it. In fact, the Maestro had been right to declare, 'You belong to me now.' *Now!* That was the operative word, for before that she had belonged just as completely to Aunt Charlotte, from the day she had become her ward.

The truly frightening aspect of all this was that acceptance of the situation, which was embedded in Max's personality. She was stunned by her body's tyrannical hold over her. She was like a young animal permanently coming into heat. Every night, tormented by shame as she was, helplessly she indulged in the solitary irresistible pleasure to be found with the purring Night Rider – in spite of the scalding ignominy she endured each morning at Holger's hateful grin and the Maestro's knowing smile.

The vision of the Maestro's coupling with the lovely Meena flashed constantly before her, and the chief sensation it aroused was one of pure burning envy. Why not *me*? Why won't he make love to *me*? Screw me? Fuck me? Shag me? Never mind what ugly or euphemistic term you used for it. She wanted him to have her, to possess her utterly, to be the first to do so – the way he had surely possessed every other facet of her nature.

Even under Aunt Charlotte's strict regime, Max had never felt this sense of being owned. Not like this. She guessed it was because she was so completely alone here. Before, she had always shared her bondage with Toni. He had been her fellow slave, they endured everything together, even the complicity of their willingness to be enslaved. Though, in truth, Toni had always nurtured a secret spark of wilfulness, hidden deep within, that had alarmed and disturbed her. Sometimes she had felt that on his own he would have rebelled. It was for her sake, to be near her, that he put up with it. But he was not here now, knew nothing of this new enslavement. She longed for him fiercely, had asked time and again when he was coming. The promise had always been given that soon he would join her, that they would take up their life together, as before. Now, for the very first time, she began to wonder, to doubt whether she really wanted him to be here, to be part of all this strange, frightening yet fatally seductive environment. Her devotion and former closeness to Toni might feel uncomfortably close to disloyalty, a betrayal of her powerful feelings for the Maestro.

She held her instrument by its slender neck at her side and pointed the bow, with its silver tip on the ground in front of her painted toenails, like a saucy dancer's cane. 'That's fine. Now, enough cheesecake! Stick your fiddle under your chin, love, and look serious. We want the little girlie genius at work now, right? Serious, soulful. Starkers and doesn't even notice.'

The photographer advanced again, and moved the violin slightly. 'Don't hide your tits, sweetheart. That's what we're really flogging, eh? Ginny!' He beckoned to his intense assistant. Her skull was shaved so that it showed palely through the finest stubble. It made the head look even huger on the slender neck. It should have been grotesque, but it added in a strange way to the delicate beauty of that childishly innocent face. 'Use the ice cubes, will you? Bring those tits up again for me. How's the arse? We'll be shooting the backside next. Those bruises not coming through, are they? No? Good.'

They had smeared Max's bottom with the tawny body foundation to hide the evidence of the Maestro's playful but painful spanking. Now she gasped as the girl hefted her breasts, and rubbed the dripping ice cubes over the tingling nipples, which rose to renewed rubbery hardness. Ginny dabbed quickly at them with a tissue to absorb the liquid. 'There you go, Terry!'

'Thanks, ducks. Right. Soulful, Max. You're giving it your all, right? Getting off on Beethoven, or one of that bunch!'

On cue, the music swelled up. He moved behind her, crouching, the camera pointing up at the rounds of her buttocks, then came and sat on the floor, almost between her legs, which he parted even further, pointing his lens like the barrel of a weapon directly up at the line of her labial divide. Next, she was sitting on the stool before the music stand, while his hands held her by calf and ankle, placing one foot way out in front, curling her other leg back under the seat, pointing her toes, intimately pushing at her inner thighs to ensure she did not conceal her sex.

Desperately, she concentrated on holding back the tears, acutely aware the whole time of those other eyes mercilessly fixed on her – the Maestro and the grinning Holger. The diminutive shaven-skulled Ginny hovered, darting in with the powder puff, dusting her in clouds of talc so that she was in grave danger of sneezing explosively. It was a timeless ordeal, by the end of which she felt hot and drained, but, at last, it *was* over, the dazzling lights were switched off, the camera put away. Now her mind could focus on what was happening, and had happened, beyond this room in which she spent so much of her time.

Aunt Charlotte brought the disastrous news that Toni would not after all be joining her within a day, as she had been told. Her soul mate had defected. Gone, disappeared, run away!

She was ordered to go upstairs and take a bath, to wash all the plastered paint from her, and was greatly relieved when neither Holger nor the leering Davies was ordered to accompany her. All four clearly had more important things to discuss. Obediently, she padded out to the hall and the wide stairs, where the photographer and the girl helper were still carrying their equipment out to the van. Ginny, her small breasts attractively outlined under a black sweater – and the rest of her equally desirable in a pair of faded skin-tight jeans and solid boots – came in puffing after struggling with the heavy floodlights. To Max's astonishment, she advanced boldly to her and seized her in a passionate embrace. That wonderful mouth clamped over Max's still-glossy lips, and a narrow tongue plunged possessively into her. Max felt the rough contact of the girl's clothing on her skin as she held her locked in the kiss.

'There! I've been dying to do that all fucking afternoon!' the dark-eyed girl giggled.

103

'I dunno! You sodding lesbos!' the photographer said affably, shaking his head. 'Come on! Let's be having you!'

Helplessly, Max stood there and watched them open the front door and pass out through the porch. She could hear the traffic noise momentarily.

Run! Run after them! Beg them to take you with them! Or just run away! Anywhere! Like Toni! Max stood there, staring at the reclosed door. The tears came, flowed thickly, smearing her face with comic runnels of black dye. She turned away and made slowly for the stairs, feeling the thickness of the carpet under her feet.

'You've let me down very badly, Charlotte. This photo shoot was for some very important people, and I mean important! And it was supposed to feature *both* our little virtuosos. The matching pair! That's how I've sold them. I think you deserve to be punished, don't you, Charlotte? And as for that lesbian servant of yours! Don't worry. Holger will take good care of her.'

Charlotte glanced towards the door, her heart fluttering. The Maestro had just dismissed both servants. Davies had glowered truculently, looked across at Charlotte enquiringly, ignoring the Maestro's apparently pleasant-enough suggestion that Davies should go with Holger to the privacy of his quarters for some refreshment and to await the conclusion of the business between the professor and her mistress. Charlotte's pulse had raced with alarm at Davies' defiance, and her head had jerked urgently towards the door. 'Yes, do that, Davies. We won't be long.'

Now, she wondered briefly just what that bastard Holger had in mind. Well, he was in for a shock if he thought he could get one over on Davies. He might be a tough cookie, but Charlotte knew just how capable Davies was of handling herself in even the roughest of tight corners, against the toughest of opponents. Then she forgot her subordinate and was once more fully concerned with her own fate, as the Maestro came to her with his most winning smile and seized her hands. She felt that old familiar draining of willpower, the liquid melting of her muscles – so untypical, so disturbing, and so exciting – that only this compelling figure could arouse in her.

She was wearing a full-skirted black evening dress. Its stylish femininity, the low cut bosom, as well as the scanty bits of lace and sheer nylon stockings she wore beneath, had drawn scathing comment from her maid, but Charlotte had answered her roundly. 'Listen! We're in big trouble, believe me! Wait till I get my hands on that little shit!' The fact that the Maestro had added the proviso that she should bring Davies with her indicated the seriousness of the dilemma. But now, Charlotte shook with fear only for herself.

On his quietly voiced command, she slipped down the scrap of lace and nylon that was her knickers, balancing awkwardly on one leg, then the other, holding onto the furniture as she tugged the tiny garment over her high-heeled shoes, which he ordered her to keep on. He did not move, and she had to endure the humiliation of bending over the back of the sofa, spreading her legs wide apart and hoisting her dress up over her back to bare her buttocks for her punishment. Still it did not come, and she hung there, her muscles braced, her head touching the chintz-covered cushions.

'So you've no idea where he might be?' The Maestro's voice was perfectly modulated.

'No, Maestro.' Her reply was muffled by her doubled-over position and her head being way down in the depths of the sofa. 'There's no one he could go to, I'm sure. I don't see how he can have any money. They've scarcely ever been out of the house unaccompanied.'

'Clearly, you gravely underestimated him. Shame on you, Charlotte.'

His earlier cold fury seemed to have dissipated altogether. He sounded almost amused, yet she knew he was highly disturbed. She was well aware of Labat's unique place in the highly privileged and secret society he moved in. She had known it all along, even before the death of her sister and Richard. He was indeed a gifted musician, and an excellent teacher, having developed and honed the skills of a number of top-notch musicians and singers. But he was not as celebrated as he might, and should, have been. His circle of fame was small and highly select, dependent, not on musical talent alone, but on the powerful sensuality that guided his nature. The glossy photographs of Max which he would circulate, and which should have consisted of both her and her equally beautiful partner, would be erotic masterpieces to be possessed and cherished by a few choice and extremely wealthy individuals in the uppermost ranks of a cosmopolitan coterie. Just as, later, when they had been fully moulded to his will, the heavenly pair would be enjoyed in the flesh by some of those highly privileged clients, who would pay enormous sums to gratify their refined pleasures. Which was why that foolish boy, the shameful and secret bane of her life over so many years, had so mightily cocked things up by his untimely vanishing act. And why she was here, bent over, arse in the air, to bear the brunt of his foolish action.

At last the Maestro moved. She tensed, the muscles in her limbs quivering, the swells of her bottom clenched, forming deep hollows in the splendid rounds. She dared not lift her head to discover which instrument he had selected. Somehow, she had anticipated a whip. The first whistling cut of the springy thin cane startled her. It seemed to bounce cleanly off the resilient globes, yet it had bitten deeply, witnessed by the straight red line of fiery pain laid symmetrically across the centre of her cheeks, at right angles to the central divide.

In spite of all her efforts, she could not keep her head and shoulders from lifting, or the shrill scream from bursting forth.

'I think Mrs Maybury or one of her girls might still be working in the kitchen. If you wouldn't mind?'

Through her streaming tears, she saw that he was smilingly holding out the tiny pair of black knickers. Gasping, she took them, and wadded them inside her mouth. The strip of lace and satin was scarcely practical as a gag, but she was able to bite down on it, and, by a supreme effort of will, to muffle the cries.

Pain flared afresh at the rough invasion of his fingers on her smitten flesh prising apart the burning cheeks of her behind, and a great surge of desire flickered. She felt the slimy tip of his engorged prick stab deep into her cleft while his searching fingers groped for then found the wet and palpitating crevice of her vagina and spread the ready lips at its entrance. Then she shuddered in pain and joy and fulfilment at the plunging possession of her spasming passage that followed. He thrust furiously, utterly selfish in pursuit of his relief, but she was more than ready, and welcomed his battering rage, enfolded it, soared with it, and finally cried wildly in matching ecstasy, spitting out the limp ball of cloth at the flood of his release and her own shattering climax.

* * *

Davies hated the unaccustomed fear that was knotting up her insides, and strove hard to dismiss it. She eyed Holger with plainly hostile suspicion. 'What's your fucking Maestro want me over here for, if he's sent me off to the servants' quarters with you?'

Holger grinned infuriatingly, and shrugged. 'Who the hell knows? Perhaps he wants you to be around to take care of her after he's given your mistress a good seeing-to.' He saw the anger bristling, the fierce scowl on the plain features. 'Come on. Relax. I won't bite you. Here, have a drink. This wine's excellent stuff. Know anything about wines? Or are you more a pint of bitter type?'

She grunted derisively, but took the glass of rich dark liquid he held out to her. She sipped at its full-bodied flavour and nodded coolly. 'It'll do.' He was right, she would have preferred a beer, but she wasn't going to let him know that. He was working hard to make friendly conversation, but she could feel the familiar contempt and hate mounting acidly within her. She just couldn't stand men of any description. Especially thick hunks of beefcake like this one, showing off his muscled torso, grinning at her, thinking how superior he was to this pathetic dike. They were all so ludicrous, with their barnyard strutting. And as for that ridiculous tube of flesh hanging down between their legs or, even worse, more often than not sticking up like a pole from their hairy bellies, she'd like nothing better than to take a razor-sharp knife and with one swipe put an end to all that macho posturing.

Her anger and her unease made her swig the wine faster than she should, and soon she had taken several glasses and her head was getting heavier and heavier, her senses dulling. What was wrong with her? Christ, she could take more liquor than this. She could drink better men than this oaf under the table! But not tonight! Her head was going, it felt like lead, she could feel it wobbling on her neck. Worse than that, she had no willpower to fight away the fog that seemed to be drifting over her mind, nor the weakening lethargy stealing over her limbs.

The wine! For a brief second, like a clanging alarm bell, came the realisation that he had doped her, but then that terrible melting weakness seized her, enfolded her once more, and she sat there, her own heavy breathing thundering in her ears. She blinked down foolishly at the top of his fair close-cropped head. As short as hers, she thought distractedly.

What was he doing? She couldn't even frame the question in words, nor move to stop him, as, with a hatefully masculine chuckle, he knelt at her feet and began to unlace her boots. 'You've had a real skinful, Davies. Now it's time to enjoy ourselves, yes?' Amazement stirred her at the ease with which he lifted her feet and pulled off her boots. She tried to protest, to move, to plant a well-aimed kick. She could do nothing! Still she gaped as he slowly drew off the thick grey socks. He held her bare foot, tugged playfully at her toes, and, to her horror, she felt thick tears well up and form on her eyelashes, then trickle down her cheeks.

He was up now, behind her, pulling the dark sweater up over her head. She was lost in its stifling blackness, then it was clear of her, and she felt her arms flop uselessly to her sides. He bent and clutched her about the waist, in terrible intimacy, and she could do nothing to prevent him as he lifted her from the chair and plonked her down on the edge of the long wooden table. Roughly, he unbuttoned her shirt, tugged it out of the waistband of her jeans and dragged it off her shoulders and arms. She was crying audibly now, sniffling like a child. She tried to raise her arms, to fold them over her breasts, hating herself for even thinking of such a pathetically feminine gesture, but she couldn't do it anyway.

He was lifting the hem of the singlet, taking his time, enjoying every second of his power over her. Then the thin vest, too, was gone, and she was naked to the waist, slumped on the edge of the table, unable to protect or conceal herself from his mocking gaze. 'My God, look at you. I think I've got bigger tits than you, eh? Nice pecs, babe, but not exactly Page Three stuff, is it?' He tweaked the small nipples over the hardly discernible swellings.

She managed a tortured groan as he pushed her down on her back, stretching her out along the length of the rough wooden top, before his fingers delved into the fastening of her jeans, tugged at the zip of the fly, and fought them down over the prominent thigh muscles, to draw them off her feet. All she wore now was a pair of plain white underbriefs. They had a broad band of elastic at the waist, just like a man's undergarment. The only concession to femininity was the lack of any opening in the triangle that covered her crotch.

He took his time over the removal of this last garment, peeling it slowly off her, grinning at the exposure of the springy black bush of her pubic hair which came into sight over the top of the disappearing pants. He left her stretched out there, naked, and she wept as she strove to move. Her head lifted, with tremendous effort, then fell back against the wood, and she sobbed bitterly. 'Bastard!' she groaned.

He moved away, then came back. Through her blurred vision, she saw that he was carrying a small basin in one hand and what she at first thought was a knife in the other. She only realised that it was in fact an old-fashioned barber's razor when he began to lather the triangle of her pubis with a thick fragrant shaving foam. 'A beautiful little lady like you shouldn't have all that hair down there, sugar. Bald pussies are all the rage now, my lovely! Better keep still. I'm not so skilful at shaving ladies' beards.'

She felt, and heard, the scrape of the razor over her skin. He rinsed the area, then lathered it again, and repeated the process. Caught in the nightmare helplessness of the victim, she felt his fingers scrabbling intimately at the folds of her labia, stretching the sensitive tissue as he wielded the blade at the very brim of her sexual fissure. Eventually he declared himself satisfied and gave the smoothly denuded pout of her mons one last wipe with a towel. 'I'm sorry, my love. So far it's been all fun for you, but, you know, you and your mistress have been naughty girls, haven't you? I'm sure the Maestro has made your mistress sorry for her carelessness. Now it's the maid's turn.'

He rolled her over. Hating herself, she heard her voice pleading with him. 'No! Please don't! Let me go, please!'

He shook his head, grinning wickedly, then bent low, his lips moving against her ear. 'You'll love it once you get used to it.'

Eleven

'Are you sure you don't mind my not fucking you?'

Polly shook her head inadequately, in an effort to express her giddy delight at the pleasures he had already brought to her. 'Of course I'm sure. When I think – when you do those things you do to me . . .' She shivered dramatically, but with genuine excitement, at the thought of the wonderful lovemaking he had given her. Then guilt stabbed at her again, this time for a very different reason, when her mind dwelt on her selfishness; the way she simply lay back, opened herself, took all that hectic loving until mind and body spun wonderfully, deliriously, out of control. 'I just wish – there was more I could do . . . for you . . . to make you . . .' In spite of their intimacy in the cocooned world of the flat, her shyness held her back from expressing her wish more specifically. 'I seem to do nothing . . . except take all the time,' she finished lamely.

'Bollocks!' He rolled over until their naked bodies were once again plastered together in the tangled sheets. His hands on her bottom pulled her belly close against his. She could feel the cold wetness of his squirming penis on her, so close to her own sore but throbbing centre of desire that, in spite of her brave words, she felt a great yearning suddenly to feel that very penetration she had just denied concern over.

She had been shocked to her very foundation at first by this strange boy's frankness, his utter unself-consciousness about sexuality, both his own and hers. He had confessed in great detail the ambivalence of his sexual inclinations. 'Most of the time, I'm closer to a girl than a boy in the way I feel. With Max – I know she's been dying for me to fuck her ever since we were kids –' he grinned at the wide-eyed horror on Polly's face, her gasp of outrage '– but it just never bothered me. I've often wished I was a girl, too, then we could have a superb lesbian relationship. I used to love dressing up in her things, using her make-up. Not that she was allowed much, or that we had much chance to get up to anything really wicked! They were nearly always around.' He gave an exaggerated shudder. 'Especially that bloody dike, Davies!' He grinned again, shaking off the instant of sombreness. 'I always used to imagine I was Max when I tossed off.'

His speech was punctuated by another soft squeal of shock-horror from his listener. Polly was still in a daze most of the time at how her world had been turned upside down by this entrancing boy. She could scarcely believe that they had been together only two days. 'Listen,' she pleaded now, kissing him avidly on the lips, and disengaging herself from his embrace. 'I really have to get up. I can't afford to miss work today. It's a full day, morning *and* afternoon.' She was teaching at one comprehensive from 9.30 until noon, then at another across the city, after lunch. She stood, trying not to use her arms to shield herself from his gaze. 'Bring me some cereal in the bath. There's a good boy.'

'Yes, Mumsie!' She squealed and ran, as he pursued her across the short passageway into the gloom of the little bathroom. He smacked her bottom resoundingly and she yelped, then moaned as he gathered her to him and sealed off her mouth with his in a long kiss.

'Please, Antonio! Don't! I can't – it can't happen any more. So many times last night! Then first thing this morning . . .' She shivered at the memory of waking in the grey dimness of dawn to find herself sprawled, her legs lewdly spread, and that devouring heavenly wicked tongue exploring her sexual orifice, rousing the tender tissue to yet more dizzy heights of passion and loss.

He insisted on jumping in with her, sending the water splashing over walls and lino-ed floor while he washed her from neck down over every curve, plane, hollow and cleft, until her body, which she thought had been sated beyond her wildest imaginings, was thrumming with urgent hunger yet again. But even that hot melting desire was an exquisite torment she would be glad to endure through the drearily interminable hours of the day without him, until she could return to this private world she never wanted to leave. Even her fear of the wicked pair who had ruled the two young people's lives was held in abeyance by her rapture at having him so completely to herself.

Away from him, sitting wearily on the crowded morning bus, dark specs sensibly in place, dark hair discreetly parted, dressed in neatly unexciting two-piece, thick black tights and flat black shoes, her reeling mind went over the incredible events of the last few days. A blush tinged her cheeks at the recall of his teasing words after he had first made love to her. 'Perhaps you're a lesbian, Polly. After all, I'm only doing girlie things to you. Max could give you just as good a time.' Her blushes deepened at the disturbingly titillating thought.

But it was true. When he used his mouth on her, 'ate' her, as he so graphically put it, it drove her wild, the orgasms she experienced were more shattering than *she could* imagine. She was sure she would never need a man – or a woman – to do anything other than that to her. She had, shyly, offered to let him 'do it properly' to her. Her embarrassment was, at least temporarily, forgotten in her shock at his forthright reply.

'I don't know if you've noticed, Polly, my love, but my willy evinces great reluctance to burrow into even your virginally narrow hole, and would indeed fail to do so, I am certain, should we attempt to bring them together. I think we'd better let perverse nature take its course, don't you?'

Which was, more or less, what it was doing, as, after she had left the flat, Antonio lay face down on the narrow bed. His legs were primly together, the narrow hips scarcely moving; only the clenching and hollowing of his tight buttocks indicated the excitement mounting unstoppably through him, that, and his ragged sighs as impetuous nature finally *did* take its flowing course and erupted in the ejaculation which stained the sheet and stickily coated his lower belly and the small patch of his pubis.

Newly bathed, he wandered back into the bedroom, his nose wrinkling fastidiously at the tell-tale hint of spilt semen on the air. Ignoring the wet patch on the rumpled sheet, he went to the dressing table and liberally doused his body in Clinique perfume from the bottle there. Eagerly, he began opening drawers, searching through the tops and tights, scarves and socks. He found the bras, examined them, confirming what his eyes and exploring hands had already told him: that her breasts were no more impressive than Max's modest mammaries. And a good job, too, he assured himself. Nothing could be more grotesque than those massively inflated balloons the Page Three bimbos paraded before them.

He spent more time with the knicker drawer, riffling through the plain workaday briefs, in black and white cottons. One or two were more adventurous – a pair in deep red, another in pastel blue, several with a floral print over them, reminding him of the kind Max wore in her early teens. Not that Max had had any say in the underwear that was supplied for her. He was surprised that Polly 'Mouse' should have been so daring as to have found herself a flat and a life (if you could call it that) so far from her parents. Even though that life was as dull as ditchwater – or had been until he had re-entered her drab existence!

Aroused by his thoughts, in spite of his recent satiation, he felt his prick flutter. He explored once more, reaching into the further depths of the drawer, behind the pile of knickers, and, to his delight, found some filmy silken garments very different from the prosaic cotton briefs he had thus far discovered. Several pairs of naughtier knicks – a scarlet pair, with an exotic lace trimming; bikini briefs in shining satin, black and red, and a deep yellow-ivory; a thong in midnight blue, and another in vivid flame colour! Oh Poll Mouse! I'll make you give me a fashion parade tonight. Then his fingers felt the edges of a box. Secret love letters? Eagerly, he slipped it out, opened it – and laughed aloud in amazement at the glittering gold vibrator nestling coyly within. Well well. The mouse was a secret sex kitten after all!

Excited and restless at his discoveries, he could not resist slipping the thong over his feet and drawing it up. It fitted snugly enough, the satin triangle hugging his prick. He eased the bootlace-thin straps about his hips, fitted one into the crack of his bottom. It looked good. He felt the electric tingle of response in his loins. He found a pair of sheer nylon tights, sat on the edge of the bed and rolled them on, with some difficulty, fitting them up over his feet and ankles, knees and thighs, then stood and eased them into place over bum and crotch. He was thankful that he so closely matched his darling Max in size for, had he been any taller, Polly's tights would not have fitted at all. He stood and surveyed himself in the exotic garments. He searched, found a white silk camisole top, and slipped it on over his head. It was a bit tight, true, but once it was on, the caress of silk, the straps at his shoulders, felt good.

Pulsing with excitement now, he began a thorough search of her wardrobe and found a pretty, demure blouse and a dark grey skirt, almost mini. Damn it, he always said he had legs as good as Max. They looked formidable in the sheer nylon. Confident now that he would be successful, he ferreted through the modest collection of shoes and found a pair of strappy heeled sandals stowed away at the back of the cupboard and clearly little used. Almost frivolously tarty for our Poll! He fastened them on and paced uncertainly about the flat, tottering a little at first. Shorten your step, pillock! he admonished himself.

Now for the hair. Fortunately, it was as long as Max's. Anyway, most girls wore their hair short nowadays. If he brushed it forward, then swept it across, the way Max did . . . some lacquer . . . that's it. Just a touch of make-up. Lip gloss. There! He smiled seductively, pursed a kiss at his reflection. 'Hello, Toni, darling. You're quite a chick!'

Heart beating fast, he pulled on a light fleece – not quite the outer garment he would have chosen to complete the get-up, but it looked breezy outside. Outside! Polly had warned him earnestly not to set foot outside the flat, not even to be seen at the windows. But hell! Who would know? Besides, this

117

was the adventure of a lifetime. His female alter ego had sprung miraculously to life. Let's go, baby! Picking his way uncertainly down the staircase in the unfamiliar heels, he opened the front door and stepped into the outside world, and the blessed kiss of the wind on his transformed personality.

Davies whimpered softly as she forced her aching body to move. She clambered stiffly off the hard table and winced at the pain that lanced through her buttocks. She realised she had been sniffling quietly, probably from the moment he had climbed off her after their savage coupling.

'What's your first name? I refuse to call a woman I've just shagged by her surname.'

'Bron.' She murmured it spiritlessly, only mildly shocked at her own readiness to answer, to obey. But then she felt a different person altogether from the confident butch personality who had entered this room – how long ago now? A lifetime, it seemed. She noticed that he was dressed again, and she writhed with inward shame at her own nudity. She glanced about her and moved like a crone, gathering up the bits of clothing he had flung carelessly on the floor. She stumbled, then hissed with pain as she hauled up her knickers and they made contact with her flayed backside. Aware of his amused gaze, she struggled into the rest of her clothing, gasping as she sat on a hard chair to draw on her boots. She hung her head to avoid his mocking eyes as he tossed a twenty-pound note on the table in front of her.

'The Maestro says you're to take a taxi home. He's keeping your mistress here tonight.' She kept her head down as she took the money and heaved herself to her feet. 'Hey! Just a minute! Come and say goodbye.' She stopped, feeling herself trembling with loathing, but also with something else, something darker, frighteningly perverse – another surrender of will that was shockingly thrilling. He took her in his arms, crushed her to him, and covered her mouth with his. Sobbing, she nevertheless parted her lips submissively and received the plunging invasion of his tongue – as shiveringly possessive as that steel-hard prick of his – in a kiss that left her breathless. Out in the night-time street, every movement sent jolting pain through her as she walked to the taxi rank.

In the back of the cab, she found the tears rolling down her face again, her chest and shoulders heaving in racking sobs. ' 'Ere! You all right, love?'

She met the cabbie's curious eyes in the dim reflection of his mirror through the open partition. 'Fuck off!' she managed hoarsely, and was grateful when he merely shrugged and slammed the partition shut. She slumped back on the cold seat and let the misery wash over her, reliving each moment in tortured solitude.

She knew that proud German cockster probably considered himself the first bloke ever to give her a good shafting. She had even failed to argue when he had said as much. But now her mind drifted helplessly back over the years, almost twenty of them, to the days of her youth and her brutal initiation into the world of heterosex.

She had always felt different, even from early schooldays, aware of her physical prowess, her delight in tomboyish rough and tumble, her good-natured contempt for the wimpishness of the members of her own sex. Then, as she moved into adolescence, she became aware of a difference in her attitude; the effect of pretty girls on her, her admiration for their looks, their softness, their femininity, none of which she wanted for herself. She envied the boys' rangy toughness, their macho leathers or ragged denims, their cropped or gelled hairstyles. She began to emulate them. Their company excited her, but not in the way they wanted. When they began to come onto her, she was shocked and secretly dismayed. She harboured secret guilt that she hadn't done 'it' when so many of her female contemporaries clearly had and spent most of the time talking ecstatically about it.

Then, when she was sixteen, drifting far afield from her own home, she met Carol: big brown eyes and long straight white-gold hair framing a flawless face, a stunning combination that left the young Davies literally breathless, her guts churning emptily. In her narrow faded jeans and scuffed leather bomber jacket, she thought she looked pretty cool herself. And, to her amazement, it appeared the golden-haired girl thought so too, for she blushed and smiled shyly and clearly loved every minute of the awkward chat-up.

'Bron. That's a funny name. Sounds foreign.'

'It's Welsh,' Davies answered. 'Listen, can I see you home?' With another cute blush and a little nod, Carol agreed. As soon as they were away from the club, she shyly offered her hand and Davies, her head reeling, held its softness reverently. She asked questions non-stop on the walk through the busy streets, and Carol was happy to answer, gradually overcoming that attractive shyness. They reached the end of the shabby terraced street where Carol lived.

'Better not come any farther. Don't want my old man – or my brothers – to see us. I – I don't go out much with boys,' she confessed, glancing down with touching childlike awkwardness. 'But you – you're different. Can I see you again?' It wasn't until she offered her mouth, tilting it trustingly, and put her hands on the leather shoulders, that Davies, her head spinning, realised the startling mistake this lovely innocent girl had made. She thought her new friend was a boy! Shocked as she was, Davies seized the slim figure, pulled her close, and they kissed, open-mouthed, in raw passion.

Davies vowed to herself she would end the deception. But she didn't, and they met regularly, and she courted the golden girl until both of them were ablaze with physical desire. The intimacy grew, Davies always taking and holding the initiative, as most boys would, until she experienced the rapturous delight of caressing Carol's small but beautifully rounded breasts, released from their flimsy cover, and tasting the sweetly engorged, pale little buds of the proffered nipples. Inevitably, there came the night when, in the bedroom of one of Carol's friends, Davies' hands made further inroads, until the unsteadily searching fingers slipped inside the elastic of the damp nylon knickers, eased them off the slender virginal hips, and finally claimed the dewy slit of her lover's vulva, damply ready to be surrendered to the throbbing male conqueror Carol was clamorously waiting for.

The conquest was not as the weeping girl had anticipated, though shattering enough, as Davies put loving hands and worshipping tongue to their heady task. But afterwards Carol sobbed brokenly, and could not be comforted by Davies' more restrained and tender kisses. 'Don't – don't you want to?' the blonde girl sobbed bitterly.

And, tormented by her own desire, and her real love for the distraught figure she held, Davies at last confessed. Seizing Carol's limp hand, she guided it to her own wet and throbbing crotch still hidden beneath her clothing. 'I'm just like you, my darling. I'm a girl!' The piercing screams of rigid hysteria pursued the fleeing transgressor all the way down the stairs and out into the street.

Forlornly, Davies strove to get in touch, by phone and by letter, all to no avail. It was while she was coming home from her job in a local factory that the four young men attacked her, dragging her into an old banger of a car, before she had time even to scream, and pinning her down on the floor while they raced to a patch of woodland on the edge of town. 'Fucking lesbo perv!' She had already realised the reason for the kidnap. Two of her abductors were the beloved Carol's brothers. Knowing that did not lessen the trauma of the brutal events which followed.

Her clothes were ripped from her and she was pinned to the leafy ground, face down, limbs spread-eagled. They used thin branches plucked from the bushes around them. Soon her pale skin was lacerated by thin red angry lines, but the agony went on and on. They had stuffed one of her socks into her mouth so that her cries of agony were muffled.

Then came a new nightmare, as they swung her over onto her stinging back. And something else, a new surrender, deep within; she sobbed now, her screams dying, shamed by the treachery of her battered flesh as excitement mounted, fanned by the very brutality it was being subjected to. The laughter and shouted obscenities had stopped. All she could hear now were the savage grunts, and her own in response to the pounding weight on her. She raised her knees and wrapped her thighs about him, thrilled by the feel of his bare skin on hers. Her ankles crossed behind him, her heels drummed on his humping back, and her cries mixed with his and rose to mingle with the small woodland sounds and the muted roar of distant traffic.

Twelve

'Please, Maestro. You don't really need me for this. Can't I go?' Charlotte's voice was husky, soft with its unaccustomed submission. She blushed as she recognised the triumph behind his broad smile.

'No, of course not. This is all part of the mess you and your dike maid caused. Besides, the child might just know something that will help us. And you may recognise it far more easily than I do. A name, a place. In any case, what makes you think I've finished with you, my dear?' The smile broadened, and she felt the blush seeping hotly upwards, and hated herself for her complicity in her own servitude. He had amply demonstrated the magical power he still held over her, which he had wielded all the years of their association. As though to highlight acknowledgement, she felt her body's pulsing response to these thoughts. She had not put her knickers back on after his latest proof of that dominion, and she was acutely aware of her bareness under the black gown, apart from the sheer stockings and the garter belt.

Her reflections were interrupted by the opening of the door and the appearance of her niece, led by Holger, who was holding her by the arm. The naked girl gave a little gasp of surprise at seeing Charlotte and her hands moved automatically, first to her denuded loins, then to her breasts. 'Oh! Aunt Charlotte! I thought you'd gone.'

'No, my dear. Your aunt is staying here tonight. We want to try and get this unpleasant business sorted out as soon as possible. I'm sure you do, too. You want to see Antonio safely home again, don't you?'

She stared at the Maestro, her eyes wide and fearful. 'Yes – yes, of course. But I don't – I haven't any idea . . .'

'Oh, you might be surprised, Max, at what you know, when you really try. We're going to help you. Come here.' Her nervousness betrayed in every step, Max advanced across the polished floor and stood before him. 'Turn around.'

She obeyed. She felt his hands moving her short hair at the nape of her neck, then the sealing velvet pad descended over her eyes, she felt him adjusting the elastic, and she was enclosed in soft blackness. 'Please!' she whispered abjectly, her body visibly trembling.

His breath was warm at her earlobe, his lips tickling her. 'It will help to concentrate your mind.' She flinched at the sudden touch of a hand at her breast, and her own hands came up automatically to meet it. 'Holger.' She felt her arms captured, pulled down behind her, and her wrists bound together by cord. The hand was still playing with her breast, stroking gently, then a finger and thumb teased and pulled at the nipple, rolling it between the pads until it budded to erection. She tried to remain motionless as the hand transferred to her other breast and swiftly roused its nipple, too, to peaked hardness.

All at once, she detected a subtle female perfume, and guessed that her aunt had come close. Then she jerked, giving a cry of startled pain at the bite of some object on her right nipple. She recognised Holger's huge hands, rough now, holding her upper arms. She squirmed, and yelped again as her other nipple was clamped in an equally fierce grip. She began to weep in short panting sobs, hunching her shoulders forward to ease the tight pressure nipping at both breasts now. She could feel the hanging weight of the clips that had been placed on her sensitive flesh, and she breathed shallowly against the biting pressure. 'Oh please!' she begged. 'It hurts!'

'A little pain can help clarify the mind, too, my dear,' the Maestro's smooth tones declared. She felt hands at her back and her thighs, lifting her with firm gentleness, and the world tipped dizzily as they laid her carefully along the length of the desk. She could feel its edges on the backs of her knees. She lay awkwardly, her arms trapped beneath her, her bound hands digging into her buttocks.

She felt the silk skirt of her aunt's dress brushing against the front of her shins and dangling feet, then the scratch of Charlotte's nails pushing at her thighs. 'Open your legs, girl!' Muscles rigid with anticipation, Max was too afraid not to obey, and she spread her thighs, exposing her bare sex cleft. She recognised the long immaculately manicured nails as her aunt's thumbs pressed firmly on her labia, either side, peeling them open to reveal the gleaming pink of the inner surface.

'Exquisite!' The Maestro's voice, deep with his appreciation and carrying also a hint of rich amusement, sounded closer, and the mortified girl visualised him bending over her, peering at her belly. Charlotte's thumbs pressed a little harder, the nails digging painfully into the soft flesh. 'So freshly perfect, so unspoilt.'

Her aunt's hands moved, and now pinned her brutally to the desktop by the tops of her thighs.

Max's buttocks flexed against the unyielding wooden surface beneath her at this new ordeal. And now, in torturous refinement, fingers – the distraught figure had no idea whose – sought out the uppermost fold of her vulva and explored the slippery tissue, peeling it further back to seek out the throbbing sensitivity of the clitoral hood. Blubbering blindly, Max gnawed at her lip, feeling the wild beating of her response to this stimulation.

Her three tormentors gazed enraptured at the pale body pinned to the desk, watching the quivering little darts of the gaily coloured plastic pegs at the breasts. 'Oh, please!' the blinded girl sobbed, no longer struggling now, her movements purely a reaction to the fierce excitation caused by that wickedly knowledgeable caressing. 'I can't – oh, oh! Let me go – please!'

Max gasped at the deeper intrusion, sensually stroking, caressing the slippery flesh, adding to the fires of passion already blazing. Somehow, Max knew it was the Maestro who was thus intimately possessing her before she felt the pressure of his clothed body leaning lightly over her, his mouth close enough for her to feel his breath on her upturned face. 'How's your memory now, Max?' he murmured. 'Sharpened yet? Think, my dear. Who in the world does Antonio know? Who could he possibly turn to for help? Think hard!'

And now, the worst agony of all, those fingers were abruptly withdrawn. 'That girl! That – the one who taught us for a while. At the house. Last year! Polly! Polly Smythe!' Max seemed to hear the urgent words as though coming from another person. She was startled at the way they popped into her mind and were torn from her working throat. At the instant she screamed them out, she felt a wave of guilt, of

126

betrayal, at once superseded by an urge to beg for the fingers to return to their intimate explorations.

'What?' Charlotte's exclamation rang with disbelief, and then shock, as she realised how completely she had forgotten the wretched little mouse whom she had employed briefly as a tutor. And all at once she realised how, absurd as it was, it might make sense. How that pathetic creature might well have come to Antonio's aid, for hadn't he continued to receive tuition from her at the academy after Charlotte had dismissed her as Max's teacher? The timorous creature had looked quite distraught when Charlotte had given her her marching orders. She could well imagine how such a drab little wallflower would be dazzled by her contact with two such exceptional talents as her two wards. And Toni's effete sensitive looks, his insouciant charm, would probably have a powerful effect on such a little miss nobody.

The Maestro was staring at Charlotte, his eyebrows raised in enquiry. Clearly, he had never heard of Polly Smythe. And why on earth should he? The creature was as insignificant in the music world as she was in every facet of her puny existence. Quickly she explained. He nodded crisply. Smiling, he let his fingers play briefly over Max's captive flesh once more, this time with a deliberately teasing manner, before he pulled them away a second time. 'Excellent, my dear. You see? I told you you would surprise yourself. We have no secrets from each other, eh, Max?'

'I don't know if – if – I just thought – I know she liked Toni –'

'And you, my girl!' Charlotte chuckled lewdly. 'She was as eager to get into your pants as his. And why not?' With playful viciousness, Charlotte tweaked the pegs attached to Max's nipples.

'Ow! Please! It's hurting so – please, let me go!'

She sensed their withdrawal from her, and her body relaxed. She lay limply, her feet hanging over the edge of the table while the hard surface dug coldly into her back. She wept quietly, sniffling, feeling the familiar wetness of the pad across her eyes. She heard movement, their voices, then the soft swish and click of the door closing. 'Please! Can I go now? Please?' Silence, except for her snuffling sobs. 'Is anybody here? Can I go?'

She rolled painfully onto one side, struggling, her legs kicking to lift herself up. She rolled off the table, feeling the sharpness of its edge dig into her, then she was standing, swaying, her hands still tied behind her. She shuffled forward a few uncertain steps and whimpered anew at the discomfort of the nipping clamps at her breasts. She bent her shoulders a little, breathed as shallowly as she could to ease the pain. 'It hurts,' she croaked blindly. 'Can someone untie me? Take these things off, please?' No one answered and, crying softly, she carefully lowered herself to sit on the rough carpeting, her knees drawn up until she could feel the plastic pegs that dangled from her nipples brushing against the front of her thighs. She waited dumbly for release.

By the end of the afternoon, Polly could feel the clinging wetness of her desire and the weakness of longing in her limbs. The loud clicks of the thick black pointer marking off every jerking minute on the wall clock seemed endlessly spaced. The sniggering insolence and insults of the two slovenly fourteen-year-olds slumped at their keyboards flowed by her almost unnoticed. She trembled and ached with her hunger to escape from this noisy hellhole back to the insulated magic of the flat, and Antonio's magical presence. The hour-long waiting and the two bus rides would be the final test of endurance before utter happiness could be realised.

Buffeted by the jostling swearing crowds, swept along the corridor of the school like a piece of flotsam, Polly did not even go to the staff room at the final bell, but headed straight for the exit. Lost in her own urgency, she was heedless of the crude obscenities, the raucous laughter surrounding her. Then she was out into the grey afternoon, and halted on the wide steps leading down to the school yard, gaping in dumb wonder at the vision waiting there for her, grinning impishly at her drop-jawed amazement. 'Max?' she managed to gasp at last to the spectacle of the lovely dark-haired girl. Her heart lurched, both with instinctive appreciation and with thudding alarm. 'How did . . . what are you doing here?'

The girl laughed, reaching out to take her hand, and Polly's heart hammered even more violently in shocked recognition. 'Antonio! For God's sake! What –'

'Shuttup!' the laughing figure hissed, the dark head dipping so close it nuzzled Polly's untidy brown locks. 'You want to get me arrested? Let's get the fuck out of here, quick!'

Bewildered, Polly noticed the familiarity of the clothing the girl was dressed in. She let Antonio take her firmly by the arm and lead her swiftly through the jostling throng of youngsters, and finally out to the safe anonymity of the busy street.

'You're crazy!' Polly gasped at last. 'I told you not to – what on earth do you think you're doing?'

The dark eyes flashed with mischievous joy, and Toni hugged the startled teacher even closer. One or two of the students still thickly surrounding the pair stared curiously. Polly blushed fiercely. 'Don't you think I make a pretty stunning girl then?' he chuckled. 'And if I keep my voice down to a husky whisper, I think I sound pretty sexy, too! Come on! Where do we get the bus? Let's get out of here before these adolescent hunks rape the two of us!'

They sat together on the upper deck of the bus during the long ride in towards the centre of the city. Polly was gradually calming down a little, though she was still very apprehensive. 'What do you reckon to my legs?' he teased. He grabbed her hand and held it to the smooth nylon-clad thigh much in evidence below the short grey skirt. Polly snatched her palm away from the contact, glaring round her wildly.

'Don't!' she squealed in panic. She stammered, and her eyes beneath her spectacles brimmed with threatening tears. 'What if someone sees? We must get back to the flat! You're mad! This is so dangerous!'

'Stop squirming about! You look as though you're going to pee yourself! Relax, will you? Who the hell's going to take any notice of a couple of chicks in all this?' He waved his hand at the bustling crowds and the traffic outside the window. 'I just had to get out of that flat! I've been cooped up for ever. It was doing my head in.' He gestured at his slim body. 'And it's pretty effective, don't you think? Cool, eh? Look! We're right in the middle of town now. No one would ever find us here. Let's go somewhere for a drink. I haven't had this much fun in years!' He stood up and turned down the swaying aisle of the slowing vehicle. With a gasp of annoyance and fear, Polly followed him.

'Here! This looks quiet enough. Come on, Poll! Buy me a drink.' He led the way in from the street. They found themselves in the dim comfort of a rather old-fashioned bar with discreet lighting. The faded furniture consisted of heavy, deeply upholstered armchairs around low, solid wooden tables with glass tops. In contrast, the long counter itself was brightly, almost theatrically, lit. Its brass foot rail gleamed, and a row of narrow high stools was ranged before it. To Polly's horror, Antonio made straight for these and clambered up on one, displaying a great deal of his shapely nylon limbs as he crossed them and arranged the short skirt over his thighs. Crimson-faced, Polly climbed up beside him and smoothed down her far more decorous and lengthier skirt about her.

'What are you going to buy me, darling?' Antonio lisped in his husky tone. Polly's eyes blinked at him, wide and terrified, from behind her glasses. Her mouth opened and shut helplessly. 'How about a glass of white wine?' he prompted, beaming his glossy smile, and batting his mascara-ed lashes provocatively. 'Two, please,' he whispered at the barman, who was staring at them with rapidly increasing interest. He served the drinks and stood there, waiting. 'Polly!' Antonio prompted. Belatedly Polly realised what the barman was waiting for, and, blushing even more, she hastily grabbed at her purse and fumbled out a note to pay for the drinks.

They had scarcely taken more than two sips of the cold wine when two figures materialised from the dimly lit background of the almost-deserted pub. 'Hi. You girls all alone? Don't mind if we join you, do you? What are you drinking? White wine? Can't I tempt you to something a little more adventurous?'

The speaker was a solid-looking man with short fair hair and the thin line of a slightly darker moustache. His face was red, with a weather-beaten look. His frame hinted at a lean fitness, and his dress – a dark sports jacket and lighter grey trousers with knife-edge creases – suggested a note of formal conservatism. Military rather than business, Antonio deduced. He was not wearing a tie, but his white shirt was immaculate and well pressed, its collar standing stiff and high inside the lapels of his jacket, highlighting his tanned complexion.

'Why, thank you. That's very kind. I'll have a gin and tonic, if I may.'

'My name's Dave. And this is Darren. Pleased to meet you.'

'Hello. I'm Antonia. But my friends call me Toni.'

'Right then – Toni. Cheers. Bottoms up, as they say!'

His companion had already moved around to stand beside Polly, who was still staring mutely, like a frightened rabbit. He seemed content to leave the initiative to his more talkative friend.

'I can't believe a pair of good-lookers like you two are all alone. Seems our luck is turning at last, Darren, mate. Don't mind if we stick with you for an hour or two? We're only in town tonight. We're off up north tomorrow.'

'You must let us buy you a drink now,' Antonio insisted, and ordered another round, ignoring Polly's admonishing glance. She was hastily calculating whether she'd have enough to buy another after this one, should she be called upon to do so.

'I must go to – er – excuse me!' Polly muttered, after they had finished their second drink. She felt Darren's firm grip on her arm as she slid off the stool. Antonio gave another swift flash of leg as he, too, dismounted, with Dave's eager help.

'I need the little girls' room as well. Make room for some more!' he whispered, leaning in to Dave, whose hand rested briefly but with intent on Antonio's buttock. 'Won't be long!'

It wasn't until they were through the door at the

far end of the bar and facing the entrance to the Ladies' that Polly gave an outraged squeal. 'You can't come in here!'

Antonio giggled, and gestured at himself. 'What do you reckon? I should go into the Gents'?' Impatiently, he pushed her through the swing door and into the toilet. He went into the compartment next to Polly and turned, hiking up the skirt and tugging the blue thong down onto his thighs before he sat at the pedestal and let the urine flow, with a shudder of relief. The action, and the novelty of sitting there, of the unusual situation and the female clothing, thrilled him powerfully. He felt the desire flaring, his prick stirring, so that, for several seconds he reached down and stroked it, his excitement mounting. He thought of the two men, of the unsuspecting Dave, waiting out there. He was probably aroused, too, thinking of what he hoped would happen later. What *would* happen? Nothing, Antonio assured himself, but there would be the opportunity for some private laughs along the way. And what a story he'd have to tell Max when ... he felt the tide of self-disgust at his desertion of her, his cowardice in fleeing as he had. Then he desperately pushed these thoughts away.

'Let's just get out of here! Now!' Polly's face was wild, reflecting her fear. 'They – they think – they want to stay with us. Let's leave before we get into trouble. There must be another way out!'

She whimpered with fright as he grabbed her and forced her against one of the washbasins, bending her back until her head was touching the mirror. Their bellies and their thighs, their lower limbs, were pressed intimately together. 'Come on, Polly Mouse!' he breathed, his gleaming lips moving slowly towards hers. 'Live a little, eh? You're only young once, baby! I won't let anything bad happen to you!' Their lips met. Polly's strangled cry was smothered as his tongue glided in, taking possession of her, and she trembled against him. 'We won't let them know we're dikes just yet!' She was panting, gulping for breath, and gazing helplessly at him when he released her.

The two men watched the two girls approaching them, their arms linked. 'I reckon we're in with a chance here, Darren, mate!' Dave murmured, appreciating every movement of the slim forms coming towards them. 'That Toni bird may sound like a feller, with that deep voice of hers, but she sure as hell don't look like one! She's in for the ride of her life tonight!'

Thirteen

'Hey! Take it easy, all right?' Antonio gasped against the roughness of the hand ripping at his blouse and thrusting through the gap, clawing at the silk of the camisole over his breast. He felt faint with fear, but also with an overwhelming excitement. 'There's no need to be so rough!'

The hands plucked him upright and slammed him against the hood of the car, bending him over it backwards, holding his thin wrists out above his head. Antonio's head was still ringing. He felt as if every fibre of strength had drained away from his muscles. There was a weird sense of relaxation, a strange almost-acceptance of his helplessness, which was at one with the throbbing excitement he could feel at his loins. His chest was heaving, the breath rasping in his throat. The blouse had been torn open to the waist. The silk of the camisole was exposed, the thin strap and the narrow trim of lace at its bosom. The silk shimmered in the faint light from a distant lamp. Antonio gazed up, not speaking now, suppressing his sobs, his lips slightly parted.

Dave's face flamed above him, the breath hot on his face. 'You fucking – I really thought – you look like a fucking girl!' The voice cracked with desperation. He sounded close to tears himself.

Antonio was still curling his lower lip, holding his mouth open, tasting the sweet seep of his blood, when the hands plucked at him again and drove him down on his knees. He sensed a movement in front of his face, heard the hiss of the zip being drawn back and the scrabble of the frantic hand. All at once, with his renewed panic, strength of movement returned. He pushed himself upwards and, as he did so, brought his right knee up with devastating force into the exposed and gaping groin, his attack unhampered by the short skirt which had ridden up around his hips.

Dave let out a choked-off grunt and doubled up, just as Toni's right shoulder caught him powerfully under his bowing head. He fell back on the wet tarmac beside the car, his groans intermingled with the sounds of violent retching.

Less than fifty yards away, in the dampness of the narrow patch of grass screened by sombre bushes, Polly was oblivious to all but her own fear. She lay resisting feebly now while Darren, this stranger to whom she had scarcely spoken more than a few words, struggled to haul down her black tights and the white briefs. She wept desolately, wondering in her reeling mind how on earth it had come to this: the terrifying scenario she had so vividly pictured, with a growing sense of helplessness, over the past two drink-laden hours, and had so thrilled to in the solitude of her bedroom, with her golden vibrator, for so many nights.

She had endured his kisses, his increasingly brutal passion, until, in the trapped darkness of this sordid little piece of land, with the traffic humming all around them, she had known it was too late. 'Please don't! I'm a virgin!' she sobbed, and his incredulous bark of laughter had been a further scourge to her shame.

'Fuck off!'

'I am! I swear! I've never – never done it!'

'You're a prick-teasing little liar, you slag!' She had fought feebly then, until he became really rough, and dragged her to the ground. 'Liar!' He repeated the word, hissing it in her ear as his hands scrabbled and clawed under her skirt.

'No, no!' Her brown head swivelled madly, she shook and wept at his potent animal lust. This was it! The first possessor of her body, the first man about to bludgeon into her, was this anonymous sweating drink-sodden creature rutting at her like a dog. Despair and a kind of useless fury overwhelmed her until she could feel the need to scream dementedly, to howl like the bitch she felt she was, clogging her throat.

Then, through her despair, she heard Toni's frantic call, heard his threshing charge somewhere close at hand, and she screamed out with all the frenzy of her desperation in answer. 'Here! Help me! Toni! Oh God! Help me!'

She was fighting again, with more vigour now, and her shrieks penetrated Darren's drink-fired urgency. 'For fuck's sake!' His hands fell away from her and he squirmed back, staggering to his feet, adjusting his own clothing. 'You mad bitch! You'll have the whole neighbourhood up!' His eyes widened at the sudden apparition of the other slim figure, clothes half torn from her, who loomed up like a white ghost, yelling. The voice? It was wild, shrill, but harsh, cracking. Like . . . like a *bloke!* The world was spinning crazily. He lurched away, making for the car park, fearful of being caught like this, of being accused. Meanwhile, the young chick, the one who called herself Toni, had grabbed the other one, and they were both fleeing, racing away through the bushes hand in hand.

Toni gripped the sobbing Polly tightly. They ran crashing through the undergrowth of the small enclosure, blundered out into a still-busy lamplit street, plunged dangerously through the line of traffic to the other side, then ran on, both gasping for breath now, and into another larger enclosure with grass and taller trees which they finally realised was a park. Still they ran, on and on, until exhaustion forced them to pause, and they hung there, doubled over, coughing and retching, their breath coming in agonised wheezes. It was some minutes before they had recovered enough to take note of their surroundings, and their dishevelled state.

'Oh God!' Polly blubbered. Her hair was a wild mess, her face streaked with tears and sweat and mucus. She had a great hole in the left knee of her black tights. 'He – nearly – he was going to rape me!'

Toni was in an even worse condition. The white blouse gaped, torn completely from one shoulder where the thin strap and the shining silk of the lace-fringed camisole showed. The sandals had gone and the sheer tights were a mass of holes about the feet, where the darkly painted toenails were poking through. The torn blouse and undergarment were liberally spotted with the blood which had dripped from his lower lip, badly swollen and still bleeding a little from Dave's furious assault.

The overwhelming terror swept over Polly once again. She started to shake violently, her knees could no longer support her. She sank into the wet grass, curled up, keening desolately. 'Oh, Toni! How could you? You crazy, crazy little fool! It's all your fault! Oh God! What's going to happen to us?' She looked up at him, her face ravaged with her grief. 'I – I've lost my bloody glasses! You little fool!'

He stared down at her, blinking, as though he was seeing her for the first time. Her sensible skirt was covered in mud, the jacket hung open, a button missing, her blouse gaped like his own. He could see her bare skin in the gap above the skirt. He saw the muddy paleness of her knee thrusting through the great hole in her tights. He began to laugh hysterically. 'His face! You should have seen his face, Poll! When he – he tried to feel my tits. Then he put his hand up my skirt. Felt my knicks! He nearly died!' His laughter sounded like sobs, he shook his head helplessly, the tears streaming down his cheeks, the mascara running in dark channels.

Polly struggled to her feet, her fury helping her to find some strength again. 'You stupid little fool! What you did – you could have got us killed! I was about to be raped back there! And you! What did *you* want? Did you want . . .?' Her squeamishness at her own thoughts stopped her. But then anger came once more as the force of her fear, the vivid recall of it, drove her on. 'Are you really – a – queer? Is that it? You like men, don't you? That's what it is! Why you can't – do it! Why you can't make love to me properly – the way a man should! I should have known. Just look at you.'

Her intense soiled face was screwed up now, her eyes shining, transformed by the terrifying experience she had just endured. She flung her arm at him, dressed in her torn ragged finery. 'You make a wonderful girl!' she screeched suddenly. 'Those bastards were right. Fucking gorgeous!'

She was startled at the swiftness with which he sprang at her. She swung her head away, flinching, expecting him to lash out, to strike her, but, instead, he caught her by the arms and pushed her back against a tree. She gasped and felt the air expelled from her at the force with which he thrust her against the thick trunk. His hands were round her wrists, then he was forcing his face against hers, his mouth open, demanding. She heard him gasp with pain as his fatly swollen lip met hers. His thumb and fingers were tight pincers about the sides of her jaw as he pinned her face there. She was forced to open her mouth to breathe, and she yielded to him, and felt his tongue thrust deep into her. The strength ebbed once more, she went limp, unable to offer the slightest resistance. His body battered her against the solid tree and all at once her despair and shock were displaced by something else, some weird throb of excitement at the novelty of this passion – this boy-girl figure in the torn blouse and silk camisole, the tiny scrap of skirt, the torn nylons. Her arms came up around the slim shoulders, she leaned into him, her body flowing into him.

His hand clamped once more like a manacle on her wrist and dragged it down between them, then his narrow hips moved back, away from her belly. He was thrusting the captured hand under that short, tight band of a skirt, dragging it up until she could feel and see the distorted shape of the dark-blue thong, the rearing penis which bulged, then finally erupted into pulsing view as it freed itself from the restraining scrap of lace and satin. It was hot, and smooth as satin itself, and lubricious with the flow of his arousal.

She felt her body melt in answer. She wept and moaned with an altogether new need. Entwined, they sank to the ground and she felt the roughness of earth and stones and wet grass beneath her, then new coldness as his hands dug into the waistband of her tights and briefs and hauled them down, off her thighs, then down further, over her knees. She lay, her limbs falling slackly open as he fought with and tugged off her sensible shoes, then completed the removal of the banded tights and knickers. She raised her white limbs joyously and parted them about his plunging body. He removed nothing, but the feminine clothing offered no hindrance to his rigid enflamed manhood as he drove forwards and, with her guidance and lifting acceptance, entered her. It was the first time for both of them, and neither heard the gasp and grunt and sigh, of pain and of ultimate long-awaited fulfilment, as they came together.

Dazedly, they had no idea how long afterwards, they disentangled themselves and climbed slowly to their feet, still holding on to each other, wincing with stiffness and pain, and sighing with pleasure. 'You all right?' Antonio asked. In answer, she gave a little shake of her head, but, intuitively, he knew it was a shake of wonder and not negation. There were no words for it. Not yet. All at once, she turned to him and laid her head on his chest, and he held her by her heaving shoulders. Finally, they separated again. She bent and picked up her still-entangled knickers and tights from the grass. She stared at the little band for a second, then stuffed them in her bag.

'Would you believe it?' She stared wonderingly at the dark-leather shoulder pouch. 'How on earth have I still got this with me? After all this mayhem? It's a miracle.'

'Is there any money left?' Toni asked, his smile disfigured by his swollen lip. He gestured at his ripped clothes, the gaping holes in the sheer nylon covering his feet. 'I don't think I'll go down too well on the bus and tube looking like this.'

She smiled crookedly. 'Never mind. There's more at home. I can nip in and get enough to pay the taxi.' She came close and slipped her arm through his. 'Quite a night, eh? The night I lost my thirty-one-year-old virginity!'

'And to a figure of your wildest fantasy! An eighteen-year-old chick with a prick!'

'Oh!' She squealed inadequately, and her eyes lowered, while her dirty face was steeped in an involuntary blush.

'Glad to see my little Polly Mouse hasn't gone for good. Come on. Let's get home and into bed. I want to see if I can give an encore without dressing up in your sexiest undies!'

'Ah! Please! No! Aunt Charlotte! Please! Stop!' Max's head tossed wildly, lifting from the desk as her back arched, bringing the flattened breasts clear of the surface with the violence of her struggles.

'Why didn't you tell me earlier?' Charlotte hissed, pausing to seize the short black hair and drag the agonised girl's head backwards until the slim neck was bent acutely, the artery standing up prominently on the smooth milk-white skin, the long throat muscles rippling visibly.

'I swear – I didn't – I – I didn't know! Polly – her name – just came to me! I don't know! I don't know if he's there. I don't know where she lives.'

Charlotte struck three more times, with a measured pause between each stroke, savouring the hiss and crack, the fresh marking of the flesh. She stood for a moment, breathing deeply. The door opened and the Maestro was there, that all-knowing smile on his face at once, as though reading every facet of her mind. Immediately, she felt the beating hunger of her loins overwhelming her. 'Do you know where this Polly creature lives?' he asked politely, ignoring Max's subdued weeping.

Charlotte shook her head. 'No,' she managed. 'But I can soon find out. I know who she works for.' Her eyes were riveted to his, begging eloquently. Suddenly she didn't care if her niece should learn the truth about her aunt's subservience, the power of this man over her. In fact, she wanted him to take her now, to fuck her there, in front of the helpless girl.

Again he smiled. 'You look all in, my dear,' he said, with cruel concern. 'Why don't you take Max upstairs and see to her? Then get to bed. The blue room. I'll see you in the morning. We've all had a busy day.'

Silently, holding in her feeling of bitter disappointment, and the sudden despicable weakness that brought her close to tears, she dragged the still-weeping girl upright and hustled her, hands about the slim waist, towards the door.

Polly's breasts jiggled and her shoulders heaved at the remnants of yet another shuddering sigh that swept through her thin frame. She winced at the contact of the cold wood on her bottom, and crouched on the edge of the chair, shoulders hunched forwards, elbows rested on the plastic cloth spread over the small kitchen table. Antonio's hands were still unsteady as he passed across one of the two mugs of cocoa he had made for them. He sat gingerly, and the two naked figures faced each other in the harsh pool of the overhead light. They had just shared a soothing bath, sitting cramped together, knees drawn up in the tub. Their bodies were fragrant, the bruises standing out on the pale skin.

'You've got to go.' Polly's voice was a croak, flat with tiredness and despair. 'You've got to leave in the morning,' she went on over the murmur of his protest. 'You've ruined my life. Turned it upside down. I don't know who – what I am any more. I can't stand it.'

'Poll! Darling! Come on! It's just the shock!' His voice was slow, thick with persuasion. He levered himself up, came round the table, and bent over her, his arm gentle round her stooped shoulders. 'Let's get to bed. Cuddle up. You'll feel better –'

'No!' She began to cry, the tears pouring, the shoulders jerking, blubbing like a child. 'No! You – you're crazy! You could – we could've been hurt – maybe killed.' Her voice grew strident, moving towards hysteria. 'I was – that was the first time for me! You're just a boy! Eighteen! I was old enough to have a baby myself when you were born!'

'What? Thirteen? Come on! Some girls, maybe. Not *you*, Poll!' He seized both her hands, squeezing harder, pushing his forehead down against her, nuzzling the delicate ear. 'It's all right! We survived! Here we are, home again! And it's over now! And we did it! About time, eh?' He managed a shaky laugh. 'It was a pretty exciting evening all round, eh? Those hairy macho bastards! We had them going for us.'

His words, his embrace, and, above all, that laugh, shredded what little measure of control she was still managing to exert. Her head was whirling crazily. She had gone from wild euphoria at the fact that they had at last succeeded in making love, to the quivering wretched assault of fear once more at the whole insanity of the past few hours and the way this strange enchanting terrifying youth had turned her staid existence on its head.

She tore herself free of his hold and flung herself upright. 'What?' she screeched. 'You *are* mad! Absolutely insane! I mean it! Bloody crazy! How – how dare you! You stupid sick – oh!' Her words spluttered into an incoherent shriek of pure rage and frustration. Her own eyes wild now, she turned on him, her fingers bent into weapons, and struck out, using them as claws, going for his face, and he swatted her away, backing off. She came after him, sobbing and swearing, raked his chest, scratching at him ineffectually. He laughed and turned, fleeing through to the bedroom and the still unmade bed, and she pursued him in a frenzy, noting even in her wildness the exquisite beauty of his slim body, the rippling grace of his divine little buttocks, the movement of his shoulders, the hollowed back.

He flung himself headlong on the bed, turning as he fell so that he landed on his back, and held out his arms to take her body that slammed down on him like a projectile. She was punching inexpertly, and he took one or two feeble blows to his upper arms as he reached out and grabbed at her narrow hips and lifted her above him, pulling her forwards so that her spreadeagled thighs landed on his upper chest, and the curl-capped crest of her mons, the hardness of her pubic bone, bore down on his very chin. She felt the immediate powerful thrill spark through her, and jerked her loins automatically against the hardness beneath her. His fingers hooked into the tenderness of her inner thighs and drew her wickedly upwards, lifting her to his upturned face, his burrowing mouth, and a shudder of pleasure passed right through her. She felt the bite of his teeth on the tender sex lips, and the wetness of his mouth, his seeking tongue, and all at once there was a flow from her, an ejaculation of her fluid he could taste. With an elemental howl, she jerked again, and her fingers fell between her sprawled thighs and clawed at the dark head buried there, holding it to her as she jerked madly and thrust the fissure of her sex crushingly against him, feeling the cartilage of his nose bending and filling the narrow cleft.

Unaware of her action, she stretched her left hand behind her, felt his lifting belly, and seized his prick in a convulsive grip. The short column was hard, the helm reared in an erection she had never felt or seen until that night. With a brutal thrill and a sense of power she had never known, she reared, raised her genitals clear of his gasping face and bent over him, moving her body, all the while holding onto that wildly throbbing penis. She put it to her, slammed down, and heard his cry of pain and her own hoarse grunt of triumph as the slippery helm slid into her fissure, and she impaled herself on the small jutting shaft, feeling it slide truly into her.

It was heaven! No burning brutal sword stabs, just an enchanting filling, a contact with her that made her come as it fitted home, and erupted simultaneously, filling her with the sweet essence of his fluid which coated both of them in the brief perfection of their unity.

'We did it! We actually made love – again! You and me!' Polly's face was transfused with the joy of her experience, her gaze luminous with it as she blinked myopically at him on her return from the bathroom, where she had gone to clean herself and carry out repairs after the storm of cathartic weeping had died away.

Fucked, you mean, Antonio supplied mentally, as he beamed benevolently at her from the bed. But he was still too stirred by his own sense of shock, and whirling emotion, to be cruel to her now. He held his arm accommodatingly, and she climbed in, fitting herself tenderly about him, her head resting on his shoulder. 'We sure did! And now we're both the same.' She lifted her head in enquiry, and he bent his lips to brush her tousled hair. 'Both lost our cherry, and in the same night, eh?'

He felt her shiver. She clung closer to him, and squeezed his thigh convulsively between hers. 'I want to forget about everything else. Everything outside this room. I love you.' She nuzzled his breast, and he kissed the cloud of her hair against his face. 'I want to stay safe like this forever. Night-night.'

They were both deep in sleep, still in each other's arms, when the world exploded into terrifying dazzling consciousness, and a light blazed down on them as they stared up in mute horror at two black silhouettes. 'Well well,' a deep voice chuckled. 'What have we here? Not at all what I expected from either of you. Lesbians and gays shagging one another! Whatever next? Welcome back to the real world, my little deviants!'

Fourteen

'Here. Let me help you with that, my dear.'

The deep purring mockery of Holger's masculine tones made Bron Davies burn from head to toe with scalding shame, and she squirmed at the novel sense of weak inferiority this gave her. To divert herself from her discomforting thoughts, she gazed down on the pale form in the boot of the car and, in particular, the huge pools of the terrified tear-laden eyes staring up at her. The thick black tape stretched over the mouth. The thin ankles were taped tightly together, the hands, also taped, were hidden under the buttocks. She reached down and grabbed the ankles as Holger bent forwards and slipped his red hands under the arms. Together, they plucked the figure easily out of the confines of her imprisonment and stood her briefly on her swaying feet, until Davies bent and thrust her shoulder into her captive's midriff, folding the girl over her shoulder and hoisting her, clapping her right hand over the curve of the pale haunch to steady her. Swiftly, she carried her through the door of the garage and up the short flight of stairs which led to the interior of the house. Meanwhile, Holger bent, slipped his hands under the shoulders and the thighs of the trussed figure lying at his feet, and carried him in his arms like a tender parent in the wake of the stomping Davies.

They deposited their burdens side by side on the wooden floor of the brightly lit, deserted music room, and left them there. Dawn was not even showing yet through the curtains of the long window at the end of the corridor. 'I won't wake the Maestro and your mistress yet,' Holger grinned. 'We'll get our pat on the head later. Come to my room for a drink.'

It was not a question. He put his hand on her wrist, and she felt herself blushing. She struggled to speak, suddenly short of breath. She looked at him, her pale eyes shining. 'I – I'm lesbian.' It sounded like an appeal.

He shook his head and laughed thickly again. 'No, you're not. No more than that randy slag of a mistress! She's panting for it, too.' Suddenly, he slammed her against the wall, knocking the breath out of her, and his iron hand seized her squarely by the crotch. The thumb and fingers squeezed, digging in painfully to her throbbing flesh through the thickness of her jeans. 'See, Davies? No balls, my dear! Not a sign! Come!' He released her, took hold of her wrist and pulled her rapidly along in his wake.

In his small, impersonally neat room, he pushed her down on the narrow bed. He lay across her, pinning her down on her back. His mouth was close to her ear. 'You can fight if you want,' he chuckled. 'Maybe we'd both enjoy it more that way.'

The shaming tears were stinging behind her eyelids. Her throat was closing. 'Fuck off!' she grunted. She thrust up impotently against his crushing weight, and he laughed again, pressing her loins down into the creaking softness of the mattress. She felt that insidious weakness, the perverse thrill of it seeping away deep within her, stealing her resolve. He captured a foot, tugged off her boot, then the other. His fingers dug into her waistband and hauled her jeans down, off her hips. He pushed the thick checked

148

shirt up, clear of her buttocks, and, with cruel deliberation, slid his fingers into the elastic of her grey cotton underbriefs and wrenched them down, to lie stretched tight like bonds with the jeans across her thighs.

The cruellest humiliation of all was him reaching out for one of his leather slippers by the bed, and the way he turned her and slapped her with it, crisply cracking blows, playfully, with only enough force to cause a tingling sting and a gradual blush of red to spread over the quivering flesh – a parody of a spanking that was no more than lovers' foreplay. But she did not put up any resistance, not even when his hands worked at her lowered jeans, and her briefs, and slowly eased them from her limbs, leaving her naked below the waist, except for the thick, grey ankle socks.

His fingers carried out a slow and teasing intimate exploration. She began to cry then, ugly raw sobs that shook her frame. She lay there with her legs wide apart, enduring his leisurely examination. But when his fingers moved, insidiously gentle, opening up her labia, seeking out the beating inner folds, and slid into the narrowing wet funnel of her desire, her belly lifted, purely in response to his stimulation, and she was clamorously ready to receive him when he raised her hips and slid his hard penis home inside her.

He controlled the coupling, moving only slowly and gently at first, hardly at all, until, helpless at her own beating need, she tightened her buttocks and began to thrust back into him, in more and more urgent rhythm, grunting between her sobs, wanting only to impale herself on the rod of his masculinity, and he held her off, his fingers clamping on her hips, restraining her movement until he knew she was at crisis point. She was moaning, the cropped head tossing back and forth, the tears flowing faster.

'NOW!' she screamed, and he released her, and rutted madly, pounding into her at the rise of his own climax, and she cried out harshly, her body arched, every muscle rigid as she came before he did.

'Ah, Max, my child!' Labat's voice purred with affability. 'I thought you'd want to see our latest arrivals without delay. And I just wanted to thank you for making this reunion possible. Without your help, my dear, I doubt if we'd ever have found them. Thank you!'

At that moment, the Maestro's words hardly registered at all as her eyes widened at the scene before her. The two pale naked forms were stretched upright in the centre of the large room, one male and one female, facing each other, so close that they were almost touching. They were fastened by their outstretched arms which were raised high above them, secured at the wrists by thick padded bands attached to long chains which were suspended from a metal girder in the high ceiling. 'Toni!' As she cried out his name, she saw the dumb expression of pain and betrayal on the beloved face, and the import of the Maestro's words smote home to her.

'Max!' he gasped.

As she made to dash forwards, Holger's hands closed like bands around her arms, but, at a nod from the professor, he released her, and she flung herself at the pinioned form. It was impossible for her to embrace him without intimately brushing against the slim body tethered so close to him, and Max recognised the tragic tear-stained features at once. 'Miss Smythe! I'm sorry.' She began to cry, then clasped Antonio, kissing him on the mouth and on the throat, sobbing, until he tried to jerk his face away from the kisses.

She recoiled as though he had struck her, and wept desolately over the Maestro's gentle reproof. 'Come

come! Aren't you pleased to see your cousin, my boy? After all this time!' He moved forwards, took the desolate Max by her shoulders, and led her to a hard wooden chair near the low stools where they usually sat for her music lessons. He forced her down into it. 'Stay there and sit still. Not that I think you would dream of leaving!' the Maestro chuckled teasingly. 'But these two delinquents must be taught a lesson, mustn't they, my dear? And I insist you see it. I'm sure you would want to, anyway, after the way your beloved Toni deserted you. And that's not all! I'm afraid he has been doing all kinds of naughty things under his new teacher's able instruction. Eh, Miss Smythe?'

She tried to crouch away from him, then squealed as his hand shot out quickly to her loins and seized the dark springy little curls of her pubis between thumb and forefinger. He tugged, and the white flesh stretched out like elastic, the thin hips jerking. He released his hold and she sagged, head down, sobbing wildly. Her little breasts shook, their contours highlighted by the way in which her arms were reaching high above her.

'Oh, please, sir! Let me go! Please! I didn't – he came to me – I didn't know anything – he asked me to take him in. I didn't know – you – you . . .' Her voice tailed off, choked by her desolate weeping. Her chin sank to her chest.

'Oh, come now, Polly!' His voice was soft, tinged with affectionate regret. His broad hands rested on either side of her face, pushing against the tangle of her wild brown hair, holding her cheeks, lifting her so that her features, shining with tears, were within inches of his own. 'That's not true, is it? And you must learn to tell the truth. There must be no secrets between us. Not now that you have become part of our world. Once you learn to accept it, you'll enjoy it here, Polly. You'll have fun!'

151

He let go of her, stepped back and clapped his hands together crisply. Both pale figures flinched at the sudden noise. 'But we must have discipline. One of our golden rules here. Obedience at all times. Eh, Max? You've learnt that already, haven't you, my star little pupil?'

In the pause, she knew he needed her reply. She cleared her throat, the tears running silently down her cheeks. 'Yes, Maestro,' she croaked.

'Of course. And here beginneth the first lesson!' He laughed pleasantly and moved away to a large cupboard against one of the long bare walls. He called for Holger to join him, then approached the two naked figures with what looked like several broad canvas belts. 'Oh, and by the way,' the professor's pleasant tones continued, 'you can make as much noise as you want. As well as the excellent acoustics, this room is entirely soundproofed.'

He advanced on them carrying an extremely thin pliable cane, which whistled terrifyingly as he made several vigorous cuts through the air. 'You can't –' Polly stared, goggle-eyed. Toni gazed in silence. His fine features, too, showed fear, but not surprise.

The Maestro nodded, his eyes dancing with delight. 'Oh, but I can, my dear.'

Holger, meanwhile, grabbed them and thrust them intimately together. He slipped a canvas band around their necks, fed its tapered end through the heavy buckle and drew it tight, until their heads were forced into contact, their faces touching, bound by this communal collar. They had to turn their faces sideways, cheeks resting together. 'You can kiss if you want to,' the Maestro urged, then turned in mock concern towards the seated Max. 'Oh, that is if you can bear that, my dear? Or will you be consumed with jealousy?' He held out the cane towards her. 'Perhaps you might

152

like to take a turn yourself later? Though it will be easier if the two of you can learn to share this delightful boy.'

Holger bound them by another broad belt around their waists. It cut into the hollow of their backs, and forced Polly's breasts to nuzzle companionably against Antonio's pale chest. The last belt went around their thighs, about six inches below their taut buttocks. 'What a good job you're not taller, my boy,' the Maestro observed. Their bellies, upper thighs, and knees pressed in intimate contact. 'Right. Let's begin. Ladies first, they say.'

At the first whistling cut of the cane, Polly screamed shrilly, transfixed by the ice-fire of torment flowing through her from the thin clean stroke of the cane rebounding from her clenched bottom. Their frames rolled and rubbed obscenely together, they teetered and swayed, moulded to one another. She was gulping, sobbing, then whimpering, while the Maestro waited implacably for them to regain their balance. With an expert horizontal stroke he delivered an equally crisp and agonising blow to Antonio's behind, and his hapless shriek was scarcely less in volume than that of his partner in the ordeal.

The cuts came with the same lengthy deliberation, with pauses after each whistling torment, to allow for the screams and the sobs and the madly twisting, conjoined bodies to settle down again. Their tears mingled, the sweat ran down between them, they blubbered and begged for forgiveness, for a cessation to this nightmare. It came only after six identical strokes had been delivered to each quivering backside.

The screams ended and they hung there, their sweat-slippery bodies leaning into each other along their length, their frames shaking in the sobs that racked them.

'There now!' Labat said, like a teacher at the end

of a satisfying lesson. 'That's just the beginning. Now, Holger. Why don't we leave these three youngsters – oh, forgive me, Miss Smythe! You're not exactly a teenager, are you? Well, anyway, you're going to be spending a great deal of time with my twin protégés, so I suggest you all start getting to know each other. Although you've already made quite a start in that direction with young Antonio, I gather!'

When the door closed, leaving the three of them, there was nothing but the sound of the sobbing, and Max's quiet sniffles, until the abominable stinging of the behinds eased.

'I'm so sorry, Poll!' Antonio whispered. Their faces felt glued together by the mix of tears and saliva. His words were indistinct, his lips twisted against her cheek. He could feel her nipples rubbing against his breast. They were hard, and his reaction to them shocked him at first. He felt the beating in his prick and realised, with yet another shock, it was pressing with growing firmness against the top of her vulva, and the crest of springy curls.

He expected her to be horrified, or to exhibit a hysterical outpouring of vituperation at this sick reaction to their ordeal, but, to his astonishment, he felt her belly move, and her thighs, seeking an even closer contact, and she rubbed against his throbbing penis in unmistakable arousal. Their bodies began to thrust rhythmically together, with increasing awareness of their physical hunger. His prick was stiffening now, its red helm pressing against her cushioning softness. In turn, Polly could feel her vaginal muscles contracting fiercely, and the lubricious hunger of her sex to feel him enter. She lifted her open mouth, searching, and they kissed fiercely, tongues twining, thrusting against each other until the chains chinked at the swaying movements.

'Christ!' Max didn't know if she had spoken aloud as

she watched the writing couple, bodies and mouths glued together. She was wearing the heavy burgundy gown which the Maestro had made her wear for so many of her lessons, and that had featured in several of the photographs. She had taken to wearing it as a housecoat before she dressed and, though it was the only garment she was wearing now, she felt positively overdressed as she stared at the spectacle of the entwined figures hanging there. For an instant, she felt an anger that made her wish she could mete out the violence the Maestro had issued, still vividly in evidence from the matching red lines scored across those clenching buttocks. 'Stop it!' she gasped in outrage, then blushed in confusion. 'I mean – they might come back any second!'

The gnawing mouths broke away. Polly's tear-smeared face looked even more ashamed and as confused as that of the lovely girl in the dark gown. But Toni was glaring at Max. 'Get us out of this!' he hissed.

Max's eyes widened, then glanced across at the door at the end of the room. 'I – I – don't know . . . they'll come back.'

'What's the matter with you? For Christ's sake, untie us, will you?'

'I daren't.' Max began to sniffle, then to cry. She nodded at their intimately bound bodies. 'You've seen what they're like. What it's like here.'

Polly's voice joined theirs, rising in shrill hysteria. 'But – but – they can't do this! This is – it's against the law! They kidnapped us!'

In spite of her tears, Max gave a bitter little laugh. 'There's no law here. Only the Maestro's. You have to do exactly what he tells you. *And* that brute of a manservant!' Her head turned again towards the door, and they could sense her fear, and knew that they, too, were now a part of it.

Fifteen

'There you are, you see. Nothing simpler! I'll have someone post this from Greece.' Labat passed Charlotte the letter, written in Polly Smythe's square ingenuous handwriting, to her parents in the north of England. It sounded absolutely genuine, full of bubbling enthusiasm, telling them of her sudden appointment, and departure, to tutor a bunch of rich youngsters at a private school in the Hellenes. 'And we've also got her letter of resignation to the local authority, and to the agency.' He pointed to the address at the top of the letter she was holding. 'That's one of ours. Any correspondence will come directly to us.'

Charlotte put the letter back on his desk, and walked over to the window. The heavy drapes were pulled back, tied to the wall. Through the thin net stretched across the glass, she could see the garden, drab now with its near-winter deadness. The narrow strip of lawn between the house and the high brick wall was still spotted with clumps of black dead leaves and black twigs from the leafless trees beyond.

As she gazed, the old wooden door in the wall opened, and three tousled figures in dark tracksuits entered. The trainers and the bottoms of their pants were spattered with mud and heavy with wetness.

Immediately on their heels came two burlier, taller figures, whom she recognised as the Maestro's man and her own Davies.

It was the sight of her maid that brought to her troubled mind the addendum of 'other things'. The insulated, easy and well-defined relationship she had known with her maid for the past ten years was being threatened more and more by the pervasive influence of this magnetic figure and his loathsome henchman. Charlotte had always valued the unique closeness of her relationship with Davies highly: the lovers' intimacy, which they had shared from the outset, yet with the unexpressed but clearly acknowledged bounds of mistress and servant, which had never been crossed. Now, it was teetering dangerously, hung in the balance, was a hair's breadth from being destroyed altogether by these two men who were coming to hold such a pernicious influence over both their lives.

'What the hell's wrong with you?' Charlotte had demanded the previous night, when, badly in need of Davies' brand of aggressively feminine loving to counteract the sickening attraction of Charlotte's own subservience to the Maestro, her maid had churlishly failed to 'deliver the goods'.

'You! You and your damned Maestro! And that great hulk of a man of his, that great German prick!'

Charlotte had at first done nothing more than blink in undisguised amazement, then horror, at the sudden blazing tearful outpourings of woe and weakness from this rock of butchness.

Now, she turned from the window and faced the Maestro, the colour mounting in her face, the trembling betraying her emotion. 'I don't like it. This is nothing less than kidnap! The letters – everything! They've been forced from the wretched girl. We can't keep her for – for ever! Against her will!'

'Is it? Really?' He sat there like an oracle behind his desk, the compact strength showing in his immaculately garbed frame, the large hands forming a steeple before his craggy face, the black hairs visible on his knuckles. 'In fact, it took relatively little persuasion to get her to write them. It's all a little game, Charlotte, my love. Dangerous, but tempting, too. Believe me, I've made promises to her of things to come that will revolutionise her dreary little existence. She's already glimpsed some of them. What we've really done is simply to give her the opportunity to realise what her true nature is. Just as you have allowed your niece and the boy to realise their true nature. I've shown them what lies deep within – the desire – nay, the *need* they share, and poor Polly Mouse, too, to be dominated, to surrender to a will they recognise as superior to their own.'

Charlotte shivered visibly, as though his hands had touched her physically, intimately. The colour mounted, she felt the constriction of her breath. She was staring at him. 'No!' she whispered. 'It's not – I didn't –'

He stood, came slowly round from the desk, and advanced towards her. She was still staring fixedly, with a haggard expression of fear and of acknowledgement. Yet she still continued to deny it, in that strangled whisper, as he turned her implacably until once again she was facing the scene in the dull garden. His hands moved round her, under her arms, and closed over her rising and falling breasts. She felt the heat of his loins as they pressed into the curve of her behind, and her own beating response.

His lips moved against her ear, his breath tickling her, his rich voice, like a deep purr, passing through her. 'That's what life is, Charlotte. You've always known it, haven't you? A recognition of those superior wills.' His chin on her shoulder, he nodded at the three figures disappearing round the corner of the house. 'They're realizing their destiny. As we all must.'

As he spoke, his hands left her breasts and dropped to the sides of her nylon-clad legs. She felt the hands moving upwards, over the sheer material of the stockings, pushing under the hem of her heavy dress, lifting it until her thighs were exposed. The hands moved over the cool skin between the stockings and the lace edging of her knickers, the fingers pausing to pluck with brief playfulness at the thin elastic of the stocking tops, then on, closing in on the curve of her belly, seeking the undergarment, sliding in, fanning through the cap of her pubis, down to the upper folds of the vulva. Charlotte leaned back weakly and felt the rising beat of his prick settling into the clenching groove of her behind; the corresponding wet flow of that narrower cleft, the outer lips of which those fingers were now peeling back with slow sureness, unfurling the gleaming inner depths, seeking the centre of her urgent arousal, fanning the damp flames so that she spasmed and rutted against their caressive touch. Vividly, she pictured the shape of his hands, the ridges of his powerful knuckles hidden but contoured by the rippling silk. She leaned her head back, stretching her neck, resting on his shoulder as though on a pillow, and with a soft sob surrendered entirely to that consuming sensation, let herself go, soaring into the mindless climax that sent her juices thickly over his fingers and gave the lie to her former pathetic denial of the truth he had just whispered to her, and demonstrated so powerfully with this possession of her body.

She returned to awareness as she felt him wiping, cleaning his fingers on the silk of her knickers before he withdrew his hands from beneath her dress. He turned her by the shoulders, gently, with a beatific smile, and kissed her on the lips. 'Get me the tawse from the drawer.' His voice was as gentle as his touch, as tender as a lover's. She moved at once to obey. Still with that dreamlike slowness, heavy with the sweet weakness of her climax, she handed it to him and placed herself over the desk, turning her head, tossing her straight hair aside, settling herself as on a lover's couch. She lifted the material of her dress up over her behind, slipped her thumbs into the elastic of the knickers that still clung wetly to her, and eased them down off her buttocks, whose generous contours dimpled deeply in anticipation.

When the beating was over, he turned her body over. And then she felt a great upsurge of profound joy and gratefulness as she felt the sharp edge of the desk cutting into the bottom of her spine, felt him slipping the shred of wet silk from her thighs and lifting them high, fitting her legs about his shoulders as he stood fully clothed, only that rampant penis bared, briefly, until it, too, was hidden, driven to the hilt inside that narrow passage which, despite its recent satiation, closed rapturously about its invader.

Antonio lay on his back on the high narrow table and stared apprehensively at the Maestro. 'You and Max are so alike. Except for one or two minor differences.' The deep chuckle resonated as the professor reached out and delicately shook Antonio's prick with thumb and forefinger. 'So we can't have any needless distinctions, can we? This is Meena. Isn't she beautiful? She's already bared Max's cute little mound – and that's not all she did, eh, Meena?' The deep laugh reverberated, and the girl in the white smock looked suitably embarrassed.

Antonio experienced the throb of excitement and appreciation as he stared at her. It overcame the apprehension which had been his chief emotion. He was no longer certain of how long he had been a prisoner here. Two weeks? Although he had spent a lot of that time in Max's company, they had had virtually no opportunity to talk frankly together, for they had never been left alone. A great many of their hours together had been spent in very serious, and very sustained practice, so that, eventually, he had become used to the erotic novelty of their near or complete nakedness, he at the piano, Max standing at his side, or seated on the low stool, the Maestro moving freely about the huge airy room or looming over them, a heavy arm draped over their shoulders, an iron hand slapping at their tender skin when irritation overcame him. But, during these hours of musical tuition, he never beat them – a fact Antonio had come to appreciate very quickly, for at other times he had suffered frequent punishment – not at the hands of the Maestro himself, except on two or three exceptional and memorable occasions, but at those of his able assistant.

Antonio had swiftly come to fear and respect Holger, even to dread his incarceration with the redoubtable manservant, who had apparently been given free rein to exert his authority over his new captive. Toni's subservience towards him was not feigned. He had swiftly realised that any spark of resistance, however subtle or disguised, would be recognised and punished with even greater severity. Perfect submission was demanded, and Antonio gave it. Which was why, he hoped now as he lay motionless on the table, the initial phase of his captivity and subjugation might at last be easing.

The Maestro had talked of a photography session arranged for the morrow. Toni did not need the evidence of the deep blush which spread over Max's features to know exactly what this would entail. He could still recall all too vividly the splendid erotic artistry of those prints he had seen at Aunt Charlotte's. He had thought that this present summons to this beautiful stranger had something to do with facing the camera. And he was right, but not quite in the way he had anticipated.

Like everyone who came into contact with the professor, including, to Antonio's private amazement and delight, Aunt Charlotte, this pretty, brown-skinned girl showed that deference tinged with a hint of fear. Though now, she flashed an enchanting smile from those full promising dark lips as she came close. His penis leapt as she laid her immaculately groomed velvet hand lightly upon it, and giggled. 'I'll just tape your todger to your thigh here. He seems determined to stick his little head up to see what's going on. Wouldn't want him to get in the way and hurt himself.'

Antonio was sure the thrill that passed through the squat column transmitted itself to the delightful girl, for he saw those limpid dark eyes flash their own mischievous message to him, and he smiled back, and lay still while she taped his member down onto his right thigh.

The procedure of removing the small cap of his pubic hair, with the glue and the strips of waxed paper was painful, then even more so when she taped his cock up onto his newly denuded belly and applied the same treatment to his exposed scrotum, and, most uncomfortable and embarrassing of all, the deep cleft at the base of his ball-bag, around the anus. Finally, he was made to stretch his arms above his head and his armpits were dealt with, though, as they were practically hairless to begin with, this took only seconds.

'There now! Smooth as your enchanting twin!' The Maestro bent at Meena's side, and closely inspected the slim body. His large hand settled over Antonio's genitals, cupping them in the warm palm, and pressed the red helm and the wrinkled shaft beneath it, up onto the belly, then rolled it back and forth. The hand, with its sprouting thickets of thin black hair, covered the beating prick completely.

Antonio bit at his bottom lip, stirring, thigh and belly muscles tightening at this powerful stimulation. The Maestro felt the organ's fluttering arousal beneath his palm. The fingers of his other hand brushed tenderly at the locks of dark hair falling across Antonio's brow, then caressed the smooth pink cheek. 'You could almost be your exquisite cousin lying there.' The palm moved, continuing its gentle stroking, and the thin frame shivered responsively. Antonio's lips parted, he sighed, and a delicate blush mounted. 'But not quite, eh?'

Antonio was breathing more heavily now, his chest noticeably rising and falling, his mouth open. He gave himself to the throbbing physical pleasure the Maestro's strokes were causing. He could feel his prick swelling within the confines of the cupped palm, knew that already the tiny mouth at the crest of the helm would be glinting with emission. His pink heels rubbed against the thin sheet which had been laid over the wooden surface as his lower limbs made an instinctive tiny scissoring movement.

'Max has assured me many times that you have never slipped this little fellow –' he shook the part in question in his firm grasp '– inside her, or any other female, as far as she is aware. Meanwhile, your friend Polly has earnestly assured us that you and she *did* undoubtedly couple, on at least one occasion, and that, in any case, during your brief but hectic association, you made a fantastically effective lover.'

Antonio gazed up at him and made a helpless little shrugging gesture. Suddenly, he was uncomfortably aware of the beautiful girl standing wide-eyed by the Maestro's side. 'Perhaps we should make one more test,' Labat observed affably. He turned to Meena. 'If you wouldn't mind assisting, my dear?' Though his voice rose at the conclusion of the remark, it was not a question but a command, and, as though awaiting it, the dark-haired girl at once unbuttoned the white overall and slipped it off. Her breasts were bare, and the well-defined pout of her crotch was minimally concealed by a white G-string.

She came forward and the Maestro stepped back with a theatrical flourish, inviting her to take his place. Toni felt the fire soar as his prick was seized tightly in her small fist and her enchanting mouth closed over the gleaming helm before swallowing dome, and almost the entire shaft, into the ultimate sensation of that warm sucking cavern.

He must burst, explode with the force of the release he could feel rising within him, but then, once again there was a transformation. He saw the vision of the brown beauty rising high, facing him this time, the knees jutting, the muscles on the brown thighs ridged, and the long dark cleft of the bared sex-lips descending, taking in the beating length of him, swallowing him as shatteringly as those other lips had claimed him, devouring him, pounding, driving the breath from his lifting belly as he managed one last cry, and then he was lost, engulfed in that ocean of warm wet enveloping brown flesh, and his world exploded in a gushing eruption.

Sixteen

'My my! As you know, sugar, I'm not one to go for blokes of any sort normally, but this little mate of yours is enough to turn me straight, I swear!' Max could feel the breath warm on her ear as the speaker bent close to whisper her comment. Ginny, the shaven-headed assistant of photographer Terry, winked a boldly mascar-ed eye at Max, who was standing with legs obediently astride while Ginny dusted her down with talc. They were both watching Terry carefully arranging Toni's body in a provocatively draped pose along the piano, and giving every indication that he was enjoying his task immensely. 'Come on, poof!' Ginny called in her husky London tones. 'You spend much longer fiddling with the poor lad's bits and pieces, you'll have him coming over all queer! Or should I say, *a* queer?'

'Saucy mare! You have your fun and I'll have mine!' He nodded over to where Ginny's hands were equally busy about Max's naked frame.

It was clear how noticeably everyone had relaxed now that the others had quit the music room, leaving Terry and his diminutive helper to finish off their assignment. After closely supervising the long and tiring photographic session, involving the skilfully lit and artistically valid poses of Max and Toni at work with their instruments, the Maestro and his cohort had departed, with his cheerful admonition to Terry to 'finish off with some cheesecake and hard core – the sort of thing that would please your run-of-the-mill customers and get their fists flying. Have fun, little ones!'

The youngsters were astonished at this sudden easing of the strict supervision they had endured over the past two weeks. Since Toni's capture, they had scarcely had the opportunity to exchange a word in private. When they were not closeted in the music room, working under the relentless autonomy of the Maestro himself, they were watched over by Holger or Aunt Charlotte and Davies, who seemed to be spending all of their waking time if not their nights there. Even meals and bath times were closely monitored, and the young people were steered into their respective bedrooms with firm instructions not to stray across the corridor that separated them. Holger's brutally effective way of emphasising his point with the aid of a three-tailed tawse caused Toni quickly to accept the harsh house rules, while, to his private dismay, he saw that Max had already been well and truly broken in to the regime.

Consequently, there was almost a holiday atmosphere in the music room after the unexpected departure of the Maestro and his little entourage. It was heightened by the unusual circumstances of the work still in hand and by Terry's easygoing, frank approach. 'Now, Maxie, luv, I'd like you sprawled out along the top of the joanna, sweetie. Up you get! That's right, Ginny'll give you a hand, won't you? Or even two, eh? Happy in your work, Gin? On your front, Max. That's right. Round a bit. Want that little arse of yours well up. Lift it just a shade, that's it! Lovely! One foot up – girlie pose, right? Heel up, curly toes. *Thank* you, Gin, you can take your hands off. Now – you on the piano, Toni. Just lean forwards towards her, heads close. Max. Inch up a teensy bit. Tits forwards, let them just poke over the edge, under his nose, that's the ticket. Toni, lean forwards slightly. Right leg up a bit.' He hurried forwards, moved Toni's pale thigh, then stepped back and squinted. 'That's it. Just hides your toggle and two. Kinda sexy and – you know?' He stretched out his right hand, fingers spread, palm down and waggled it. 'What's the word I want, sweetheart? Sort of ladyboy touch, yeah? Now hold it. Big smiles. Flash your gnashers, OK? Luvverly!'

When this final photo shoot was finished, Toni looked around, reached for the discarded robes and drew his on. He carried the other across to Max, who was standing chatting to the girl with the cropped skull. He reflected on how at ease Max had become with her nudity here. She raised her eyebrows almost in amused surprise as she took the robe and slipped it on. 'Listen. We've got to make the most of this. To talk, I mean.' He glanced significantly at the other girl, and the pretty face took on a blank expression.

'Don't look at me, mate! We only work here!' But she took the hint and strolled over to where Terry was packing up the equipment.

'What's going to happen to us?' he asked Max, making no effort to disguise the urgency in his voice. He threw an anxious glance towards the door. 'Do you know what they've got planned for us?'

Max felt a strange reluctance to respond to his seriousness. It had been a kind of defense mechanism she had adopted since being brought here, and it came almost naturally to her now. Live for the moment, live *in* the moment. Most of the time it seemed to work well enough for her, but now, seeing the tension in Toni's face, she was aware how much she had let herself slip, let her independence of mind be eroded. But then, it had largely been that way, at least with the outwards circumstances of their life, all the years they had been under Aunt Charlotte's authority too. It was only in the private exclusive world she and Toni could share that they had retained a measure of inner freedom. Since they had been separated, since she had come under the dominion of the Maestro, even that secret and limited liberty had been taken away.

She gazed solemnly at him, and gave a little shrug of her shoulders. 'I don't know, honestly. Except that the Maestro is planning some private concerts for us, I think. Some kind of private performances for high-powered clients. To do with all this.' She nodded at Terry and Ginny, and the paraphernalia they were dismantling. 'I guess that's what all these pics are for. Some rich letches will be sitting drooling over us, whetting their appetite for the real thing!'

Lady Letitia Laycorn quivered with physical pleasure. She was aware of every centimetre of her body beneath the silver gown, which clung to it like a second skin. She knew the diminutive panty liner, under the gauzy transparency of the G-string briefs, was being tested to the full. The rub and scratch of her nipples, straining against the confines of the cups that scarcely hid them, and from which they threatened to pop at any second, indicated their rock-hard arousal. She leaned back against the striped upholstery of the Regency couch, crossing her legs under the glistening thin material of the gown, and squeezed her thighs convulsively together. She relished the sweet ache of unfulfilment, acknowledging it as part of her pleasure, as she watched the two divine young bodies under the brilliance of the light beaming down on them.

Max and Antonio had been plastered, literally, from crown of head to toe, in a thick white paste, which, when it quickly set, transformed them into living statues of shining alabaster. Even their downcast eyelids as they fixed their gaze on the music before them were white. Max stood, facing the audience, one leg bent slightly inwards, unconsciously reminiscent of the 'Venus Rising' pose, though the right thigh, which fractionally overlapped its companion as it nestled into it, did not hide the hairless little curving mound with its merest hint of the beginnings of the sexual orifice beneath. The maidenly slightness of the breasts, jiggling enchantingly at the vigorous sweep of arm and dipping shoulder as Max sawed away, added to the picture of virginal purity.

As for her partner! Lady Titty's breath caught at his beauty. He was sitting in profile to the select group of viewers, bending and swaying to the stirring music he was producing from the superb grand piano. His slenderness was still highlighted, but Titty could not dismiss from her mind the heavenly vision he had presented as the pair had walked on, hand in hand, shyly uncertain at the collective gasps and cries of admiration that greeted them. He looked startlingly like the 'Boy David' come to life.

She glanced about her with surreptitious satisfaction at the wealthy and distinguished group of onlookers gathered for this very special concert. They were exclusive even for the Pleasure Dome, as the solid Victorian country house, officially titled Laycorn Court, was known to its carefully chosen familiars. Full use had been made of the discreet network which brought such events to the attention of the clientele who frequented the Pleasure Dome. Titty had pored admiringly over the artistically presented brochure, with its beautiful colour and black-and-white photographs advertising the unique talents of the gifted young duo, which had been circulated, bringing guests to the mansion from as far afield as the USA and the rich desert sheikhdoms of the Gulf – and brought an impressive addition to her already considerable wealth, she acknowledged readily.

She reached over and lightly touched the fleshy thigh of the evening-suited figure lounging next to her. 'Maestro. Are they all right?' she whispered, nodding to the two white figures in the spotlight. 'With all that stuff on, I mean? Can their skin breathe? Isn't it dangerous?'

'Oh, don't worry. They'll be all right for hours yet. And don't forget! They have certain natural ventilation holes which haven't been sealed up!' He chuckled, and she shushed him in pretended outrage. For answer, he, too, reached out for her, but his grip on her thigh was higher and firmer, much closer to its conflux with her belly and much more explicit in its lingering caress. The thick fingers delved into the hollow between her limbs and pressed against the softness of her mons. She captured the invasive hand, to still its wickedly rousing attention, but she held it to her beating warmth.

She recalled the first time she had shared such an intimacy with the professor. More years had passed than she cared to remember since then. He had been much thinner, and his hair had been raven black. He was a name just beginning to be known in the musical world, and in that other shady world to which the young aristocratic impoverished daughter of Sir Rupert Oswaldkirk was being introduced. Before her marriage, and even her engagement, to poor Tommy – who was the heir to the Laycorn estate, but not yet the incumbent of the sixth baronetcy – at eighteen, her boobs had been modest but her own, her tight little arse nature's gift, not the sculpted orbs artifice had lately bestowed.

In spite of parental reserve, she had insisted on taking lessons with the tutor she had met through a chance acquaintance. To her delight, he had waived the expensive fee – or she thought he had, until, in the studio on the top floor of a seedy apartment block up in town, he had demonstrated that he was eager to extract payment in other ways – as eager as she was to pay. He was the answer to all a young maiden's libidinous dreams, though, in her case, the term 'maiden' was hardly an accurate one since the day of her first frantically hasty shag with a randy groom on the table of the tack room in her early teens.

But all that undignified scrambling after her lately discovered focus of pleasure came to an end with that fateful meeting with her new tutor. He opened up a new world of refined fleshly satisfaction beyond her girlish dreams; a world to which she had devoted her life, and from which she had amassed an enviable fortune, for herself and for the sixth baronet Laycorn, her hopeless befuddled husband, Tommy, who was doubtless lying somewhere in the east wing enjoying the deliciously sadistic attentions of some young attendant, male or female.

At least he had known from the start what his role would be – a role he had embraced, once she had weaned him from his predilection for professional thigh-booted dominatrices and rough-handed guards-men long enough to get him to the altar and off on a Parisian honeymoon. She had coveted both the title and the Victorian pile that went with it. To be on the safe side, she even made sure the marriage was consummated, with the help of a willing accomplice, a beautifully carved ivory-handled whip, and the bug-eyed bridegroom tied as though on the rack to the hotel bed.

She had come a delightfully long way since then. The estate was not only solvent: the Pleasure Dome provided a profit that was now teetering on the brink of seven figures. And all for immersing herself in a lifetime of what she enjoyed most. She owed no small part of her success and her happiness to this charismatic figure sitting at her side, and, in gratitude, she cupped her dainty hand over his and pressed it more firmly into the warm and seeping cushion of her sex mound.

As the last notes died away, for an instant there was a magical stillness in which the two young figures really did seem like marble statues, before they moved, and the collective sigh of the audience heralded the burst of rapturous applause and the cries of appreciation, while, arm in arm, the naked couple stood and received their ovation. The lights came on, and Titty surrendered the hand she had held to her loins, as they both rose. The still-girlish blue eyes were fixed on his, the flawless face pink.

'God! That was the most beautiful thing I've seen! I swear I've come ten times over! But I still want you, Maestro! Can we have a quick fuck? Please?' Her voice squeaked like a child's. She seized the hand that had lain intimately in her lap with both hers and shook it beseechingly. 'While the others are recovering! In Tommy's den – come on! Please!'

She tugged him urgently through the stretching chattering onlookers, amongst whom the serving girls in their abbreviated costumes were beginning to move with the trays of drinks. She barely acknowledged the compliments called out from all sides, and within seconds they had passed out of the grand drawing room, crossed the large hall, and entered a much smaller room, in darkness behind the heavy drapes at its single long window. The overhead light which Titty snapped on revealed an Edwardian male sanctum complete with carved oak desk, leather chairs, bookcase from floor to ceiling filled with impressive tomes, and a tall glass-fronted gun cabinet. The scene was so faithful to the period, it had all the unreality of a stage or film set.

Titty was already hiking up her gown and dragging down the scrap of lace and satin that served as knickers, which she tossed into the waste-paper basket beneath the desk. Rolling the shimmering material of the dress up over her hips, she revealed her nakedness. A thin vertical line of light brown hair pointed like an arrow to the labial divide. 'Come on, Maestro! Unbuckle!' She perched her bare behind on the edge of the desk and spread her legs wide.

The Maestro gave a deep chuckle. 'My my! Giving me orders in your old age, Lady Titty! You're confusing me with one of your young studs, I think.'

All at once, she was a picture of contrition. 'Oh my God! Maestro! I'm *so* sorry! Forgive me, please!' She dropped to her knees, the silver gown rippling to cover her bared limbs once more as she knelt in front of him. Her fingers nimbly unfastened his flies, wriggled inside, and freed his prick from the confines of his clothing. It emerged, resplendent in its aroused state, the large helm showing proudly. At once those delicate fingers began to stroke and fondle, feather-light, feeling the throbbing response, the hardening of muscle and tissue, and swell of girth. Her nostrils quivered, filled with the scent of his masculinity. She put the round O of her lips to the gleaming dome,

173

kissed its glistening tip, and tasted the slick fluid already oozing, coating the velvet-smooth surface. The O widened. She stretched her mouth, enclosed his throbbing might within her worshipful embrace, and sucked deeply.

The golden head bobbed and bowed, and the Maestro's strong fingers dug into the piled corn-yellow hair, whose elegantly casual coiffure was soon genuinely disarranged, the curls tumbling profusely as he clasped her tightly to him. He stared down at the fine features, the long sweep of her flickering lashes, the working muscles of her delicate throat, the slender sculpt of shoulders, and beneath them the wonderful creamy swell and divide of the enhanced breasts. He felt the urgency of his response, dragged her roughly away from his beating column and hauled her upright. He saw her upturned face, beseeching, softly unfocused to everything except her own fierce hunger, her chin marred, agleam with his fluid and her own saliva. With a great surge of dominant triumph he upended her over the desk until she was flat on her back across its surface, her legs waving in the air. He clawed up her dress, pulled her hips to the edge of the wooden top, and expertly guided his prick to the fissure at the base of that narrow line of pubis. It was wetly ready to receive him.

He eased himself in with deliberate slowness, allowing only the helm to gain access, so that she cried out, and he felt her belly jerk forwards, the muscles in her thighs bunching, in her desperation to feel the potent length of him stab into her. He held himself off, moving slowly, teasing her, until she was shuddering with both ecstasy and frustration. 'I can't – I can't – Maestro! I can't wait!' She sobbed helplessly, the tumbled golden curls tossing on the dark wood.

Her legs were threshing wildly in the air until he captured her ankles and bent them back, pinning them near her shoulders, admiring the view, and the velvet feel of the backs of her thighs and the long haunches, fuller now than the taut little cheeks of the young girl he could still remember. He knew she had had both surgery and prolonged exercise with a special device to lift and enhance the curves of her bottom. She had told him so, with an honesty that had pleased him. 'Gravity beckons,' she said, when he had teasingly asked her why she had wanted a bigger arse. 'That's why I had my tits done. I don't want anything to sag if it can possibly be avoided.' She had giggled and nodded at his rearing member. 'You don't have any problems in that direction, I see!'

And he didn't. Not yet, anyway. He leaned back a little, holding onto the slim ankles, watching the squirming figure beneath him, the lovely face raised, arched, naked in its lust, lost, and with a beauty he found more stimulating than any artifice could conjure. He could feel himself, iron-hard, joined only at the base of their bellies to this divine creature. He thrust harder, deeper, hearing the grunts of rapturous response, feeling her urgent desire to be impaled on his flesh. His thrusts grew faster, he felt the climax rising, his hardness battering her. Her movements became really violent, her body arching as she screamed. The rigidity flowed out of her, and she became all softness again.

The pale dome of the rounded skull lifted swiftly at the sound of the door clicking open. Ginny Evans' gamine face assumed an expression of innocent concentration on her task of massaging the moisture cream into Max's freshly cleansed skin. Her anxiety was well justified, as she had learnt when she had first become familiar with the Pleasure Dome. Pleasure there was, to be had in plenty, while she helped to remove the white substance which had coated Max's body. Although no stranger to heterosexual activity, Ginny's proclivity for loving with her own sex had responded rapturously to the chance to be further gratified with the lovely young musician.

Struck by Max's beauty during that first photo session at the professor's house, Ginny had been excited at the prospect of seeing her again when Terry told her they had been commissioned to do a much more detailed series of pictures, this time of both the young musicians. The portfolio of erotic artistry had taken several days to complete. Terry, Ginny's camp employer, had been almost equally enamoured of Max's cousin, Ginny was sure, though he had been cruelly deprived of the chance to do anything significant about it by the unwelcome vigilance of the Maestro and his fearsomely macho henchman.

Ginny had worked with Terry long enough to be aware of what went on at the Pleasure Dome. She was flattered when, because of her skill at the special make-up required for the photographs the professor had commanded, she was invited to be on hand for the concert, to prepare the duo for their performance. The financial reward promised was breathtaking enough, but it was the sudden summons to a discreetly luxurious flat in the city, and what was on offer there, that clinched matters. Lady Titty, reclining in golden-haired naked splendour on satin sheets, put herself literally in Ginny's unsteady hands.

Only later did Ginny pause to reflect on her new level of involvement, and what might happen if she refused to participate. For instance, there was a girl at the prof's place, Polly, who seemed to be in a state of cowed terror most of the time. She acted as a skivvy to the prof, to his henchman, and to the two butch lezzes, the kids' aunt and her sidekick, who hung around. Ginny had tried to chat to her – she was quite attractive in her own skinny way – but the girl was plainly too scared to speak, other than her mumbled monosyllabic answers to a direct question.

The chance to tangle with the lovely Max, and, maybe, the exotic mistress of the Pleasure Dome herself, as well as the loot, had proved too tempting. Ginny stared now with her usual unease at the dark features of Professor Labat, who was closely followed by the agitated hostess. Her flushed appearance, cutely unkempt blonde hair, and those disconcerting china-blue eyes, indicated emotion of another kind, and from a different source.

'So!' The Maestro's voice was deep, his tone, to Ginny's profound relief, one of satisfaction. 'An excellent performance, my dears. I'm very pleased with you, Max. And you, Miss Evans.' He chuckled like a benevolent uncle. 'I must say I half expected to find you with your face buried in my pupil's genitals! Where's your cousin?' He followed the direction of Max's glance. 'Still in the shower? We must rout him out. Get ready quickly. I have some important people who are very anxious to meet you. You must be very nice to them, my dear. *Very* nice indeed! They're vital to our plans for you.'

Seventeen

The couple were distracted, and astounded, at the extent and the nature of the adulation awaiting them at the foot of the wide staircase from the guests at the Pleasure Dome. Max's toes curled in her shoes with the embarrassment that suddenly swept over her. The scores of eyes that settled on her made her all at once deeply conscious of her body, despite the fact that she was wearing proper clothing for what felt like the first time in weeks. In the insulated atmosphere of the Maestro's house, her nakedness had come to feel entirely natural. Now, the shyness she had all but forgotten flooded back under the gaze of these expensively dressed strangers, as though she were indeed standing naked for the first time before them, and in spite of the fact that she had appeared under the brilliant lights of the platform entirely unclothed. As they crowded about her and Antonio, she turned helplessly towards her cousin with a need to feel the shelter and security of his arm around her, but already these strangers were reaching out, embracing her.

A round barrel of a man, swarthy, a dark stubble showing about his lower face, an abundant black moustache hanging above his sensual lip and tapering to two precisely groomed points at his chin, showed his even and brilliantly white teeth in a wide grin. He crooked the forefinger of one pudgy and ring-bedecked hand under her chin, as though she were a young child.

'What do you think, Sheikh Hamad? Isn't she exquisite?' someone called.

'Both of them!' another voice added laughingly. 'Don't forget the boy, they're a matching pair!'

The plump hand opened and lightly patted her cheek. His eyes, a brilliant black, gazed piercingly at her. Unable to look away from their power, Max felt they touched her deep inside with a knowing and possessive intimacy even stronger than that fleeting caress. She was breathless when, at last, he withdrew a little, and she was able to pass by him, only to feel other anonymous hands on her as she and Antonio threaded their slow way through the crowd clustering around them.

'My God!' she gasped faintly, when at last they had crossed the cold polished wood of the hallway and had a little space to themselves. 'They treat us like we're some kind of animal – like pets!' She gazed at him in bemusement. She saw the red tide of acknowledgement creep slowly up his neck to stain his lovely face.

He nodded. 'I know!' he whispered. His voice sounded as awe-struck as hers. She was shaken by the elemental desire which swept right through her to be back once more in the familiar surrounds of Aunt Charlotte's, to be alone with him, and close as they used to be, sharing that bond which was half sexual, half spiritual, but which seemed so innocent compared with all that had happened to both of them since. She thought suddenly of pathetic Poll Mouse, as Toni called her. The Maestro had taken a sadistic delight in informing Max of the fact that she and Toni had been caught *in flagrante* – a fact Toni himself had not denied when she charged him with it.

She could not control the wave of pure jealousy that consumed her. All those years, all the times they had shared together, the growing awareness of sexuality, of their bodily desires. He should have done it to me! her inner voice screamed viciously. I wanted him – I *still* want him!

You want anybody! The inner voice mocked her now. You're desperate, with longing, with jealousy! You want anybody, you pathetic little creep, because you're not getting it. You've never had it, and all you get to do is to play with yourself and to watch while people are shagging all around you! Come on! Admit it! You'd even welcome Holger! No! No! That wasn't true. It was the Maestro's rejection of her that really hurt. That's who she wished for. She felt as though she belonged to him now, and she wanted his possession of her to be total. Body, as well as spirit.

Such tormenting thoughts whirled furiously through her disordered mind, tearing at nerves already over-stimulated and aroused by the erotic novelty of her surroundings and the emotional heights demanded by her artistic performance. She was still deeply distracted when she and Toni were ushered through another door that led off the great hall and into another long room, as big as the drawing room where the concert had been held, but very different in both appearance and décor.

The crowd which had been waiting in the hall – indeed, the vast majority of the audience who had listened so appreciatively to their performance – were now spreading themselves in this new venue. The room was bleak. The wooden floor was sprung, the walls appeared to be lined with the kind of material found in studios to absorb sound, though along one of the two longer walls there was fixed a row of what looked like wall bars, giving the impression of a gymnasium. This was heightened by the pieces of apparatus in various places – wooden and padded leather frames on adjustable metal legs, like vaulting horses. The ceiling was criss-crossed by a series of thin metal girders from which hung long ropes, some with loops or rings at their lower ends, again suggesting the kind of equipment used for strenuous physical exercise. However, the identical long leather couches, all in black, into which the guests were now settling themselves, indicated that whatever diversions might take place here were intended very much as spectator sport also.

These sights and impressions registered swiftly in the periphery of Max's brain, and doubtless of Antonio's, too, for their attention was centred on the spectacle in the middle of the floor under the row of brilliant spotlights in the roof which bathed the scene in their white glow. Two anonymous female figures were suspended in mid-air, arms and legs spread out. The contraptions that held them were made of shining black PVC. They looked to Max's astonished gaze like some kind of weird costume, for the lower arms, from just below the elbow to the wrist, were encased tightly in bands of the leather-like substance. Metal rings in the middle of these bands held the clips on the ends of the thin ropes that soared up to be lost in the brilliance of the lights. Similar encircling bonds covered their legs, from below the knee to the ankle, with ropes attached to them. These would doubtless have been sufficient to keep the captive bodies hanging there, clear of the ground, but, even more strikingly, around each girl's middle, like an exotic waspie, was a final broader swathe of PVC, tightly laced so that each girl's already slender waist was cinched in even narrower constriction. Two metal rings projected from the midriff of the wide strap, with the taut ropes leading upwards. Thus the prisoners were held horizontally, arms and legs spread wide, affording unrestricted view of their proffered flesh, for these central bands covered only the stomach and the hollowed back. Max found herself staring at the widely parted thighs, and the exposure of the sexual areas. Both girls had been shaved, or depilated as she herself had been, and the fissures of their labia stood out against the bareness of the curving flesh surrounding them.

The Maestro stepped forwards. He held a short-handled whip with several thin dark strands hanging from it. Moving forwards, he handed it to Max and led her to stand directly in front of one of the girls. Her face, like that of the other victim, was partially hidden by a black mask, similar, Max recognised with a shudder, to the eye mask she had been made to wear so often in the music room. Clouds of unruly black hair streamed down towards the floor. All at once, the light brown body, garbed in the strange restraints, began to thresh and jerk, arms and legs dancing, torso lifting and bucking madly. 'No! Please! Don't hurt me!' She was sobbing wildly, babbling, pleading frantically.

Briefly, Max wondered if it was all an act. Surely the helpless figure could not be a true captive? She must be an employee of this strange and frightening establishment. Or was that the right word? Was that what she and Toni were, too? They had performed for these people – naked, painted, in an erotic charade combining art with the extremes of sensuality these powerful degenerates commanded. No! Employees was not the word at all to describe what they had become. They belonged to the Maestro. They were his possessions. He did with them exactly what he liked, including putting them on show at this frightening place, for Lady Titty and her powerful friends. And they had done it. Like his good little – slaves!

The word she had been all along striving to avoid, the notion she had been trying ever since that first meeting with the Maestro to push from her mind, and which hovered always like a dark shadow on the edge of her consciousness, smote her with its full force now. He ruled her, body and spirit. Of course he could see through her, into her pathetic little sexual being! He knew how consumed she was with desire, with hunger to be truly taken by him.

'Go ahead!' the Maestro whispered, softly, irresistibly, in her ear. 'Use the wrist. Just flick. Start here.' Lost in her dream, she felt him take her by the shoulders and position her in front of those sprawled limbs, the centre of that long V. With a sob, which acknowledged her own helplessness to fight the primitive emotion coursing through her, she struck out, brought the lashes down inexpertly, but with all her strength, onto the conflux of those straining thighs, that twisting belly. And as she struck, she recognised the howling weeping features, the cascade of rich black hair, as Meena, whose beautiful body she had watched being entered by the Maestro.

The thin leather lashes bit wickedly into Meena's most tender flesh and snaked over the inner thighs. The fire blazed and burnt through her, and she bucked madly, her head flung back, the thick black hair whipping back and forth. The scream rang out, high and agonised, and its hearers shivered and sighed, melted and throbbed with the basic pleasure and fierce longing the sound aroused.

The calves in their black bonds threshed as Meena struggled to draw her legs together, and failed. Max struck again, equally wild, her vision blurred by her tears, and the sweat she could feel beading her brow stung her eyes. This time the lines of fire fell higher, some tangled uselessly in the ropes stretching from her victim's midriff, but others cracking stingingly across the swells of the breasts, leaving their thin red traces of torment on the light-brown skin with its darker circles and budding teats.

Max felt herself weeping, lost to the thickening excitement that was itself a sweet pain, like the helpless rise towards climax that sex brought, that she had indeed been gifted, by the other writhing screaming anonymous victim whose cries she could hear faintly. Her world was centred on that lifting belly, those gaping thighs. She was shaking, sweating, weeping, a victim of her passion, almost as helpless as the unknown girl whose body was in reality being beaten ...

She returned fully to an awareness of her surroundings as the girl was unhooked from the series of ropes holding her in the air. The strange bindings were left round her limbs and waist when she was first deposited gently on the wooden floor, then left to sob out the violence of her grief. The vivid weals and the shuddering groans were real enough, Max acknowledged. There were numerous willing helpers to undo the PVC straps, and to bear her gently away for more extensive repairs to her throbbing abused flesh. Mortified, Max glanced round when she had recovered herself sufficiently, and saw with new dread that, through it all, the other suspended figure had been observing in terrified silence.

Antonio, meanwhile, despite his initial shock, had been looking on with a much less tender conscience. He jumped as he felt an arm slip round his shoulder, while a soft hand brushed across the front of his slacks. Lady Titty's lips breathed against his ear. 'Come with me, you divine boy!'

He felt as though every eye in the place was on him as he obediently trailed in her wake, his own gaze fixed on those splendid undulating orbs of her backside through the shimmering skin of the silver gown. It clung so closely he could see the rolling curves and the deep divide in every detail, almost as though she were naked. He could see no trace of a panty line. He found out why when she led him to a door close by the foot of the staircase, and they stepped into a small study.

The heavy furnishings and old-fashioned wallpaper, as well as the large desk, the books, and the racked guns in the cabinet, gave it a totally masculine aura in which the beautiful shining vision of Lady Laycorn seemed exotically out of place. But then his sensitive nostrils distinguished traces of her perfume already hanging in the air, mingled with another cloying heaviness his startled senses identified as the powerful musk of sex.

His reflections were cut short as she turned, and ordered impatiently, 'Get me out of this fucking dress!'

'Yes, er – milady!' he managed, blushing at his feeling of foolishness. I sound like Mellors and Lady Chatterley! he thought mockingly. His fingers shook when she turned and he groped for the zip fastener between her flawless shoulder blades. The dress divided down to the risings of her buttocks. The beautiful shoulders twitched with even greater impatience. 'Hurry up!' Even less steadily, he eased the tight material down off her hips, unveiling the nakedness beneath. She wore no underclothes of any sort. She slipped off the dainty heeled sandals and he crouched, reverently slipping the discarded dress over her feet.

Leaning back across the desk, she pulled him on top of her. 'I want that divine little cock of yours right now! You hear me?' He felt her painted nails talon across his chest as she ripped his white shirt open to the waist and clawed it free of his shoulders. The fingers swooped to the waist fastener of his trousers and tore it loose. 'Help me!' His own hands were frantic, too, as he assisted her in stripping off his remaining clothes. Almost swooning with the ecstasy of their flesh making such contact, he lay on her and buried his head worshipfully in the proud full rounds of her breasts, with the jutting nipples stabbing firmly into his own tingling chest. His insides felt as though they had been hollowed out. 'Milady!' he gasped. 'I – I – don't know –'

With a grunt, she lifted her thighs about his waist, and gripped him crushingly, like a wrestler. 'Jesus, boy! Don't piss about –' She reached down feverishly between their straining bellies and he almost screamed as she seized his slippery penis in a vicelike grip. She pulled so hard he did indeed cry out. But then the cry transformed to a high whinny of pleasure, of fear, and of helpless excitement as he felt that unstoppable spasm and the swift thick flow of his ejaculation, over her fingers, and their conjoined flesh.

'I'm so sorry!' He raised his head and chest from hers and saw her staring down at their bellies and the sticky evidence of his ejaculation. A few thick pearly drops clustered in the thin line of light curls at her pubic mound. She raised her hand, the fingers stiffly extended, webbed by more stringy semen.

'Fuck me!' she whispered, gazing disbelievingly. Her lovely nose wrinkled in extreme distaste. 'You disgusting child!' She pushed him clear of her and struggled upright. 'How dare you? Coming all over me!' She glared about her. 'Get me a handkerchief! Clean me up!'

He glanced around, then looked at her helplessly, gesturing at his own nude body. 'I haven't – I'm sorry – your ladyship!'

With another savagely muttered obscenity, she looked about her until, stirred by recent memory, she suddenly bent and snatched something from the waste-paper basket under the desk. Antonio was surprised to see that she held a tiny diaphanous scrap of material that looked like a piece of underwear. Her lovely face set in a grimace of revulsion, she cleaned her sticky fingers, then wiped at her lower belly. 'You've let me down badly, boy! Popping your cork while I'm still fizzing away! You deserve to be punished.'

But already the anger was dissipated. He could tell by her tone and by her look that she was seized by a new excitement and anticipation. Once more she was turning, glancing searchingly around her. 'Ah! That'll do.' She moved, and Antonio watched her bend again, this time on the other side of the desk, and emerge clutching a dark narrow object. 'Tommy likes his comfort!' She had in her grasp a leather slipper. 'Over the desk, you naughty boy! I'll teach you to go off at half-cock! Oh, I say! That's rather good, eh?' She giggled, nodding at his still gleaming, now-shrunken member. 'Half-cock! How appropriate!'

Antonio took up his position, stretching over the desk, shivering at the contact with his bare skin and the sharp edge of the wood on his lower belly. When she had delivered several ringing blows, the outlines of the sole stood out in vivid splendour on the pale flesh. Titty felt her excitement rising with sweet urgency once more, her splendid breasts heavy as they rose and fell rapidly, both with her exertion and her desire. She flung the slipper aside and seized him by his dark hair, dragging him up from the desk. 'Service me, you gorgeous bastard!' She pushed him to his knees. She felt the bite of his teeth, his lapping tongue, and knew she couldn't wait. She bent him backwards, toppling him over on the oriental rug, and sat crushingly on his streaming face, thighs spread wide and head flung back as she howled at the power of the orgasm surging through her.

Eighteen

Max's overwrought nerves had been stretched to breaking point by the events of the long day. She wept as the Maestro led her from the sinister punishment room, where she had so shockingly witnessed the sadistic desires of the wealthy inmates of the Pleasure Dome. She was filled with self-disgust at the sick fantasy she had fixed on in her mind during the exhibition. How could she have allowed herself to be manipulated into such a perverse chimera? Surely it must be the fault of the man who had taken her over so completely that he could even fashion her thoughts? Bitterly, she reflected that the earlier performance with her cousin, coated in that white paint, was no less perverse than what she had just seen in that bizarre room. In fact, the concert had been worse, in its way, for their skill, their gift as musicians, which some would regard as sacred, had been sullied by its combination with the erotic display they had provided. No matter how appreciative of their talent the audience might have appeared, it was the youthful nakedness of the performers, every vestige highlighted by that obscene white coating and on display under the brilliant lights, that was the chief vivid attraction of the whole degrading spectacle. She and Antonio had prostituted their art – except, she acknowledged even more bitterly, they would reap no reward. Prostitutes worked for gain. Antonio and she worked because they were slaves, pretty objects, owned body and soul by the Maestro.

She was so wrapped up in her despairing thoughts that she had paid little attention to where she was being taken. She found herself in a long narrow room on one of the upper floors. The row of four beds, all along one wall, gave it the appearance of a dormitory. There was a low metal locker beside each bed. At the far end of the room an opening without a door led to a bathroom. The Maestro nodded towards it. 'Get undressed. Clean your teeth, wash your face. There's new toothbrushes, clean towels. Use the lavatory. You're going to bed now. You must be exhausted, you poor thing.'

He spoke as though to a child, and that was just how she felt. At the kindly concern apparent in the last remark, her eyes filled with tears again. 'Aren't we going home?' she asked quietly. A tear escaped, hovered, and rolled down her cheek.

He smiled, reached out a hand and brushed her cheek. 'No, my child. The weekend's just begun. There are much more important things to happen tomorrow. You'll need your sleep.'

She removed her dress and stepped out of the light sandals and the tiny white knickers. She went through to the bathroom. There was no door to close, let alone lock, but she was past caring now. She saw that there were two lavatory pedestals standing side by side, without any compartment or screening to hide them, just as there were two washbasins, two adjacent bathtubs and two shower stalls. She relieved herself, washed and cleaned her teeth, as bidden, aware all the while of his smiling observation of her. He led her to the bed nearest the door, and folded back the sheet

189

and the blankets. Suddenly, her heart started to thump and she felt the familiar weakness of sexual hunger stir her deeply. She could feel the hot blush staining her neck and face. She was hoping he would stay with her! Hoping that at last he was going to possess her body. But then she gaped in astonishment and dismay as he reached into the locker and took something out.

'Here. Let me fit this on before you jump into bed.' It was a triangular shape, like a G-string or a cache-sex, except that it was made of much more substantial material. The pouch, which fitted over her genital area, was thickly padded with cotton on its inner surface. The outer surface was of strengthened leather, the dark brown smoothly polished. A thin strap coming up from its base fitted so deeply into the cleft of her bottom that it was hidden from view until it joined the thicker belt that passed around her, just above her hips. The Maestro drew this belt in until the pouch fitted snugly over her mound, then snapped the catch shut. A catch that could only be released with a key, she realised, as he tested it.

'There now!' He grinned at her. 'That should ensure you get a good night's sleep. What's left of it!' He grimaced good-humouredly, looking at his watch. He flicked his fingernail at the hard leather triangle. 'A modern version of the good old chastity belt, my dear! I'm afraid we've been far too lenient with you in the past. Your move here marks the beginning of new things. You must learn restraint from now on. And it's no good searching for your night-time comforter, my dear! You'll have to learn to do without it – or him, or her, or whatever your libidinous little fancy used to dictate. There are some rather uninhibited guests wandering about here, as you've seen. Oh yes! And it will act as a formidable

190

deterrent just in case that hot-headed Toni should manage to slip into your boudoir, eh? I've a feeling he's learned enough of the wicked world lately to want to change that sweet innocence that has marked your relationship for so long. And perhaps he's not the only one, eh, my sweet?' The dark eyebrows lifted, and he gave a deep chuckle. 'Good night , my darling. You played well tonight, by the way. And you looked beautiful. I was very proud. Good night.' He bent and kissed her full on the lips. She opened her mouth, seeking to turn it into an embrace full of passion. With gentle firmness, his hands encircled her thin arms and eased her away from him. 'Someone will be along to unlock you in the morning. In you get!'

She climbed in, and lay still while he tucked the bedclothes chastely under her chin. 'Night-night, Max!' He bent and kissed her again, this time on the brow, like a parent putting a child to bed. He switched off the light and closed the door, leaving her alone in the unfamiliar darkness.

She felt the tears trickling down her temples, clinging in her hair. Very faintly, she could hear music. Sometimes the sound of laughter swelled louder, and shrill cries. She heard a scream of genuine pain, and her body stiffened. There were several more, then they were cut off abruptly. Why had the Maestro put the chastity belt on her? Why stop her masturbating, when he had given her Night Rider and knew how frequently she had used it? She felt her insides hollow as she recalled his use of the phrase 'the beginning of new things'. She knew this momentous evening marked a watershed in her life, in the weird isolated existence she had lived since coming under the Maestro's influence. Was her youthful beauty to be sacrificed to someone like that fearful Sheikh Hamad?

She was shocked to discover how easily she could accept the degenerate nature of the spectacle she and Toni had provided – as long as the Maestro continued to rule over them himself. She would prostitute her art – and even her body – if that was what he wished. Just as long as she – and Toni – could remain his. But then, belonging meant exactly that. She was his 'thing', he could give her to whomever he liked. Certainly, he himself didn't want her. Not in a sexual way. He'd made that abundantly clear.

She shivered, and cried anew at the way her body was responding. She became aware what a refinement of cruelty this new symbol of subjection was. Apart from this hard little seal so effectively denying her vital access to her sex, she was completely naked – and aware with cruel sensuality of every inch of her body. The caress of the cool sheet on her skin was a sweet torment. She could not keep still. She twisted from side to side, her limbs threshed, she felt her nipples harden, she could not keep her hands from caressing her breasts. She could feel her vaginal passage stirring, the muscles clenching, the dampness beginning under the obscene little shield of the device he had locked her into. Impotently, she tried to push it off her mound, to tug the belt down over her hips, and only succeeded in hurting herself in the process. The weeping fit came again, and her frame shook with its brief violence, even though she despised herself for giving in to it. When it had passed, she thought again of the way he had treated her just now, the gentleness of him. In a way, that rarely revealed tenderness was another refined cruelty, it added to her helpless longing for him to possess her bodily. She recalled the way he had tucked her in, kissed her. Just like – daddy!

The word went off like a firecracker in her head. She knew the Maestro had been mummy's lover, even from the time before she had met daddy, when she was just a young girl, no older than Max herself was now. Aunt Charlotte had lately been at great pains to let her know, to impress upon her just how infatuated mummy had been, how much she was under his spell. And afterwards, after the wedding – in fact, right up to the tragic end of her life, Aunt Charlotte said – mummy had continued the affair, continued to be entirely under his spell.

'Your poor father –' Max could hear the contempt in her aunt's voice '– couldn't do anything about it. He was never any match for the Maestro, and he knew it! Whenever the Maestro showed up, Dicky would disappear. Crawl back like a little lap dog when he'd gone again!'

What if . . .? Her mind spun like an overloaded machine with the enormity of her conjecture. What if daddy were not her daddy at all? What if her real father was the powerful magnetic figure who had just put her to bed, whose bondmaid she undoubtedly was?

Somehow, eventually, despite the torment of her troubled thoughts, she fell into a deep sleep. She woke in the dim greyness of early dawn, to feel an icy figure fitting its nude body tightly about hers, the hands intimately exploring her own warm flesh, exclaiming with astonishment at feeling the hugging restraint of the protection snugly shielding her genitals. 'What the fuck?' hissed Toni's voice in her ear.

'It's to make sure nobody can get at me,' she whispered. As she spoke, his lips closed over hers, and his tongue drove into her wetness. His hands were still roaming possessively over her pliant body, and she shivered at the arousal of his caresses. 'Where've you been?' she demanded. 'I've been in bed ages. On my own!' she added significantly.

She felt a tremor pass through him, and heard him wince as she passed her hand over his behind. 'Ouch! Careful! Lady Titty's been having her wicked way with me! And I mean wicked!'

All at once, she remembered the turmoil of her thoughts, and all that had happened to both of them recently. She thrust her concealed loins hard against his. 'Yes! Well, *you* can't have your wicked way with me tonight!' She jabbed the leather guard aggressively into him once more. 'Not properly, anyway! But then, you never have, have you? Even when you had the chance, you never even tried. And it's too fucking late now! Never mind! There's nothing to stop me having my wicked way with *you*! What's a little incest between twins? That's what they all think we are, you know – this bunch of rich sickos!' She reached down and grabbed at his cold flaccid prick, and gave it a vicious tug. He squirmed helplessly. 'Lie back and think of England! Or Poll Mouse! Or Lady Fucking Titty!'

The horse bucked nervously at the suddenness with which the black-garbed figure stepped out of the bushes at the side of the path, and Titty swore profanely as she fought to control it. The other riders were already disappearing through the leafy trees which fringed the narrow trail, and she glanced ahead with dawning apprehension. She wanted to cry out, to attract their attention, but failed to do so. The tall burly man in the dark tracksuit already had hold of the animal's tossing head, holding it steady, until the movements calmed a little.

'What the devil are you doing? Do you realise this is private land? Let go –'

Her alarm gave way to irritation as she recognised him. 'Holger! What on earth do you want? My guests –' She gestured ahead with her crop, and made to pull the horse round, to carry on. 'Whatever it is, it can wait. See me up at the house –'

'No. It can't wait, milady,' he answered, with an insufferable grin. 'The Maestro wants a word with you. In private. Now.'

She bridled at once at his tone. 'The fuck he does! Tell him I'll see him after breakfast. Now get out of –'

She gave a cry of alarm as the powerful figure pulled savagely at the bit, preventing her from moving her mount round him. The animal backed off, snorting, the white eyes flashing, and she had to cling on, fighting not to slide from the saddle. The world spun crazily, and suddenly she was indeed free from her seat, dragged clear by Holger, who let her fall heavily onto the hard earth. The contact momentarily knocked the breath from her. The mare whinnied and skittered out of the way, blundering off through the trees, where it came to a halt several yards into the woodland.

'How dare you?' she panted. She glared up at him, more astounded and angry than afraid. 'You insolent bastard! I'll –' she let out another squeal as he bent and pushed her down flat on her back by her shoulders. His hands seized her waist, gripped the jodhpurs and tore them open. She heard the fastenings rip, then he was hauling them down, over her hips, freeing the billowing white shirt, beneath which peeped the pristine and conventionally respectable white sports briefs. He tugged the riding breeches down, fought them over the tops of the polished boots, and left them clinging there. They acted as effective bonds, hobbling her, while he strode off and confidently took hold of the still nervous mare and led her back to the path.

Titty was still trying to struggle up and clear herself of her ridiculous restraint when Holger

unceremoniously hauled her upright, and with one
heave plucked her off the ground and tossed her, face
down, over the saddle. In a trice he had bound her
wrists tightly in the leather reins, which he dragged
under the horse's belly and tied to the breeches
clinging about her feebly waving legs. She hung there
like a sack, neatly tethered and utterly helpless. 'You
fuck-pig!' she fumed impotently, red-faced, her words
muffled by her undignified stance. 'Let me go! Untie
me, you – you –!' She spluttered into incoherent rage,
twisting and turning. Her horse gave a few skittering
steps before accepting the dominance of Holger's grip
and allowing itself to be led along the bridle path.

'Mustn't keep the Maestro waiting!' Holger grinned maddeningly. The jouncing of the animal beneath
her rendered Titty's comments mercifully incompre-
hensible.

When they stopped, she recognised the shed that
stood at the edge of the woodland, where paraphernalia for the feeding of the pheasants and the rearing
of the chicks was kept. At their approach, Labat
appeared in the doorway. In spite of the rural
surroundings, he was dressed formally in dark suit and
tie. Titty's fury seemed to melt away at his formidable
presence. She remained silent at his mocking greeting.

'What? Were you reluctant to meet me, your
ladyship? Bring her inside, Holger, will you? Then
take the animal up to the stables. Someone might be
anxious. We wouldn't want them to come looking for
you, would we?'

Quickly, Holger untied her, slung her over his
shoulder and, with jodhpurs still dangling around her
boots, carried her into the mustiness of the little hut
and dumped her on the piles of old sacking that
littered the floor. With a grin, he nodded at her, put
a mocking finger to his brow in a final salute and left.

Titty cleared her throat. She lay propped on her elbows. She made no attempt to pull her breeches up. 'What the fuck is the idea, Maestro? Why did your man debag me and sling me about like a sack of potatoes?'

'You've no idea, Titty?' The dark eyebrows were raised in amused enquiry, the sensual lips stretched in a wide grin.

'No! Of course I haven't!' But, despite the aggressive tone, she could feel the red tide of guilt flowing into her face, and was helpless to arrest it.

'Several little birdies tell me you've been having confidential talks with some of your illustrious guests – like Willard Koln, for instance?'

'It was nothing – I was going to tell you – I just wanted to see –'

'And Sheikh Hamad,' he went on, over her gabbled interruption. 'I heard you were trying to organise something of an auction. For *my* property! Surely I don't need to remind you that the Heavenly Twins belong to me? Entirely to me? And I'm perfectly capable of negotiating on my own behalf. You've done well enough out of them already, Titty. Thanks to me! And this is how you repay me!'

'No, no, Maestro! I swear! I was only setting things up. Seeing how the land lies. I just wanted to see if there was some proposition – I could bring to you –'

He looked at her pityingly, and shook his head as he clicked his tongue in gentle reproach. 'Really, Titty! I think you've got too used to handling prickless little pervs like your Tommy, you naughty old tart! What *are* we going to do with you?'

'Please!' She began to gabble frantically. 'It could be such a huge deal, Maestro! I know we can –'

'*We*, Titty?' He laughed richly. 'Come on. Let's get you up!' He bent, put his hands under her shoulders, and lifted her to her feet. There was a solid wooden table against one wall. It was covered in filth. A pile of wickerwork cages rested on top of it and he swept them off before dragging it to the middle of the tiny space. 'Over you go!'

Her blue eyes wide with tearful anxiety, she glanced at him before obeying. She was craven now, her voice breathless as a child's. 'Please – Maestro! Don't hurt me. Please! I'd never do anything – you know –'

'Shut up, Titty,' he said pleasantly.

She began to snivel. Her voice was no more than a husky whisper now. 'Please. My arse – it cost a fortune. Be careful –'

He had hold of her riding crop, and he used it to carefully lift the tail of her shirt. Then he eased her white knickers clear of the resplendent globes, moving them down carefully until they clung about mid-thigh. His palms cupped, he explored the wonderfully enhanced curves, feeling the firm heaviness of the rounds, lifting them to expose the faintness of the telltale tiny scars in the creases, evidence of how nature had been improved upon. 'A beautiful job!' he chuckled. 'I'm sure they'll stand up to a good whipping. I just hope sensation hasn't been deadened at all. I know how much you always enjoyed a good thrashing. Why don't you stuff this hankie in your mouth, my sweet? Just in case! We don't want any intruders, do we?'

She obeyed him. He saw the long haunches clench ready for his assault. He brought the crop down smartly. It cracked against the cheeks, rebounding from the resilient flesh, and he watched the thin red line rise, darkening against the milky flawlessness of the skin. He sighed with appreciation. He could hear her muffled cries against the makeshift gag, heard the breath whistle through her nostrils. He struck again with the same clean stroke, and admired the quiver of shock that ran through her bottom, then the jerk of her entire frame, the gasp as she fought to keep herself prostrated across the dusty table.

He paused for a few seconds between each stroke, allowing time for her to experience to the full the initial flare of pain, then the burn and sting that spread through her hindquarters, stirred her nerve ends, and sent its ripple of agonised movement throughout her frame before she sagged limply, and waited weeping for the next blow. There were many such before he stopped.

She lay, unmoving except for the heave of shoulders at the sobs tearing through her. He removed his jacket, unzipped his flies and took out his penis, which strained mightily, its purple head massive, agleam with his emission. She spat out the handkerchief and groaned as she felt his thumbs pressing into the hot abused cheeks, parting the deep cleft, his fingers, wet now with saliva, seeking that hidden puckered slit. She gave a soft cry of protest at the insistent pressure of the probing finger, then a sharper higher sound at the thrust of the wet helm, before the steel-hard shaft drove in to fuse pain and pleasure for both of them in their melding.

Nineteen

Polly stared fixedly at her own image reflected in the full-length mirror on the wall opposite. She looked thinner than ever, like some starved refugee waif. And, most shocking of all, was the complete hairlessness at the base of her belly. The depilation of her pubis, carried out with the strips of waxed paper by the beautiful foreign girl, Meena, had been painful. It had been followed by similar treatment to her legs and arms, including the tender armpits, after which Meena had donned a pair of special gloves, meant to be used in the bath for exfoliating the skin. They were of a texture as abrasive as the roughest emery paper. Polly's supine body had been coated with an over-poweringly sweet thick cream, squeezed all over from a large tube, and then massaged vigorously into her flesh by Meena, wearing the gloves and causing Polly acute discomfort. Her skin burned, then tingled. For most of the time, her distress was heightened by the eager observation of Charlotte Behr, and Davies, her fearful maid. Not to mention Holger!

Afterwards, she was put into the shower, where Meena joined her, and, still wearing the rough gloves, rubbed her down, from neck to toes, until her skin glowed pinkly. After the spectators had departed, and when the jets of tepid water had been turned off,

Meena began to make love to her, holding her down on the wet tiles, coiling her own brown body around the paler pinker flesh. Those gloves became the instruments of both fiercely kindled excitement and sharp pain as Meena cupped and caressed the slight breasts, playing with the pale nipples until they stood up, throbbing and smarting under the abrasive touch. Then the invasive hands passed over the smooth bareness of the belly, scratching at the tender insides of the victim's thighs, pushing them apart to gain access to the beating furrow of flesh nestling between them.

Polly yelped at the intrusion of those fiery pads at the entrance to her sex, and Meena, with a guilty and, Polly suspected, duplicitous laugh, finally peeled them from her skilful hands. A finger penetrated through the slippery tissue into the spasming vagina itself. The helpless girl felt her excitement growing, throbbing ever more urgently, both the recent pain and the arousal blending in a strange union which brought her almost to the brink of climax – a release that was for a long while denied to her, for which she was uncertain whether to be glad or sorry.

She had endured similar treatment several times now, and not just from Meena. From what had initially been a nightmare unreal world of terror, she had drifted into an existence in which the fear had receded, and blended into an existence of fantasy become all too real. Her skin was as soft and smooth as satin. She could not help touching herself whenever she had an opportunity to do so, and her own caresses never failed to arouse her. Even when, in that long chamber she had come to associate with the strange fusion of pain and pleasure, staring at the image of her own sprawled body, arms akimbo, feet apart, she shivered, and felt that overpowering urge to gratify the beating sexuality stirring deeply within her. The leather circlets of the restraints at wrists and ankles chafed her. The short links of chain by which they were fastened to the stout hooks in the wall chinked softly, and she wept at her inability to touch herself and ease the fires of sexual need burning through her.

She was being transformed by her captivity into a sensual creature, whose only value lay in her physical attributes. Already she felt separated by a lifetime from her former world, the world of freedom, of work, of clothes – of solitude. These days, although she spent some time alone – as when, for instance, they left her chained to the wall, to stare at her naked self in the mirror – during such periods she felt she was only waiting; waiting for the next person to make use of her, to demonstrate total mastery over her captive body. She realised this was all she was to the small circle who ruled her life now – Professor Labat, Holger, the dreaded Charlotte and her terrible companion, Davies.

It was in the presence of those two harpies that her chief fear still lay. She had been afraid of them even in those earliest days – in her former life, as she was rapidly beginning to think of it – when she had first met Max and Antonio, her Heavenly Twins. How innocent those entrancing hours seemed now, when she had tutored them, and fallen head over heels in love with both of them.

After those magic afternoons, she could scarcely wait to get back to her lonely little flat. She would sit in the anonymity of the crowded bus, aware of every throb and quiver of the engine passing through the worn seat, up into her limbs. She would squeeze her thighs tightly together, short of breath with desire, her fists clenched in her lap with the effort not to stroke herself in that beating centre of her hunger where she could feel the wetness seeping through her knickers and the tights. Her body was pungent with it and, as soon as she was safely behind her own locked door, she would feverishly strip off her clothes and hurry through to the dingy bathroom to slide into a tub of foamy fragrant water, as hot as she could bear it.

Still deliciously torturing herself, she would strive not to arouse herself sexually, delaying that exquisite moment, denying herself the relief of the passion drumming through her every nerve. She did not always succeed, but she fought hard, lying back, savouring the embrace of the warm liquid, the scent and the feel of the suds, their fragrance, as long as she could, before she rose, wrapped herself in one of her best fleeciest bath sheets, and moved to the bedroom. Letting the damp towel drop to the floor, she would sit at the cluttered dressing table, devouring the image of her nakedness in the mirror, still struggling desperately not to touch those areas of her body shrieking for her attention – the aching breasts, whose nipples felt as though they would burst at any second; the throbbing vulva, nestling beneath the soft damp curls of pubis.

'No, no! Not yet!' she would whisper, pleadingly. If she could summon up the resolve, she would reach for her make-up, and, with painstaking slowness, work on her face with the eye-liner and cream and lipstick, the dusting of powder, until her features took on the appearance of some theatrical mask, and she would feel the urge to giggle scandalously at the thought of how her few acquaintances would gasp with amazement if they could see the mousy creature they thought they knew like this.

But always, at this stage, or at any of the stages preceding it, she would reach into the depths of the narrow drawer. Her nose wrinkled fastidiously as she fell across the musty unmade bed, then the reality of the scene around her faded, the shaming pathos of the picture she presented, on her back, her knees lifted and parting, in the dim silence broken only by the soft purring of the device she held to the crevice of her lonely desire, and she entered the rich and vivid world of fantasy, possessed and captivated by the magically beautiful twins as they took their pleasure with her eagerly surrendered body.

That lonely world had been shattered by the events that had overtaken all three of them. Yet, somehow, she acknowledged that, in some deep part of her mind, she had been brought face to face with her innermost secret self – the self she had never wanted to admit to – the degenerate sexually obsessed being who had always lurked, in dark corners, in solitary intimacy, behind the timid respectability, the dowdiness she had presented to the world outside for so long.

Reality had become so blurred with this private inner world that her mind seemed numbed, refusing to function, to help her sort out her fragmented thoughts. For example, her fear. She realised she had never truly been frightened before. Not this paralysing fear, which could affect her physically so that her muscles literally failed, her strength drained away, she had no control over the most basic functions of her body. Shame came later, the most withering scalding shame, but it did nothing to lessen that hopeless bodily failure. That was why she had sat, shivering and naked, at the table in the Maestro's house, after only a few days as a prisoner, and written those letters, and filled in the forms, at his dictation, scarcely realising what she was doing, or how completely she was giving herself over to him. She was glad only that the beatings had stopped, along with the fear of Holger's sadistic use of her.

And even that – in the midst of all that pain and fear – had shaken her. How even his taking of her could set her ablaze, set her senses clamouring with helpless need, send her soaring to those mindless shattering explosions of release he brought – and sometimes even more cruelly – denied her.

The Maestro had told her, in that devastatingly implacable voice of his, that she now belonged to him. The notion was too immense for her to get her mind round – it only added to the sense of unreal nightmare she was plunged in. But after endless days of proof – her nakedness, the beatings, the sex – she had come to realise its truth. Holger, in one of his post-coital easy humours, had driven it home to her. 'You have only one purpose in your life now. You're the Maestro's, and your only aim is to serve him. To obey. If you don't, you'll be got rid of, believe me. It happens. We could have a chopper here today – put you in it, wrap you up in a tarpaulin, strap you down with great heavy weights. Fly you far out to sea and throw you out. You'd be bones long before you were ever found – if you ever *were*. So you be a good little girl and concentrate on pleasing your master. That's all you have to do. Isn't that an easy life, eh?' It was life, easy or not. That was all that mattered.

At least Holger, though he was the one who most frequently beat her, was also the one who made love to her. Fucked her, she corrected herself bleakly, for she had given up all rights to love when she was taken prisoner. And even in that, as far as she was concerned, he had told her, he was the agent of his master, who was her master, too. That was why, he asserted, poor Max was finding it so hard to accept her status. The poor little slag couldn't get it into her head that she was his property, just because he chose not to fuck her. Holger had laughed, and Polly felt her heart ache with compassion for the lovely girl and recognition of her status. 'Randy little cow's dying for him – dying for *anybody* to shag her now! And she's still a virgin! She won't know what's hit her when she finally swaps the machinery for a piece of real meat!

Well, Polly certainly didn't have to worry about that problem any longer. How many times had she privately tormented herself with the spectre of her own unclaimed virginity, the unnaturalness of never having had sex at the ripe old age of thirty-one? Was it really only a few short weeks since she and Antonio had shared that strange sweet interval together in the flat? She felt again the embarrassment she experienced at its recall. Though it was in its own way precious, their relationship could never be classed as normal. The lovely boy's sexuality had been too ambivalent for that. The way he had made love to her, thrilling as it was, was not such as a man and woman usually shared. Even now she blushed at the recollection of his kisses, all over her body, his hands, exploring, opening her, his tongue . . . he might well have been his own cousin in the way he aroused her, as, indeed, she had imagined sometimes in their love-play.

And then their sexual congress, when it was finally achieved. Her eyes moistened with regret and tenderness for the happiness she had undoubtedly found in being with him, in being so close together in those few days they had shared. Now, she had no idea how many times Holger had taken her – and roused her to such wild excess. Nothing romantic or sweetly insubstantial about such fierce coupling. No cloudy tender loving – just the heat of animal rutting, pure and uncomplicated in its way, and with such catastrophic results.

To her own shame and confusion, she found herself praying now that Holger would continue to assume his surrogate mastery over her. She would accept it gladly, punishment and all. Her heart had sunk after their capture, when Miss Charlotte and her fearful subordinate had shown up, and, instead of immediately accompanying the twins to their new venue, the

Pleasure Dome, Polly had found herself being wrapped in a long black coat that enveloped her from shoulders to ankles, her feet forced into a pair of tart's shoes, all shiny black plastic and five-inch heels, and hustled into the back of a car. The cropped head of Davies and the solid square shoulders occupied the driving seat. Polly sat in the back with Charlotte. The busy early evening scene of the city only inches away, through the thin glass, served to reinforce her sense of nightmare. Ordinary people, crowds on foot, cars, buses, all flowing unknowingly by this naked prisoner. It was mind-bending. She kept urging herself to do something, make some desperate attempt to escape, to fling herself clear, back into that world from which she was sealed off, for ever. As if reading her thoughts, Charlotte had flung open the concealing coat, exposing her nakedness, and with clutching hands explored her body with all the blatant right of ownership demonstrated so forcibly by the Maestro and his man.

She had been left alone, scarcely able to register any coherent thought through her fear. Davies had fastened a leather collar round her neck, fixed a short chain to it and manacles to her wrists and ankles and tied her like a beast to the wall. She had little idea how long she crouched, shivering and whimpering, the faint noise of traffic only emphasising her isolation, before the door of the room suddenly opened, and Polly's heart raced. She wished fervently that the torture of the waiting she had endured could go on, as she stared in horror. Davies was dressed in a pair of shining black lycra shorts which came almost to her knee, and clung like skin to her muscular unattractive frame. She wore a white singlet hanging loose outside the waistband of the shorts. It was sleeveless, and thus revealed the strength of the muscled arms in full. In contrast to the plain and butch athleticism of her maid, Charlotte Behr was dressed in a full-length sheath of black, starkly yet elegantly simple. It was an off-the-shoulder evening gown, and its low cut bosom emphasised the imposing swell of the substantial breasts and the flawless smoothness of the pale shoulders. Beneath the dress, her waist was nipped in to an impressive slimness, again highlighting the generous swell of the hips and the curves of the buttocks, and the shapeliness of the long legs outlined beneath the clinging material. Matching heeled shoes, elegantly stylish, completed the outfit. She wore no jewellery of any kind, not even earrings, and there were no rings on her fingers. Even in her quaking terror, Polly could not help noting the power of the impression this imposing figure made on her.

The elegant mistress appeared content to play an observer's role. She moved to one side of the long mirror and leaned against the wall, while Davies advanced on Polly with a grin that fanned the fear already causing the chained form to shake visibly. 'Well, well! Poor little Poll Mouse!'

Polly tried to keep still. Her breasts shook as a huge loud sob escaped her. The fear mingled with undeniable frissons of desire as Davies' gentle fingers invaded her. Polly could feel them toying wickedly with the hard little nub of her excitement. She was close to coming when the sweetly enervating torment ceased. Davies' gruff chuckle of satisfaction showed how well she was aware of her victim's condition. 'Why should you have all the fun, sexy?'

The hands swiftly unbuckled Polly's manacled wrists and ankles and unchained the collar. The naked girl slid down the wall to crouch at Davies' feet, whimpering softly. 'Don't hurt me, please!' she whispered. Part of her frightened brain was already dealing with the problems of survival, telling her that this cringing subservience was what her captors demanded of her. Not that her terror wasn't genuine, the melting trembling of her weakened limbs any less authentic.

'Kneel!' Davies commanded, then seized the weeping figure impatiently and positioned her, thrusting her by the neck down to the floor in the centre of the room, pushing the head down further until it rested on the folded arms. The pale haunches and curving back were thus presented as a prime target for the punishment to follow.

The instrument chosen was a whip and the wielder was an expert. The lash curled around the narrow hips, after the first vicious bite of fire across the twitching buttocks, adding a cruel refinement to the pain. The blows were laid with precision, until Polly could no longer hold herself in her foetal crouch and moved, spreading herself, trying vainly to escape the burning sting of the blows.

'Enough, Davies!' Charlotte had to repeat the command. She saw the look of hate stamped upon the plain features, swiftly followed by one of guilt. Davies let her hand fall to her side, the coils of the whip trailing on the floor beside her. Through the thin cotton of the top, her small nipples thrust sharply as the curves of the almost masculine chest rose and fell with her exertions.

Charlotte felt again that cold clutch of fear and uncertainty at the thought of the future – and even the present, for their lives were changing, had, indeed, already been altered, by the return of the Maestro into their lives – and, especially for her maid, the influence of that hulking brute of a man of his. Davies was no longer that rocklike character she had loved and relied upon for so many years. The strong figure displayed a brooding moodiness, a bewildering variation of temperament, that was so foreign to the stolid personality Charlotte was accustomed to.

'We don't want to mark her, do we?' she added now, lightening her tone to take away from the sharpness of her previous command. Polly, stretched out face down on the carpet, was too wrapped up in her private world of throbbing pain and weeping misery to be aware of the exchange, or of the muttered imprecations by her punisher before she swept angrily from the room.

Polly was surprised at the gentleness of the hands with which Charlotte drew her to her feet, led her along to the bathroom nearby, and helped her to bathe her stinging flesh. But in the soft lamp glow of the bedroom, Polly's heart fluttered again with alarm when Charlotte ordered her to help her undress. Beneath the long gown she was wearing a black body, tightly encasing her torso. The sheer stockings were fastened to it with long lacy ribbons of suspenders. Polly's fingers shook as she stripped these delicate garments from the still shapely frame, yet, strangely, this time there was none of that frightening brutality Polly had anticipated. The touch with which she placed Polly's quivering body on the bed, and placed a cushion under her to lift the belly and thighs, displayed all the tenderness of a generous and skilled lover.

Polly's head rolled back and forth on the counterpane, not with fear now but with urgent ecstasy. She was no longer the hapless virgin taken by force. She was another creature altogether, one whose existence depended solely on giving gratification such as this, and, shatteringly, she was discovering that she could be the recipient also of such sensual delights.

Twenty

'Well, gentlemen, I think that concludes our business. Shall we drink to it? No hard feelings, I hope?' The Maestro beamed. He felt an extra glow of satisfaction which he was careful to hide from the two men, who were struggling to conceal their own feelings of intense annoyance and frustration. Sheikh Hamad was used to getting his own way, and he knew he had failed. In his kingdom of Qumshah, he was autocrat absolute, and even in watering holes of the wealthy throughout the world, east and west, he was one of the most powerful of playboys. The fact that he had just failed to buy the thing he most coveted at the moment did not sit well on his swarthy bristled features, or his rotund frame.

He tried to tell himself that he had at least achieved a compromise, had won a partial victory. The infidel, Labat, had agreed to lease the exquisite twins to him for two or three weeks so that he could enjoy them in the seclusion of his desert palace, and exhibit their formidable musical talent to an exclusive gathering of his cronies. It would be a supreme coup for him, he knew, for, even in the elite circle in which he moved, nothing like this heavenly boy and girl had been seen before. And he had the added comfort of knowing he had outbid the disgruntled figure sitting beside him.

Willard Koln, as tall and saturnine as the sheikh was round and bland, would be smarting inwardly at having lost the race to host the next erotic concert by the beautiful duo. The fact that Labat had smoothly agreed to let the American have the couple at some future date, after their trip to Qumshah, would scarcely lessen the gall Koln must surely be feeling.

But Hamad had wanted that divine pair. He had known they would be something special. He could not fail to be moved by the glossy pictures sent to him, the excited speculation which had preceded this painstakingly screened and carefully prepared meeting at the Pleasure Dome. But as soon as he had beheld them, in all their perfection, shining white, ethereal under the spotlights, no less so in the unadorned flesh, which he had gazed on and touched briefly afterwards, his portly frame had quivered and his heart had beat with a fierce desire to possess them for himself. Totally, as his own, in the way this accursed Maestro owned them, and refused to let go, in spite of the unprecedented munificence of the four million dollars Sheikh Hamad had offered. As it was, it was going to cost him over a million for the pleasure of entertaining them in his home for a mere two weeks.

The dark mirror glasses he habitually wore in public helped to hide his true feelings. He had learnt to play the game to the rules these urbane foreigners had created. He watched the flawlessly groomed features of Lady Titty as she rose from the depths of the armchair, and saw her wince almost imperceptibly, her hand moving instinctively towards those pronounced jutting rounds of her bottom, splendidly outlined by the clinging material of the dark-red tight little dress she was wearing. When she sat, cross-legged, the hem was so short it slipped to the very top of her thighs, revealing her long legs, bare of any covering, to their full extent. As she stood, she delivered the merest flash, almost a mirage, of the shaded triangle of her sex, an infinitesimal glimpse. Bare also, covered only by nature's adornment, those silken curls? Or snugly caressed by satin? Who could say?

His admiration, however, was soured by his recall of her confident words to him in much more intimate circumstances, two days previously, in the luxury of one of the mansion's many bathrooms. She had sunnily promised him success in his heartfelt wish for ownership of the cousins before putting her mouth to a much more rousing use. But now he felt bitterly disappointed at her failure to make good on her promise. 'Oh, Titty,' he exclaimed, as she brought him his drink, 'you seem a little stiff, my love. Have you been riding too hard?'

'Or been ridden?' Koln grunted acidly. He was far less skilled, or concerned, about hiding his irritation. The thought soothed the sheikh a great deal.

Titty herself was feeling less than delighted, for she had promised both these men success in their quest in order to fan the flame of healthy competition, and had failed to deliver to either – unless they counted this scheme of using the gorgeous youngsters as rent boy and girl a success. She doubted it very much, though the Maestro must be laughing like a drain at having hooked them.

Her behind was still sore, as the Arabian letch had noticed behind those black glasses of his when she stood up. She pictured the lines, bruise-dark now and standing in hard ridges, under the thin material of her dress. The Maestro had really flogged her, damn him. And it had infuriated her even more to admit that the whipping had literally whetted her appetite for the equally frantic battering he had given her elsewhere immediately afterwards. Such rough treatment, on both counts, had always held its own uneasy thrill for her. However, after the fortune she had spent on her 'arse job', as Tommy insisted infuriatingly on referring to it, she was hesitant about indulging in such treatment. Not that the Maestro had given her any choice, sod him! That was what was so maddeningly fascinating about the bastard, that dominance against which she could still feel helpless. Like now, when she should be spitting blood with rage at the chance he had thrown away – a chance to make himself, and her, rich beyond their dreams. But all she could feel was a knicker-soaking hunger to have him impale her once more on that great dong of his, like a piece of meat on a kebab!

Her wish was granted, eventually, when, after a long interval of heavily torturous preliminaries, she knelt on her own high double-mattressed four-poster bed and presented the succulent gleaming fissure of her sex for his delectation. Her head rested on her folded arms and the heavy orbs of her breasts lay against the rumpled satin of the coverlet. Her bottom, thrust in the air, afforded him a splendid view of the weals striped across the impressive rounds. He positioned himself a little more squarely between the upturned soles of her feet, lined up his ramrod penis, and eased its dome gently through the slippery labia. For an instant, he savoured the visual thrill of the brown shaft linking their bodies, the swell of those wonderful haunches, marked with the satisfying evidence of his punishment, the curve of his own belly, liberally covered with the black curls, leading to the thick cluster of his pubis. He put his hands on her hips, and, even as she thrust her backside eagerly into him, he plunged forwards until their flesh met, and he felt his thickness squeezed convulsively in the clench-ing muscles of her sheath. She shuddered, sighed, and his hands dug in, eased her off again a little, withdrawing fractionally, resisting that backwards thrust that begged for more. He withheld the climax as long as possible, drawing out the sweet torment until her wails grew loud and she was rutting feverishly, then he let himself go and battered into her, thudding into her softness, hearing the scream ring out, the mantra of obscenities spilling forth as the crisis went on and on. His own release came at the point when he felt her slump, every muscle in her driving frame sagging with exhausted satiation.

When they had both recovered, Titty reached up behind her and pressed a hidden button. The Maestro smiled at the apparition which entered a minute later carrying a tray with two tall glasses on it. It was a naked man whose scrawniness was made incongruous by the little potbelly. The white skin was hairless. A short thin greying thatch covered his skull, and over his upper lip hung a grizzled drooping moustache. In contrast with the pallid body below the neck, with its hugely visible Adam's apple, the face was florid. The beaky nose was rosy, the eyes had a washed-out appearance and were surrounded by wrinkled puffi-ness, the undersides heavily bagged and of a dark purple that was almost theatrical.

The most striking feature was the thin penis, stretched tightly onto his belly, like an arrow pointing upwards. It was held there by what seemed to be a thick silver ring passing right through the base of the helm, though in fact it did not pierce the tissue, but was held in place by a powerful spring, which was perhaps why he spoke only in the huskiest of short-breathed whispers. This ring was attached to a broad leather body belt, cinched tight and fastened by three narrow buckled straps in the small of the back. Beneath the prick, also stretched and uplifted, the testicles were hidden, clamped in a shining silver sphere of metal.

'Ah, Tommy!' The Maestro greeted him affably. 'How are you? I haven't seen much of you this weekend.'

Titty's husband carefully handed them their drinks. The contraption he wore helped to ensure his humble stooping mien. 'Very well, thank you, Maestro,' he wheezed.

The Maestro nodded at his loins. 'Been having fun, I see,' he laughed.

Tommy nodded towards the reclining figure beside the Maestro. 'And you, Maestro.'

'Take these with you, Tommy.' She flung small soiled towels at him, and he gathered them in.

'Yes, dear.' He turned, shuffling, and lapsed into his most cringing menial mode. 'Will there be anything else, milady?'

She giggled. 'Not that *you* can give me. Run along.'

'Yes, milady. Maestro.' He gave a slight bow, which made him grimace slightly.

When he had gone and they had both taken long pulls from their ice-cold drinks, Titty said reflectively, 'I know you were mad at me, Maestro, for interfering –' her hand moved expressively over the scars on her bottom '– but I still think you're making a mistake not taking Hamad's offer.'

He gave his deep laugh, reached out and tweaked her right nipple. He felt the artificial firmness at the summit of her breast. 'Ah! There speaks the soul of the eternal whore! You have no artistic blood in you at all! Those two aren't just a matter of dollars. They are beautiful, Titty. And talented. They mean far more than money to me. I don't think I'll ever be able to part with them. Not permanently.'

She set her perfect face in a deep pout, though she was not at all offended by his words. She snuggled up to him, lifted one leg and laid it over his. 'Don't you think *I'm* beautiful? I –'

'You're a great shag, Titty. One of the best.'

'Listen! You can talk all you want about the soul and artists and all that shit! Those music lovers down there are interested in only one thing. That cute little cunt of hers, and his tight little arse! And don't try to tell me different!'

'I'm not peddling flesh!' he answered sharply. 'I'm not some pimp trying –'

'And what do you think Shekh Hamad will do with them while they're over there? Have them playing to his guests over dinner? You think that's all he wants? You think he won't fuck the pair of them till their eyeballs rattle?' She shrugged. She reached over and began to massage his thick penis lightly with her fingers. It started to uncoil at once. It was still tacky to the touch. 'And another thing. Don't underestimate Koln. You know how powerful he is, don't you? Just as much as Sheikhy-Baby, and a lot nearer to home. He is one unhappy guy, believe me! You'd better watch him.' She bent over him, her fist working faster now. Then her hand slowed and the blonde hair fell softly over his thighs as her tongue flickered over his swelling tip, before her lips parted, and she sucked hungrily at his throbbing column.

He lay back, stroking her bowed head, and felt his prick rear up, rock hard in her warm wetness. 'I take it all back, Titty. You *are* an artist, after all. And a damned fine one!' He wriggled and eased himself flatter on the wide bed. 'And don't worry your pretty head, my sweet. I've got a plan that will keep Herr Koln happy, and make us even richer. Yes, you'll have your share, my dear, if you help me sell it to him.'

Max stared up apprehensively at the gowned figures of the doctor and his nurse, framed between her widely parted legs, which were supported in the stirrups. The nurse's gloved hands were touching Max's vulva, held open by the curving dilator. 'Just relax, my girl. All you'll feel is the merest prick.' Max felt herself blushing, and wondered if they were smiling beneath the surgical masks. I've never felt a prick in my life – not there, anyhow! she wanted to tell them angrily. She recalled the Maestro's explanation when he told her why she was being taken to the Harley Street clinic.

'I want you restored to pristine condition, my dear. You've made so much use of that dildo of yours, anyone might think you're on the game, instead of a virgin pure.'

When the surgeon had sewn the tiny flap of skin to restore the hymen, and she had been released from the trussed indignity of her position on the operating table, he said, with a bluntness at odds with the elegant surroundings of his consulting rooms, 'You'll be a bit sore when the anaesthetic wears off, and when you pee, for a while. Nothing you can't put up with. I'll give you a few painkillers, though, just in case. Oh, and, of course, don't play with yourself – or let anyone else play with you. Not until you're ready to be deflowered.' He grinned, and she glanced down, writhing with her embarrassment and anger.

The shame and the discomfort she had known made her bold enough to question the Maestro when they met once more in the secluded luxury of the Pleasure Dome. 'Why have you – had me – my

218

hymen – repaired?' she blurted, crimson-faced with shame and with her own temerity.

'Well, you *are* still a virgin, after all,' he said reasonably. 'Aren't you?'

Her blush deepened, as she nodded. 'But why have me marked as such? You know I am.'

'And I intend to keep you that way. So no more jolly japes with your latex companion – or with the busy fingers of your girlfriends, like Ginny, for instance. Or your sweet cousin,' he added, his voice heavy with significance, while she stared in wide-eyed outrage.

'I've never –' she squeaked, but he waved her protest aside.

'No more! You'll stay intact, until I decide otherwise,' he concluded, with even crueller emphasis, which set her mind racing in frantic speculation.

Since coming to this strange place, the routine had changed yet again. Supervision appeared to be much more relaxed. Max and Toni were left alone much more – Toni had even managed to visit her in her 'dormitory' during the night, though the intimacy of these trysts had been severely disrupted by the attendance of Ginny and then Meena. Though Max had been glad of the girls' company, she had been piqued at Toni's easy and even appreciative acceptance of their presence during these clandestine meetings. 'I've died and gone to heaven!' he murmured, beaming his delight at the three naked figures sitting up in their adjacent beds. But later his words carried a sombre note of warning as he glanced into the corners of the room. 'Don't let the unlocked doors fool you. They know what we're up to all right. They've probably got their eyes on us right now!' He was probably right. Max began to feel that hidden eyes, or lenses, were fixed on them the whole time.

They were even allowed to wear casual clothing, too, and those chill and gruelling early morning runs had terminated. 'We're being softened up for something!' Toni surmised and, though his voice was light with fatalistic acceptance, it made Max shiver inwardly with foreboding.

When they were left alone to practise in one of the long drawing rooms on the first floor of the mansion, Max told Antonio all that had happened at the hands of the doctor and nurse. 'I've been stitched up.' She gestured towards her loins. 'What does he intend to do with me, Toni?'

Her cousin stared at her. His slim shoulders shrugged. This time he did not voice his own speculation that her virginity, or, rather her defloration, was to be part of the profitable package the Maestro was negotiating with the sheikh. If he could have overheard the conversation taking place in another part of the grand house, he would have discovered that he was wrong.

Willard Koln's craggy features, and the gleam in his normally hooded eyes, betrayed his excitement. 'You are proposing I pay a million dollars, for one fuck?' His tone was a mixture of incredulity and scorn. 'You think I can't buy a dozen virgins, all over the world, if I should desire it?'

'This is not just any virgin. This is *my* virgin. I do not give her lightly.' Labat's voice was even in tone, as always. He could detect the responsive flicker in the American. Besides, he knew already, from Titty's skilful work on him, that Koln, despite his parade of indifference, was afire to take the unique opportunity to possess Max's body. 'I love her. And the boy.' The Maestro's voice was confidential, deep with sincerity. 'Like all of us, I have my weaknesses, my foibles. My desires. I cannot do it myself.' He raised his fingers quickly, as though Koln had spoken. 'Oh no, it is not impotence.' He laughed softly. 'Though, in this case, perhaps, it might actually come to that, if I tried. She is precious to me. That is why I could not part with her, not permanently. And why I do not want the gallant sheikh to be her first *lover*.' He gave the word a savagely satirical emphasis, accompanied by the merest shiver of distaste. 'No, I could not bear that. But you – you are different. I know that. And I want to be there.'

The Maestro knew he had him. His senses told him so, even though Koln laughed disparagingly and strove to project an air of condescension. 'All right,' he said at last. 'I'll save your maiden from the monstrous sheikh. I'll be part of an exhibition, if that's what you want. I'll even do it in public, and you can extort even more money out of the peeping Toms, if you like!' He paused, then looked across at the Maestro, the glitter of his stare reflecting his ruthlessness and power. 'But, if you're making a fool out of me – if I'm not the first man ever to impale her, then, by God, I'll ruin you! Understood?'

The Maestro bowed his head formally. 'Understood.'

Twenty-one

As soon as Max was led into the room, and saw the dangling ropes and the shining PVC restraints, she began to cry, and to plead brokenly for mercy. She was certain that she was to be whipped, and the humiliation of the ordeal was to be witnessed in public. When she was, therefore, strapped into the cradle, and left hanging there in mid-air, arms and legs spread wide, it was some time before her crying eased, and her locked muscles relaxed. It was not unduly uncomfortable to be suspended thus – the broad bands which held her took her weight without imposing any great strain on her – as long as she did not thresh about. And, apart from some initial, almost instinctive attempts to close her legs, in order to conceal her gaping sex, she remained still. She swayed gently when she twisted her head in an effort to look about her. She peered into the dim corners of the room, the long shapes of the black couches, and saw that she was alone, bathed in the brilliance of the spotlights overhead, which forced her to close her eyes against their brightness.

She could hear the muted voices and laughter, the faint background music, which told her that there were a number of guests enjoying the exclusive amenities of the Pleasure Dome. Was she to be one of the after-dinner diversions? she wondered fearfully. Tears stung her eyes once more, and she felt her throat closing with her grief. Why couldn't the Maestro keep her to himself? Why couldn't he be the one to enjoy her youthful beauty, keeping it solely for his own pleasure? She found herself wishing fervently yet again that he might be the one who would possess her body. Even in her fear, she could feel desire stirring, feel the muscles along her inner thighs hardening, the spasm of her vagina, so that the ropes moved gently, quivering like the strings of a harp. Perhaps, if she demonstrated her loyalty, her devotion to him, by enduring this public degradation and all the pain it might offer, he would take pity on her. She prayed that it would be so.

The soft click of a door opening sent the ropes shivering once more as her spreadeagled body started. She twisted her head round, heard a strange shuffling and scraping, then gaped up at the weird figure who approached her. A naked man, with a ring through his stretched penis attaching it to a wide belt around his middle, came close to her. From his meagre frame, she could detect that he was by no means young, though his face was hidden entirely by a black mask with scarlet hemmed holes for eyes, nose and mouth. It was like the kind of concealment robbers or executioners might wear, except that its blackness was dotted with numerous tiny beads of sparkling glass, giving it a grotesquely festive air.

'Don't be alarmed, my dear!' he gasped, in a thin breathless voice. 'I'm not going to hurt you.' He bent close, and she let out a cry of fear as he fumbled with her head. Her vision was cut to dramatic darkness. She recognised the feel of the elasticated velvet eye mask she had been made to wear on other occasions at the Maestro's house.

'No! Please!' She let out a tiny squeak of alarm as she suddenly felt sharp nails scratch at the tender softness of her breasts, and cold fingers exploring the small rounds, brushing the peaking nipples.

'Sorry!' Tommy croaked. He gave a smothered whimpered sigh as blood invaded his penis and it stirred agonisingly against its fetters. Doubled even lower, he glanced furtively about, and, with a shuffling run, made for the door as fast as he could.

She shivered with relief when she heard it close, but then found herself straining, her nerves tautened, for new noises. She hung there in blackness now, yet vividly aware of the spectacle she proffered, her body pinned out in the glare of those lights. The door clicked again, and again she whimpered with fear, straining to hear someone approach, and failing. She screamed at the suddenness of the hands on her inner thighs, then the fingers mercilessly peeling open her labia, invading her unready dryness, probing the tenderness of her newly sealed orifice. She gasped with pain, felt the resistance of that tender tissue against the prodding exploration. There was a sharp intake of breath, the hands withdrew, and she could make out the soft footfalls retreating, the door closing. She cried bitterly, alone and desolate, hanging there, trembling, waiting.

The next time she was disturbed, it was obvious that several people were coming in. The voices, hushed to whispers, terrified her even more. She waited in dread for the first cruel bite of the lash on her most tender flesh. When contact came, it was far from what she had expected. The hands holding her thighs were firm yet gentle, and the mouth and tongue that caressed her exposed genitals were wickedly soft and rousing. The beat of excitement flared unstoppably within her and her belly lifted instinctively in response. The tongue lapped along her fissure, the fingers were feathery as they peeled back the outer lips and exposed the inner surface for the tongue's further attentions. She was swaying now, her body lifting in rhythm to this flooding titillation, held steady only by the anonymous figure drawing such passion from her. She guessed it was a man, but she was uncertain. Could it be the Maestro himself? Surely, she would know ... wouldn't she? The thumbs were opening her, pressing on the spongy tissue, parting it – yes, a man, surely, that firmness, the calm dominance? Then she cried out, for, at last, she felt it, the sleek dome, the weeping slickness of fluid, the velvet yet potent kiss of a penis at the entrance to her sex. The helm eased in and she felt her labia desperately spasming to contain it, to grip it. Those hands were under her now, holding her buttocks, raising her, and the pounding pleasure transformed to a burning pain. She felt that fragile reconstructed barrier resisting, felt the implacable pressure, and she cried out sharply, a high yielding shout as the hymen gave, and the fierce strength of the conquering prick slid remorselessly in, filling her. The pain was one with the beating excitement, the need. She drew her tethered thighs about the strong body, she strove to lift her knees as high as the bonds would allow, to take him in completely, wanting more and more of him, wanting to obliterate herself in the potency of that living flesh.

The tall figure of Willard Koln stiffened, the cheeks of his buttocks deeply hollowed, his long hands splayed in the centre of her arching back, feeling the knobs of her spine, the supple ripple of her muscles through his palms and his fingers. The blindfolded head was thrown back below him, her mouth opened wildly at the howls torn from it at the force of the orgasm sweeping through her. He could see the shape of her breasts, stretched over her rib cage. The nipples were fiery points, darts of her desire, of the impulses coursing through her. The howls sank to deep convulsing sobs. They were punctuated by one swift yelp of agony as his limp but still swollen prick was plucked from its penetration into her.

She hung there, oblivious to the expulsion of pent-up breath around her, the envious longing gazes. It was a long while before she returned to awareness, and when she did she cried desolately for many things, not least her lost innocence. Or, rather, that it had not been lost to the one man she wished with all her heart had been the one to take it, for one thing she knew for certain: it had not been the Maestro who had fucked her. It didn't matter who *had* done it. All that mattered was who had *not*.

A long, long while later – so long that when she stirred she wondered if she had fallen asleep, or if indeed, she was still dreaming – she felt the soaking mask being removed from her, and stared up through the blur of her tears at the object of her despairing thoughts. Carefully, he unclipped the ropes from the rings in the corselet and unfastened it from her. Her skin was wet and slippery with gathered sweat where its tightness had held her. His hands supported her as she sagged, hanging by her arms and legs only. Next, he released her ankles, and again held her, helping her to stand before untying the bands around her forearms.

She was grateful there was no one else in the room. She could not stop weeping, her tears coming thicker at his gentleness, the warmth of his protectiveness. He carried her in his arms out into the hallway, past avidly staring eyes, up the wide staircase and along a corridor. In one of the luxurious bedrooms, he laid her on the bed, then went into the adjoining bathroom. She heard the sound of running taps. He returned, lifted her again, carried her through, and deposited her in the tub full of warm fragrantly foam-topped water.

Though she winced at its first contact, the warmth soon soothed her aching muscles and the stinging tenderness of her sex. As gentle as a mother with an infant, he bathed her. She moved, lifted limbs, stood with obediently parted thighs, while he washed even the most intimate parts of her. The tissue of the labia was puffed and sore, but the pain was not as intense as she had imagined it would be.

'There now!' he said, when she stood before him, newly dried and powdered. 'It's over. You know what it's like now. No more worries, no more conjectures.'

Her eyes filled with tears once more. 'I wish – it could have been you,' she whispered. 'All the time. Since I first came. I wanted it to be you.' Her breasts shook at the huge sob expelled from her.

He smiled and shook his head. 'You're still mine. This is how it had to be. It had to be someone else. It doesn't matter who. You still belong to me, don't you?' She nodded wordlessly. His smile widened. 'But, to prove to you that I am after all only human, and to pander to your sense of guilt – come.'

He led her back to the bedroom and gestured for her to lie down across the wide bed. 'No. On your front.' She did as he had bidden her. She kept her legs chastely together. She heard him moving about and did not turn her head to follow his movements. All at once, she knew what was to happen to her. 'Try and remain silent, if you can,' he murmured. He bent, and her bottom tensed as she felt him bestow a light kiss in the centre of each cheek.

He used a slender pliable cane, which cut in deeply and cleanly. The first stroke snatched her breath away. It was a flash of ice and fire, the pain flaring through her every nerve, taking the air from her lungs so that she could only gasp, a sharp intake at the lightning strike. She bit deep into the coverlet and smothered her face in the springy softness, to kill the whimper trapped inside her, at the throbbing of her buttocks, their paleness bisected by the thin rising crimson line. The blows rained down on her defenceless frame, which jerked spasmodically at each whistling crack. A deep muffled grunt came from her buried face, her hands were claws clutching at the dishevelled sheets.

When the ordeal ended, she gazed up at the figure of her persecutor. He tended her lovingly, bringing cold cloths to lay on her burning flesh, bathing the angry ridges marring her skin, though even the lightest touch made her hiss with fresh suffering. Finally, he wiped away the mess on her face. The least movement was agony, but somehow, with his help, she raised herself and staggered through to the bathroom. Though she whimpered at its touch, the bidet, filled with tepid water, eased the pain when she managed to lower herself to sit on it. He crouched in front of her and held her hands tightly. 'You know why?' he asked, and waited for her weary nod.

'To show that I belong to you, Maestro,' she croaked.

'And to show how much I care for you, my darling girl.' His mouth came close, then covered her lips and stayed there, and she leaned against him, exhausted, but overflowing with gratitude.

'Thank you, Maestro,' she whispered, when the long kiss ended.

For the next two days, Max did not leave her room. She had to lie on her stomach, on top of the covers, for the slightest contact on her bottom caused acute pain. She had plenty of time to dwell on the momentous events. What did this strange relationship with the Maestro mean? Why did he refuse to have sex with her, only to pursue an even stranger and stronger bond, to make her feel, despite her defloration, that she now belonged even more firmly to him? Once more the thought occurred to her that it could be because he knew that in fact he was her biological father. That her mother, besotted as she had been with him, even after her marriage to Richard, had kept the truth from Max, and from everyone else, including her husband. Anne and Richard had been brought together by the Maestro, had practically been put to bed together and led to the altar by him, because of their great combined musical talent. But right up to her death, Anne had been under the Maestro's spell. She would have rejoiced at bearing his child. And poor daddy – Richard – though a gifted musician, had not been endowed with the strongest of personalities. Max was tormented by her thoughts, and did not know even now whether she truly wanted to know the answers to her doubts.

She was surprised and delighted when Toni appeared and declared that the Maestro had instructed him to stay with her and tend to her. His own backside was bruised with recent beating, but he dismissed her concern. Nor would he tell her who had been responsible. 'Come on! It's not as though we aren't used to it. Though I must say our lord and master certainly gave *your* arse a good thrashing. You poor thing.'

It was her turn to be reticent now. She was startled to find that she did not wish to talk about the strange events of that day and her reaction to them, even with her cousin, from whom she had never withheld anything. She realised just how much both their lives were changing. Had already changed. She found it difficult to sort out in her own mind how she really felt about all that had happened to her. In its own strange way, the beating which the Maestro had inflicted on her had undoubtedly bound her to him even more strongly. It was different, totally, from all the previous punishments she had received, from him and from the others. It was something intimate – as intimate as if he had had sex with her! The shocking thought stirred her deeply. It was true. By that whipping, and, more significantly, by the way in which it had been administered, and by her own reaction to it, she had been bonded to him as closely as if he had been the one who had fucked her.

In fact, during her seclusion afterwards, she strove to dismiss the public loss of her virginity from her mind, trying faithfully to mirror the Maestro's attitude towards it. Not with complete success, however. Another question hovered, as uncomfortable as the throbbing ache of her bottom, during her enforced idleness. Who was it who had actually done the deed? Whose prick had been the first, and so far, the only one to enter her?

It was another mark of the change in their relationship that she did not ask Toni if he could supply the answer, even though they spent the entire night sharing the wide bed. And, if he knew the answer he was not telling. 'Here. The Maestro said this would help. Lie still. I'll be as gentle as I can.' He smeared her behind thickly with an antiseptic cream. The flesh was standing up in hard ridges where the severest cuts had fallen and, though his touch was light, she flinched at the contact. But it did soothe the soreness and, with the help of two of the tablets the Maestro had also sent, she soon fell into a deep dreamless sleep. She woke once in the night, whimpering softly, but the feel of Toni's warm body lying at her side, his arm across her shoulders, and his lips nuzzling at her neck and ear, sent her drifting contentedly into slumber again.

It was late, the sunlight was streaming into the room, when she awoke again, alone in the bed. She blushed when she saw Meena standing there accompanied by one of the maids, a pretty girl of similar complexion, but with more distinctly oriental features. The maid was carrying a large breakfast tray with food for two, which she placed on the bedside table before retreating, giving her a beaming smile and a little nod of the head.

'The Maestro asked me to look in on you. See how you're feeling. How your backside is.' At that moment Toni emerged from the bathroom, his hair still wet from the shower.

He smiled at the newcomer, entirely unselfconscious about his nudity. 'Hi, Meena. Which one of us are you after?'

'The one with the sorest arse. That's not you, I guess.' She gestured at Max. 'Let's have a look.' Max swivelled a little and rested on her elbows and her knees as she lifted her posterior for inspection. The vividly discoloured cheeks shone with the cream Toni had spread on them. 'Mm. He certainly gave you a good going-over, didn't he?' She sounded impressed as she surveyed the injured area. 'Let's get you in the bath and get this stuff off. I've got something that should help a lot more.'

Max showered, aware of Meena's keen gaze, and stood meekly, trying to keep still as Meena patted her bottom dry, then carefully rubbed in an astringent liquid. When she had finished, she washed her hands thoroughly at the basin before she left.

Much to their surprise, the cousins were left alone all day, their meals being brought to the room by the smiling non-speaking maid. In the evening, the Maestro visited them, accompanied by the glamorous Lady Titty. Max was closely attuned to her cousin, and she was aware at once of the tension within him. She realised it was not the Maestro who had caused it, but his beautiful companion. There was no doubt that, although he tried to hide it, there was something between them. It showed in Lady Titty, too – a certain subtle nuance in her tone, an extra degree of animation in her manner, the looks she cast over his slim frame.

The Maestro was his affable self, but, to Max, it appeared that towards her he exhibited that new intimacy and tenderness she had noticed only since the loss of her virginity to her anonymous partner.

Lady Titty beamed the full power of her glowing smile at her as she advanced and held her in a gentle embrace. 'Do you think I might borrow your divine cousin for an hour or two?' Her breathy voice was pleading, as if for all the world begging for a favour it was within Max's power to bestow.

Max glanced shyly towards the Maestro, who raised his thick eyebrows enquiringly. 'Er – uhm – yes. Of course!' She was conscious of the faintest pinking of Toni's complexion, the downwards cast of those long lashes, as bashful as any schoolgirl, before he followed obediently in her ladyship's wake.

Twenty-two

'I'm sorry, my darling boy, but I have to make sure you don't make a sound. You know how it is, don't you?' Lady Titty placed her full lips over Antonio's, whose mouth opened obediently to the flickering tongue which slipped immediately inside. She pressed her naked body against his and writhed sinuously, holding his loins tightly to hers, her painted finger nails digging like talons into his haunches. 'Oh Christ!' she gasped, when she broke the long kiss. 'That magnificent tight little arse of yours!' The fingers dug in expressively, and he could feel the head of his prick beating furiously, thrusting and buckling against the furrow of her sex. It was almost hard enough to penetrate her. She bit the lobe of his left ear with a force strong enough to make him yelp softly. 'See what I mean?'

At last she released him, only to approach him from behind this time. Those fingers now pushed a ball of sponge against his mouth. 'Open wide, darling!' He obeyed, and the sponge filled the interior completely, rendering him incapable of making any sound other than the faintest of muffled gasps. Thin leather straps led from either side of the sponge ball to be fastened by means of buckles at the back of his head. They secured the gag firmly in place.

She moved away and his gaze followed her, wide-eyed, his nostrils flaring as he drew in breath. She came close holding a short-handled whip, from the end of which dangled numerous bootlace-thin straps, only about two feet in length. Her lovely face was red, her eyes flashing with excitement. 'You'll love this, my darling!' she breathed, embracing him again, and letting that wicked tongue flicker across his nipples, and narrow smooth chest. 'Lie down across the bed, my love. On your front. Hide that rampant little member from me, you wicked boy! Show me your gorgeous derrière. That's it.'

She stepped back a little, and began to strike, quickly, and, at first, lightly, though the vigour of the strokes soon increased with her mounting frenzy. It was like myriad bee stings. Soon the pale skin was a glowing pink. At each stinging cut, his desire flared, and Titty groaned with bliss. The saliva ran thickly from the corners of his stretched mouth. Titty was panting, her own body shining with her perspiration. She dropped the whip and fell to her knees, hugging him by the thighs and turning him over onto his back, mashing his throbbing penis against her full breasts, between which it nestled. The helm was turned up, the fluid seeping thickly from its narrow mouth to mix with her perfumed sweat. She bent her face worshipfully, stabbed her features against his glistening dome, the slippery emission larding her cheeks. Her mouth opened and she moaned, seeking out his jutting thickness, suckling its beating length avidly.

Antonio's shrill scream was lost in the soaking gag. He felt the scrape of her teeth, felt his entire self drawn into her furiously sucking warm wetness, and he ejaculated fiercely. She spluttered and choked, was forced to pull her mouth away briefly, but then immediately plastered herself once more to the still-pumping cock. The residue flowed over her upturned face as his column went limp. His slim body lay there, shivering. The air whistled through his nostrils as he sobbed into the sealing gag.

She went into the bathroom and spent many minutes cleansing herself before she returned and finally released him from the soaking gag. He was moaning quietly, only now fully aware of the throbbing pain from his body which was still lividly marked from the beating. However, he was to be given no further time to recover. Seizing him roughly by his hair, she fell back onto the bed, spreading her thighs wide and pulling his face down unmistakably to the base of her belly.

He knew what to do and, the discomfort of his stinging flesh forgotten, he did it, drawing out her excitement, stretching it to that fine distinction between utmost pleasure and dire torment, until, with every sinew and nerve afire, her knees lifting, pink heels grazing the bed sheets in rhythmic need, she clutched at the head burrowing between her thighs and sobbed and begged for release. It came, and her pale frame lifted, bore him up with it, and she howled in the elemental fury of orgasm, the silence she had insisted on when she beat him shattered by the high-pitched scream which rang, echoing, through the corridor outside.

'Oh, I can't bear to let you go, you gorgeous creature!' Titty moaned a while later, stroking the head which nestled still, but less frenetically, between her thighs, while she sipped the drink which her exotically accoutred husband had brought in answer to her summons. 'I want you all for myself, for always!'

She said as much, hours later again, and exquisitely dressed in an elegant black evening gown, to Sheikh Hamad over an after-dinner brandy and before the night's entertainment got under way. Beneath the gown, she was wearing a transparent bra of dark net, and equally diaphanous knickers of the most minute proportions, which, she decided philosophically, Sheikhy-Baby might well have the pleasure of seeing, and, in all probability, removing. Especially when, in reply to her besotted drooling about her desire for the boy, the sheikh leaned forward, placed his plump hand on her knee, and rasped conspiratorially, 'And it might just be possible, Lady Titty, that I can make your dream come true, if you can help me with my plan. You know how much I want those two – the boy and the girl. But the boy I can keep for you – for your exclusive use whenever you desire, if you are my ally.'

He saw her pink tongue flick out and lick her already glossy lips. His prick swelled mightily in his clothing as he recalled how skilfully she had used that tongue on him a few evenings ago. She covered the hand on her upper thigh with her own, pressed it more firmly against her flesh. 'I'm all ears, Sheikh,' she breathed.

Finally Max overcame her reluctance to confess to Toni the confused and fearful speculations she had been entertaining for so long now. After all, he was the one person she *could* bare her soul to. She had never felt close to anyone else in her young life, and he was still her partner in this bizarre world they were caught up in. 'He's never touched me,' she confided, blushing fiercely even with her intimate. She remembered all too vividly those earliest lessons back at the Maestro's house, his exploring hands, and her embarrassment increased. 'Well – not really – properly. I mean not the whole hog!' She saw the curl of Toni's lip, the beginnings of his savage amusement, and she cried out, her dark eyes glistening with her tears. 'Oh no! Please! Don't make fun. Just listen.' She told him of her wild conjectures, though by the end of her tale she could not bear to meet his gaze.

'You think the Maestro could be your real father?' he murmured pensively. But he made no mocking disclaimer, there was no cruel hoot of disbelieving laughter. Instead his look reflected her sombre mood. For a while he said nothing, and Max quickly realised that he was finding difficulty in replying. He seemed unwilling to comment, but at last he started and spoke with painful hesitation. 'There's something more. I've been thinking, too. It's not the first time, but now, well, it's in my mind more and more. Has it ever occurred to you – I mean – we look pretty much alike, don't we? For someone who's only vaguely related, on your father's – Richard's – side?'

Her eyes widened, she glanced up at him, looking thoroughly frightened now. Her fist was clenched on the bed covers and he reached out his hand to lay it over hers, his fingers stroking the prominent bumps of her knuckles. He cleared his throat. 'I know nothing at all about my parents. Aunt Charlotte's my only living relative – and even she claims she's not really a blood relation. She's always told me my mum was some second cousin of Richard's – a schoolgirl who got into trouble. Nobody bothered about who my father was – my mum had me and gave me away at birth. Didn't even see me at all. That's what I've always been told. And believed. I wasn't really bothered. I just knew I wasn't wanted, whoever my parents were.

'Then Aunt Charlotte came along and took me in, and there was you, just lost your parents, and suddenly I belonged somewhere. And we had each other. That's all that mattered. Yeah?'

Max gave a sudden small cry of pain and love, and flung herself at him, and he held her close, her face pressed against his beating chest and his mouth against the fragrance of her hair. They clung silently for a minute before he eased her back with gentle firmness, so that she was forced to look into his eyes once more. Their faces were still close, the warmth of their breath mingled. His voice when he continued was even softer, almost a whisper. 'I thought we'd be together always. Made for each other. But . . . we've never had sex, have we? We've done things, played with each other. Naughties! But not Big Naughties, eh? Why not? We could have done it, loads of times. Even under Davies' evil eye!' He gave a short grunt of laughter that held no humour in it. 'Why didn't we? Eh?'

He waited for her to answer, and saw the redness creeping back into her face as she gave a little hopeless shake of the head. 'Was it because somehow, without knowing why, we didn't feel it was right to go the whole way?' he pursued. She stared at him with a strange pleading expression, almost as though she wanted him to stop. 'Look at us. So much alike it's sometimes like looking in a mirror. Except you're a girl! But even that – I feel so close to you, I used to feel I knew what you were thinking. Why? Why so close?' Another, last pause as he drew a deep shuddering breath. 'Maybe it wasn't some unknown schoolmate who got my mum pregnant! Maybe it was someone older. Maybe it was *your* dad!'

She reared up away from him, her eyes saucer-wide, her mouth agape. Her mind spun crazily. What did he mean? *Who* did he mean? Daddy? Richard? Or the Maestro? 'Oh God! Toni! What can we do?' She reached for him again and clung even tighter to him as the tears began to flow once more, and huge sobs tore through her.

'Aunt Charlotte. There's something I have to ask you.' Max's voice quavered, betraying her nervousness. Her mouth felt dry, and she choked back the

238

tears as she spoke. 'Please don't be mad with me. But I have to know. What is the truth about Toni – and me? And our parents?'

Max saw the start her aunt gave, the strange, fleeting look – of fear? Guilt? – which swept across the severe features, heard the tremor which the older woman could not disguise. 'What – what on earth do you mean? Explain yourself, you –'

'I have to know. Was Richard Audley truly my father? My *real* father?'

'What on earth are you talking about, girl? Who's been putting stupid ideas into your head? Tell me!'

Charlotte's eyes looked wild, her reaction frightening, and Max almost lost the courage to go on. 'It's just – lately – since all that's happened these last months . . . I've been wondering. Could the Maestro have got mummy pregnant? I know, you've told me before . . . even after they were married, daddy and mummy, that she . . . and the Maestro. She still used to see him, spend time with him –'

'Be quiet!' Charlotte hissed, her face livid now. She advanced on Max, who cowered away from her, expecting a blow. 'You wicked evil little slut! You think everyone's as loose as you are?'

Max began to cry. The injustice of her aunt's attack, after all Max had been subjected to, filled her with a welling sense of hurt and injustice. The harsh vituperative tones continued to assault her. 'You think he would have kept quiet if he had sired you? Of course Richard was your father! That hopelessly weak pathetic creature! You're just like him. Go on! Get out of my sight! If your backside wasn't already all the colours of the rainbow I'd thrash you till you squealed like the stupid little piggy you are!'

Max fled, and was glad to find her way back to the dormitory room where she slept. She could not rid

239

herself of the vision of Charlotte's face when Max had first voiced her doubts. There was something her aunt had not told her, some secret to do with Max's birth that was still hidden. In spite of Charlotte's firm denial of her suspicions, Max remained convinced that there was something seriously amiss about her parentage, and, as she told Toni when he came to seek her, she was determined somehow to find what the secret was.

'What on earth is all the mystery about, Tommy? Why all the secrecy, hush-hush phone calls?' The Maestro stared curiously at the slim figure on whom the expensive clothing did little to enhance his appearance. Above the pristine white collar and the old school tie, the features were as debauched and lugubrious as ever. 'That will be all, thank you, Holger.' Holger turned at the dismissal and strode out, not bothering to disguise the sneering contempt on his face for the titled individual he had just shown in to the Maestro's study.

Professor Labat noticed the stooped mien and the slight wince as Lady Titty's husband lowered himself into the proffered chair. The Maestro gave a deep chuckle. 'You're not still wearing your nut crackers, are you?'

Tommy did not seem in the least offended. He shook his head with a sheepish grin in return. The Maestro noted the washed-out wateriness of the pale-blue eyes, and the weakness that lay behind them, as Tommy glanced up at him. 'Titty thinks I'm up in town on business. Please don't let her know otherwise, or I'm a dead 'un!' He cleared his throat noisily and glanced about him again, as though he feared they were being observed or overheard. 'Fact is, Maestro, something dashed awkward has come up.

Something I feel I must warn you of – as long as you swear not to let on that it was me who tipped you off. You have to promise. It's something you ought to know about.'

'Of course you can rely on my discretion,' Labat answered with quick impatience. 'Now spit it out. What's your guilty secret?'

'Not mine, old boy. It's Titty's – and that dreadful sheikh fellow. I overheard them. Wasn't meant to, but then –' His eyes flickered away from the Maestro's keen stare for a second then back again. Behind the shame was a kind of vulnerable appeal, which acknowledged all the weakness of his decadent masochism '– they don't notice me, when . . . things go on at the Pleasure Dome. You know what I mean?' Again the Maestro nodded, and gave a low growl of testiness at Tommy's hesitancy. 'Well, I was . . . in attendance, on Titty and the sheikh, and they kind of forgot about me being there, I suppose. Anyway, I overheard them talking, plotting. Talking about your boy and girl. He's planning to keep them there – when they go out to Qumshah for this concert gig. Titty's planning to help him with his nefarious scheme.'

His thin voice quavered and his rheumy eyes displayed his naked misery. 'I'm afraid she's going to leave me, Maestro! Stay out there herself. He's promised her constant access – she's besotted about the boy, especially. Sheikh Hamad says she'll be their keeper, be in charge of them.' The voice broke, and Labat strove to hide his quickening disgust for this abject spectacle. 'I couldn't bear to lose her, Maestro! I don't know what I'd do. I'd be lost – without her. She takes care of everything.'

You miserable wormy specimen! The Maestro felt the contempt and rage swell within him until his

fingers curled, could almost feel the handle of the
whip he would love to wield on this pitiful excuse for
a man – except that the wretch would doubtless love
it as he howled for mercy! The Maestro mastered his
anger admirably, and his voice was quietly confident
and controlled as he answered. 'Don't worry,
Tommy, my dear. I'll make sure their devious little
scheme comes to nothing. Your Titty won't be going
anywhere. I think maybe it's time the little minx
learnt a rather harsh lesson on the kind of reward
infidelity reaps, don't you?'

Lady Titty screamed wildly at the agony of yet
another cutting blow from the cane. She was hanging
upside down, her ankles and calves tightly fastened in
the leather restraints to which were fixed the ropes
that held her vertical and kept her legs open in a deep
Y, even though the long thigh muscles ridged and
bunched in her frenzied efforts to draw her limbs
together. Her arms were bent, her wrists shackled
together in the centre of her back. The crown of her
head ground against the hard wooden floor, her
nipples, blood-dark, throbbed at the cruel bite of the
powerful spring clips attached to them, the stripes
across her buttocks stood in livid rows.

Charlotte, watching from the sidelines along with
Davies, Holger, Polly and several others on the
wooden bench, became aware of the damply
mounting excitement, which was doubtless shared by
most of the other spectators. She was ashamed of the
instinctive disappointment she felt as the dim realisation dawned that the flogging was, for the time being
at least, over.

Through the sweat and tears stinging her eyes,
Titty could dimly see the polished shoes and knife-
edge-creased trousers of the Maestro as he stood over

her, the cane hanging limply in his hand. She wanted to protest her innocence, as she had done throughout the hours of this ordeal. But the gag sealed her words as effectively as it had sealed her cries of pain and despair. She had no idea who had framed her, or why. All she knew was that the evidence stacked against her, implicating her in the proposed kidnap of the young couple, had been a pack of carefully planted and contrived lies. She would never have gone along with Hamad's nefarious scheme. She would have told the Maestro of his evil intentions before any of them could be carried out – and when she was certain there was nothing more she could gain herself out of her pretence of going along with his plans. She had protested with such conviction she had almost convinced herself of her commendable innocence in all this manoeuvring.

Now, swimming in and out of full awareness through the waves of undefined pain, she found she scarcely cared any more what happened to her. She would welcome anything, total degradation and submission, provided it came from the hands of the man who was standing over her. And that was what she wanted, she suddenly realised, had always wanted, in the very depths of her being: to belong to someone as powerful, as totally dominant as this dynamic figure, just as Charlotte Behr and the beautiful duo and Polly were his. She even wished, as much as she doted on Toni and Max, that they had indeed been snatched away, if, instead, *she* could be his devoted slave, his to do whatever he wanted, to serve, or to be disposed of, as he chose.

Titty recovered slowly. The soaking gag had been removed, though the cruel red marks were still livid at the corners of her mouth. She shivered violently and gave a sharp cry as she felt the ice pack applied to her abused flesh. It would be several days before she could enjoy even the gentlest of sexual pleasures after a whipping like that. But what did that matter? She had been saved perhaps from making the biggest mistake of her life. As they untied her, and she moaned softly under the gentle ministrations of the foreign girl, Meena, and the one they called Poll Mouse, she heard the deep rumble of the Maestro's voice and thrilled, despite her agony, as it seemed to penetrate right through her.

'There are going to be a lot of changes now, my dear. You will no longer be mistress here. Understand? You belong to me. You understand?'

'Yes, Maestro,' she whispered, in that breathy tone of submission which suddenly felt so natural to her.

There was a collective gasp of delight at the entrancing spectacle revealed in the brilliance of the white lights when the velvet curtains fell away. The golden cage, surrounded by the blackness, seemed to hang in the air. Inside it, the two golden statues gleamed, then came magically to life as they began to play. The boy sat at the piano, the girl stood at his side. The grand was gold, the stool he sat on was gold, the violin and bow in the girl's hands were gold – as were the heavenly naked forms, from top to toe.

The majority of the select guests were genuinely able to appreciate the music which Max and Antonio made. Max was concentrating hard. It still felt strange that she should have to do so, for normally she was lost, it took her over, the gift of her genius seemed to flow through her, so that in some ways she felt trancelike, coming to awareness of her surroundings only when the final applause rang out. But now she could feel the stiff heaviness of the paint, weighing even on her eyelids. She stared hard at the notes while the pure beauty of the Mozart melody flowed through her. Outside the cage was only blackness, as though the world ended at the edge of this golden floor, and the harsh white light. But she visualised all the unseen eyes fixed on her golden nakedness, caressing every centimetre of her exposed flesh under its brilliant coating. How they must long to touch her! She prayed none of them ever would. But then both she and Toni belonged to the Maestro – their master. And, could it be – the word trembled on the edge of her consciousness all the time now – their father? She had not accepted Aunt Charlotte's scathing dismissal of her speculation. There was something not right about her aunt's vehemence, her fierce denial.

But the struggle was far from clear in Max's mind. Perhaps she should accept things as they were. Their life now was far less severe than it had been. The Maestro was convinced that he had succeeded in bending them entirely to his will. And perhaps, she reflected, he had. Certainly they put up no visible resistance, neither she nor Toni. This was their world, this golden cage. It ended at the bars, where the light cut into darkness. They must not look beyond it. Only then could they be happy. And inside, they had each other, always, day and night.

Twenty-three

Max was sitting in front of the long mirror in the dormitory bedroom. She sprang to her feet when Toni entered and ran to greet him. She flung her arms round his neck and kissed him unrestrainedly. She was wearing only a bra and thong. Toni gazed appreciatively at her reflection in the mirror. 'My God! You can tell times have changed! Look at your bum. Not a mark on it!'

Max grinned in return. 'And I notice you're sitting much more comfortably since Lady Titty's been taken out of circulation.'

Toni felt his buttock cheeks wince in instinctive sympathy. 'Yeah. The poor old girl won't be sitting herself for quite a while, after the drumming she got!' He had lowered his voice automatically, started when he heard the toilet flush and a few seconds later a naked Polly appeared in the bathroom's doorless opening. Both their countenances reddened at the sight of each other. Toni could not help the guilt he felt every time he saw her. He was responsible for her being here, for dragging her into this whole complex existence, to which he suspected they were all condemned for a long way into the future. And for her more than most it must be traumatic, he reasoned, given the humdrum nature of her former life. His conscience had pricked him ever since their capture, and he had avoided her as much as possible. It had not been difficult to do so up to now, but, once again, the character of their living had been transformed.

The Pleasure Dome appeared to be their permanent home nowadays, while the severity of their regime had been lessened almost beyond recognition. They had a much greater degree of personal freedom – within defined limits, of course. He and Max spent most of their time together, often unsupervised. They were allowed to wear clothes, to wander about their spacious living area at will, even to spend time together in their respective bedrooms, though the communal nature of Max's sleeping quarters, where at least one of the other three beds was frequently occupied by Poll, or Meena, or Ginny, that strange little photographer girl, rather limited whatever they might wish to get up to.

It would therefore be harder from now on to avoid these confrontations with poor Polly, or the recognition of her subservient state. For example, she was the only one of the three who was naked, and not, he guessed, from choice. Yet she seemed to pay little heed to it, other than the briefest flutter of a movement to hide her most sensitive areas – a ghost of the old Poll Mouse, which already was fading from her persona. 'Hi!' he beamed, his enthusiasm partly a result of his tender conscience. 'How you doing, Poll?' She nodded in reply and returned his smile with every appearance of genuine pleasure at seeing him. She turned to Max, who was stepping into a thick pleated skirt of a heathery check, before drawing a short-sleeved jumper of the palest blue over her head. Poll's hands moved to assist her, then to tidy Max's simple hairstyle into place again. Was that her new role? Toni wondered. To act as maid to his cousin, or maybe to act as general serving wench for the exotic household, except when she was required to carry out more specialised duties for the Maestro or his privileged intimates and clients?

One thing: his and Max's role was now clearly defined. They were performers, too, you might say the star attraction, of this weird place. The golden cage was their stage, their gold-painted bodies rather than their musical talents the centre of the wealthy clientele's attention. And a devil of a job it was to get that glittering spray paint off! It got into the most awkward places! And required a deal of painstaking assistance to remove it, he recalled, his excitement stirring at the memory.

But there would not be *too* many of those specialised exhibitions. Not at the prices the Maestro and his team demanded, Toni calculated. Which meant, apart from the regular hours of practice still demanded of them, considerable leisure time for both of them. Everything was relative, after all. Better to be living in the luxurious surroundings of the Pleasure Dome, with its considerable acreage of grounds and parkland, than trapped behind the walls of Sheikh Hamad's desert kingdom, where life would have been far less pleasant, Toni acknowledged.

He was still unaware of the details of that episode, though he had heard from Tommy, 'the Bart. in the iron ball', as Toni had privately christened him, that the Maestro had forfeited at least a million quid over the sudden dramatic cancellation of the proposed trip to Qumshah. It was to have been ostensibly a trip of several weeks only, with only one 'concert', but there were rumours of much more sinister plans on the sheikh's part, hence the Maestro's drastic action. Another result, it had been hinted, was the public humiliation of Lady Titty's flogging, and subsequent incarceration somewhere in the mansion. Toni was wise enough not to be seen to be actively seeking information, but it was clear eventful stirrings had taken place. Although the young duo had much greater liberty of movement and association, it was still evident who pulled their strings, extended though they might be nowadays. And the security about the mansion and its surrounds was tighter than ever. Clearly, the threat of possible reprisal from the powerful mid-eastern figure was not taken lightly.

The young couple made their way down the wide staircase to the ground floor, where one of the large reception rooms had been converted to a mini concert hall. There was no sign of the exotic apparatus or effects that had been used for their unique performance, but it was an ideal venue for their practice sessions. The Maestro was waiting for them and they were straight into it, for over two hours of solid concentration. At the end of it both the youngsters were tired and looking forward to their escape out into the open air, despite the cold grey day. Max felt a stir of apprehension when the Maestro said, with his usual urbane smile, 'Just wait behind, will you, Max? There's something I need you for. You run along,' he added to Toni, who departed immediately. 'Come with me, my dear.'

In the book-lined study close by, which the Maestro had commandeered as his private office, he ushered her to a comfortable chair before taking his seat in the imposing leather chair behind the desk. He pressed a buzzer and within seconds Polly appeared. She was wearing a plain black dress. It hugged her slight figure, then flared from the narrow waist to a wide skirt of conservative mid-calf length: a garment of well-cut dimensions, giving her an air of tasteful modesty. Except, as Max was very much aware, beneath that respectable skirt Polly's unadorned flesh was available for anyone who cared to make demands of it. 'Show Nurse Fallon in now, Polly.'

Max's heart quickened, then her face flamed as she recognised the features of the woman who had assisted at the operation to reconstruct her hymen.

The Maestro's deep chuckle merely added to her embarrassment. 'Don't be alarmed, my dear. We're not about to subject you to a second bestowal of your virginity. Which would this time be an unadulterated lie, eh?' His reference to the momentous event of defloration pained her even further. 'All we require of you this time is for you to offer up your pretty little mouth while the nurse takes a sample of your saliva. And, just to be doubly sure, a tiny sample of your blood. All that entails is a little prick – on your thumb, let me hasten to add!' Nurse Fallon giggled obligingly, and Max was mortified. She was also puzzled.

'I've heard,' he continued easily, 'that you've been harbouring some very strange ideas about your paternity. This will remove any wild ideas you have been entertaining. I will supply a sample also, and the results will quickly prove something – not who your father *is*, but who he *isn't*!' he concluded with heavy emphasis, while Max stared in mute shock.

The nurse dealt with the taking of samples from both of them, and left hurriedly. 'The doctor will confirm the results and bring us the details very soon.'

Max sat there, feeling her face and body glow with shame, her toes curl inside her shoes. 'I'm sorry,' she muttered miserably. She was shaking, wondering how severe his wrath would be, and, more importantly, how he would manifest it. But, to her surprise, he remained in calm good humour.

'I'm flattered you should even in your remotest thoughts honour me with being your father. You have a great talent, Max. But it comes not from me – from God, perhaps, but also definitely from your lovely mother – and her dear Richard. Yes, she was very dear to me, but so was he. I was delighted when she told me she was pregnant. Delighted for both of them. Richard was in ecstasy. You must not forget we were very close, all three of us. As close as you and Antonio. I loved Anne, but I was young myself. I had plans. They were part of it. I didn't want to father her child – and believe me, I took care not to. If I had been your father, my dear, I would have acknowledged it. But you don't have to take my word for it. You'll see the results of the DNA test, I promise. And they'll prove conclusively we share no blood, my dear, joined as we are in spirit.'

She stood as he gestured towards the door in dismissal. She could feel her legs trembling, her heart still hammering. She was stunned at the uncertainty of her feelings following his announcement. As she was about to leave, he spoke again, in the same even tone. 'I understand young Antonio has been speculating, too, on the even greater mysteries surrounding *his* birth. I admit I have been lax about it all these years. But I'm going to look into it. Rest assured, all will be presently revealed. I confess the whole business of inherited genes has begun to intrigue me. The way you two lovely creatures resemble each other so closely. The Heavenly Twins, eh?' He gave a rich laugh. 'What if our dear little Dickie had hidden depths after all?' His dark eyes sparkled with cruel glee at his final barb. 'What if you and Toni should prove to be somewhat closer than distant cousins after all?'

'Hello, Polly. How goes it?' She jumped at Toni's sudden entrance and her face flooded with colour.

She turned from his bed, where she had been straightening the covers, and gestured awkwardly around her. 'I've just about finished. I've put your clean laundry in your drawers. I – I didn't think you'd be back yet.' She glanced at the clock. She was clearly embarrassed by his presence. 'It's early.'

'Yeah. Maestro kicked me out. I'm superfluous to requirements, as they say. He's going over the Mendelssohn, the dreaded *Wings of a Dove* thing! Poor Max is copping it. You remember?'

'Oh yes.' She nodded enthusiastically, and their eyes met. Toni's memory and guilt sparked once more.

'Poll! My love!' The words seemed to burst from him all at once. 'I never meant – to drag you into all this. Please! Forgive me.'

'No! Shush! Don't say a word! I – I . . .' her voice died for a few painful seconds, then she resumed, staring down at the floor. 'I don't mind, really. Not – I mean, at first it was all a hell of a shock. Terrible. I was scared out of my wits. That terrible Davies, and Holger!' Her face was flaming once again. A shudder passed visibly through her. 'But lately . . .' she sounded as though she was exploring her own state of mind. 'Things seem a little different. My life – I was missing so much before – before you came along!' She was struggling now, and looked up at him in almost helpless appeal.

Swiftly he closed the door and moved towards her. Her eyes widened. 'Toni! Someone might come in!'

'The Maestro and Max will be stuck down there for another hour at least. Davies and the German both went out in the car. Aunt Charlotte's been in London since yesterday. There's no one who matters.' He caught hold of her hand, tugged her towards the bed. 'Come on! It's been ages. I've really missed you, you know. You were my first, Poll, I swear it! Don't

252

tell me you've gone off me with all the competition that's around here. You haven't forgotten, have you? There's things I can still do for you!'

He pushed her down on the single bed, and at the same time swept the wide skirts of her dress up over her bent knees. The slender high heels of her black shoes caught in the folds of the counterpane, impeding her movement. Toni's hands pushed the dress up off her pale thighs. 'It's great to see a full head of hair again!' he grinned, nodding towards the patch of curls adorning the base of her belly, and was rewarded by her small yelp of outrage. 'It's bloody uncomfortable being bald down there! Specially when it starts to grow again! Scratch my snatch, as Max says!'

'Please!' But her protest, if that was what it was, was made in the faintest of indeterminate whispers. Her hands fell from his, her knees splayed open as she spread her legs to the glorious invasion of Toni's warm breath, and face, his searching lips and skilful feathering fingers over her clamorous flesh and she lifted her belly for his further exquisite assault.

Charlotte hung there, in the dimness. The slightest movement sent her body swaying, her sprawled limbs spread in a star, encased in the shiny restraints from which the thin ropes stretched upward towards the ceiling. The one spotlight trained brilliantly on her sacrificial frame made it impossible for her to see where the bonds ended far above. The broad belt about her middle was so tightly drawn it supported her in efficient comfort, and the shapes of the other fastenings moulded to her stretched arms and calves with such firmness that, suspended as she was several feet above the floor, she felt as though she were being cradled in the gentlest of firm embraces. Whatever else one might say, that German bastard knew his business as far as this effective method of bondage went, assisted by her own erstwhile handmaiden, Davies – transformed now, like Charlotte herself, and anyone else who came under the influence of the powerful magic the Maestro exerted. Davies, *her* Davies – Bron! She had actually seen her wearing an outfit worthy of the most girlie little tart – sheer stockings, stiletto heels, ribboned suspenders, lacy strappy sex symbols. And bowing in complete subjection to that great Germanic prick – in every sense, Holger the barbarian!

But then that stupid insipid mousy little Polly Mouse had been with them, too – another who had surrendered herself to this exclusive little world, and who would never escape, would not even take the chance were it to be offered. Which it never would.

Last of all, though, and greatest subjection of all, was her own. Charlotte Behr, once again the creature of this magician, just as she had been all those twenty long years ago, from whose spell she had never truly escaped. Witness the sprawled sacrifice of her body now, waiting for what would doubtless be terrible retribution – a retribution she would acknowledge, even as she howled and blubbered and begged for mercy under his hand. Indeed, she had brought it on herself with the confession which had put into place the final piece of the puzzle, and sent him off to find its final solution.

She lost track of time before she heard the door open and close quietly, and she knew at once he was present. No one else. She had expected an audience, perhaps even those she did not know, and now her eyes flooded with gratitude. She heard his footsteps, then he was standing over her, staring down at her. His gaze was calm but intense. He said nothing, and she knew that he knew. She tried to speak, had to clear her throat, strive to moisten her dry mouth before she could whisper. 'I'm sorry, Maestro.' The tears flowed from her eyes down into the hair at her temples. 'Please! Will you gag me, Maestro? I don't want to scream – don't want you to hear me begging.'

He shook his head. 'Oh no, my love. I *want* to hear you. All those years. Not a word. Who knows what I might have done, or had done, to the boy? Oh yes, you'll scream, Charlotte. And beg, too.'

If that was what he wanted . . . she thought of that day, so long ago, when she first discovered she was pregnant, how her plan evolved, through the jealousy that had eaten away at her for so long, at the way he had so clearly preferred her more talented sister – the gifted Anne! How he had even placed her in the bed of that milksop, Richard Audley, so that he could fulfil his weird plans for her. So Charlotte had taken her revenge – disappeared, suddenly and completely, resurfacing only when the child had been safely born, and, at the orphanage, banished from her life.

She had seen him only rarely, until after Anne and Richard's accident, when she had brought him to her home, to be the companion of the distraught twelve-year-old Max.

She stiffened and the ropes swung as she felt the Maestro's large hands, firm but gentle, turning her, readying her for the punishment, which, when it came, was a timeless burning ordeal. She was lost in it, consumed by it, threshing and twisting, spinning and howling blindly, the room and her head were filled with it, and she knew nothing else until she was once more alone, hanging there, swinging gently, and weeping with relief and gratitude that at last her greatest secret was no more.

* * *

The sweat was cooling on the Maestro's body as he made his way quietly up the great staircase in the night silence of the house. He glanced in at the dormitory bedroom and smiled when he saw that Max's bed was empty. He moved along the corridor, carefully opened the door of the bedroom, and heard the breathing of deep sleep. His sensitive nostrils detected at once the faint perfume, and the equally stirring scent of clean young flesh, of sex. There were the two dark heads on the pillow, close together. He could see, in spite of the covers hiding them, that the two bodies were intertwined, the limbs lovingly entangled. Max's head was tucked beneath Toni's chin, her slightly open mouth resting against Toni's smooth skin. Her face was red, her brow dewed with sweat.

The Maestro smiled. He bent and very softly, so as not to wake the pair, planted a kiss on the young man's forehead. 'Good night, son,' he whispered.

nexus

The leading publisher of fetish and adult fiction

TELL US WHAT YOU THINK!

Readers' ideas and opinions matter to us so please take a few
minutes to fill in the questionnaire below

1. Sex: Are you male ☐   female ☐   a couple ☐?

2. Age: Under 21 ☐   21–30 ☐   31–40 ☐   41–50 ☐   51–60 ☐   over 60 ☐

3. Where do you buy your Nexus books from?
☐ A chain book shop. If so, which one(s)?

_____

☐ An independent book shop. If so, which one(s)?

_____

☐ A used book shop/charity shop
☐ Online book store. If so, which one(s)?

_____

4. How did you find out about Nexus books?
☐ Browsing in a book shop
☐ A review in a magazine
☐ Online
☐ Recommendation
☐ Other _____

5. In terms of settings, which do you prefer? (Tick as many as you like.)
☐ Down to earth and as realistic as possible
☐ Historical settings. If so, which period do you prefer?

_____

☐ Fantasy settings – barbarian worlds
☐ Completely escapist/surreal fantasy

- ☐ Institutional or secret academy
- ☐ Futuristic/sci fi
- ☐ Escapist but still believable
- ☐ Any settings you dislike?

_____

- ☐ Where would you like to see an adult novel set?

_____

6. In terms of storylines, would you prefer:
- ☐ Simple stories that concentrate on adult interests?
- ☐ More plot and character-driven stories with less explicit adult activity?
- ☐ We value your ideas, so give us your opinion of this book:

_____

_____

_____

7. In terms of your adult interests, what do you like to read about? (Tick as many as you like.)
- ☐ Traditional corporal punishment (CP)
- ☐ Modern corporal punishment
- ☐ Spanking
- ☐ Restraint/bondage
- ☐ Rope bondage
- ☐ Latex/rubber
- ☐ Leather
- ☐ Female domination and male submission
- ☐ Female domination and female submission
- ☐ Male domination and female submission
- ☐ Willing captivity
- ☐ Uniforms
- ☐ Lingerie/underwear/hosiery/footwear (boots and high heels)
- ☐ Sex rituals
- ☐ Vanilla sex
- ☐ Swinging
- ☐ Cross-dressing/TV

☐ Enforced feminisation

☐ Others – tell us what you don't see enough of in adult fiction:

_____

_____

_____

8. Would you prefer books with a more specialised approach to your interests, i.e. a novel specifically about uniforms? If so, which subject(s) would you like to read a Nexus novel about?

_____

_____

_____

9. Would you like to read true stories in Nexus books? For instance, the true story of a submissive woman, or a male slave? Tell us which true revelations you would most like to read about:

_____

_____

_____

10. What do you like best about Nexus books?

_____

_____

11. What do you like least about Nexus books?

_____

_____

12. Which are your favourite titles?

_____

_____

13. Who are your favourite authors?

_____

_____

14. **Which covers do you prefer? Those featuring:**
    (Tick as many as you like.)

☐ Fetish outfits
☐ More nudity
☐ Two models
☐ Unusual models or settings
☐ Classic erotic photography
☐ More contemporary images and poses
☐ A blank/non-erotic cover
☐ What would your ideal cover look like?

_____

15. **Describe your ideal Nexus novel in the space provided:**

_____
_____
_____
_____

16. **Which celebrity would feature in one of your Nexus-style fantasies?**
    We'll post the best suggestions on our website – anonymously!

_____

THANKS FOR YOUR TIME

Now simply write the title of this book in the space below and cut out the
questionnaire pages. Post to: Nexus, Marketing Dept., Thames Wharf Studios,
Rainville Rd, London W6 9HA

Book title: _____

nexus

NEXUS NEW BOOKS

To he published in February 2007

SLIPPERY WHEN WET
Penny Birch

Penny Birch assembles her famous cast of naughty girls for a slippery and messy week of fun. Gabrielle, the mischievous Poppy, and their nurse Sabina (from *Naughty, Naughty*) receive a gift from Monty Hartle of one week at an SM boot camp in Wales. Gabrielle is doubtful, but Poppy and Sabrina are keen, so they go. The camp turns out to be a converted home hired for the purpose, and is run by Mistress Kimiko, a poisonous individual with a serious uniform fetish. According to the rules Mistress Kimiko has absolute authority, save for the mysterious Master. The girls are assigned to the kitchens, which is asking for trouble . . .

£6.99   ISBN 978 0 352 34091 7

THE ROAD TO DEPRAVITY
Ray Gordon

Helen's husband, Alan, has walked out on her yet again. But this time she won't take him back. Thirty years old and extremely attractive with long black hair, Helen is enjoying her freedom and she has no shortage of men after her. But Alan won't leave her in peace. When she discovers that he's spying on her through the lounge window, watching her having sex with a male friend, she's initially shocked. But she soon realises that his voyeurism is a great turn-on.

Knowing that Alan is watching, she enjoys one sexual encounter after another. Taking things further in order to shock Alan, she experiments sexually with Mary, a young blonde lesbian. And Helen's sexual conquests plunge her deeper into the pit of depravity to the point where she enjoys group sex.

Alan takes his voyeurism to the extreme by hiding in the house and watching Helen with her sexual partners. Unsure what his long-term goal is, Helen again tries to shock him. Indulging in bondage and spanking, she's not sure whether she wants to be rid of Alan or continue to enjoy his spying. Until . . .

£6.99   ISBN 978 0 352 34092 4

NEXUS CONFESSIONS: VOLUME I
Various

Swinging, dogging, group sex, cross-dressing, spanking, female domination, corporal punishment, and extreme fetishes . . . *Nexus Confessions* explores the length and breadth of erotic obsession, real experience and sexual fantasy. An encyclopaedic collection of the bizarre, the extreme, the utterly inappropriate, the daring and the shocking experiences of ordinary men and women driven by their extraordinary desires. Collected by the world's leading publisher of fetish fiction, this is the first in a series of six volumes of true stories and shameful confessions, never-before-told or published.

£6.99   ISBN 978 0 352 34093 1

If you would like more information about Nexus titles, please visit our website at www.nexus-books.co.uk, or send a large stamped addressed envelope to:

Nexus, Thames Wharf Studios,
Rainville Road, London W6 9HA

NEXUS BOOKLIST

Information is correct at time of printing. To avoid disappointment, check availability before ordering. Go to www.nexus-books.co.uk.

All books are priced at £6.99 unless another price is given.

NEXUS

☐ ABANDONED ALICE	Adriana Arden	ISBN 978 0 352 33969 0
☐ ALICE IN CHAINS	Adriana Arden	ISBN 978 0 352 33908 9
☐ AQUA DOMINATION	William Doughty	ISBN 978 0 352 34020 7
☐ THE ART OF CORRECTION	Tara Black	ISBN 978 0 352 33895 2
☐ THE ART OF SURRENDER	Madeline Bastinado	ISBN 978 0 352 34013 9
☐ BELINDA BARES UP	Yolanda Celbridge	ISBN 978 0 352 33926 3
☐ BENCH-MARKS	Tara Black	ISBN 978 0 352 33797 9
☐ BIDDING TO SIN	Rosita Varón	ISBN 978 0 352 34063 4
☐ BINDING PROMISES	G.C. Scott	ISBN 978 0 352 34014 6
☐ THE BOOK OF PUNISHMENT	Cat Scarlett	ISBN 978 0 352 33975 1
☐ BRUSH STROKES	Penny Birch	ISBN 978 0 352 34072 6
☐ CALLED TO THE WILD	Angel Blake	ISBN 978 0 352 34067 2
☐ CAPTIVES OF CHEYNER CLOSE	Adriana Arden	ISBN 978 0 352 34028 3
☐ CARNAL POSSESSION	Yvonne Strickland	ISBN 978 0 352 34062 7
☐ COLLEGE GIRLS	Cat Scarlett	ISBN 978 0 352 33942 3
☐ COMPANY OF SLAVES	Christina Shelly	ISBN 978 0 352 33887 7
☐ CONCEIT AND CONSEQUENCE	Aishling Morgan	ISBN 978 0 352 33965 2
☐ CORRECTIVE THERAPY	Jacqueline Masterson	ISBN 978 0 352 33917 1